EyeCue Productions
Presents

DUNCAN P. BRADSHAW

Hexagram First Published in 2016

Published by EyeCue Productions

Front Cover illustration by Mike McGee.
Internal and Cover Design by EyeCue Productions

ISBN 978-0993534614

ACKNOWLEDGEMENTS

Big thanks to the beta readers, George Anderson, Stuart Park, Kit Power, Rich Hawkins and Debbie Bradshaw. Was worried with this being my first undead-free novel, so appreciate you putting my mind at ease.

Mike McGee, for another fantastic cover, really nailed what I was after, thanks fella.

Neil Baker for the illustration at the end, much like the Dude's rug, it really ties the book together.

Adam Millard for proofreading this, thanks for getting it looking all purty.

DEDICATION

To Debbie, for everything you do, both knowingly, and simply by just being there, this is for you.

Mum and Dad, thank you for everything you've done to give me the courage to do this.

Stu, my brother and oldest friend, thank you, though I'm glad I didn't go with your suggestion of calling this 'Squid the Dangerous Poisoner'.

To you, whether this is your first taste of my brain, or you're a return guest, I appreciate it.

Journey's end

Unsteady bare feet struggled to find a sturdy footing on the loose shale which littered the side of the mountain. "How much further papa?" the child wheezed.

Her father, a few broad steps ahead, stopped, turned back and smiled at his daughter. "Not far now. Once we get through the mist, we'll be nearly there, look."

A long bony finger pointed to the hidden crest of the peak, wreathed in a green fog which swirled as if stirred by the Gods themselves.

"I'm tired," she whinged again, "can we stop?"

Her father walked down the slope and knelt down in front of her shivering exhausted body. "You know we can't. If we don't get there in time we will have to wait for the next one, and that won't be for many sunfalls. Come on, it'll be fine, trust me." He held out his hand, the palm as smooth as the pebbles which lay around them. Grudgingly, she accepted it, and the pair continued their ascent.

Breathless step followed breathless step. For every inch of ground they made, the mist seemed to retreat further away; she became convinced that they were walking on the spot.

From behind them came guttural howls, talons clacked

against rock, fevered snarls were followed by muffled screams. As hope began to wane, there was a crack in the miasma. A ray of light zig-zagged through the minutest of chinks.

All thoughts of exhaustion and despair disappeared in an instant. She poked her tiny fingers into the beam and, for the first time, felt true warmth upon her skin. It took the child's breath away. Her father smiled knowingly, and said, "Just wait till you see what's beyond."

He pulled on her hand gently; any notion that their journey was impossible vanished as the pair trudged up the incline. Looking up, the girl saw her father's head and upper torso disappear through the fog; momentarily she was scared of what she would see when she reached the summit. As the wraithlike fog wrapped around her hand, she felt simultaneously both hot and cold. Her face was brushed gently by the mist as it washed over her. Taking one last step, she stared into the green vapour, and then...

The sight swamped her senses. Having lived in permanent shade, she instinctively shielded her face from the iridescent light. It wrapped around her, reminding the child of her mother's loving embrace, before the monsters had attacked and taken her. Eyes, unaccustomed to the brightness, squinted and blinked. Tears welled up and trickled down her face.

Slowly, the light began to soften; a large fiery orb in the sky rolled off the horizon, and she was able to see what lay ahead. Her father stood sentinel nearby, holding her hand, and she gripped back tightly. With a smile on his face, he looked so different up here, beatific, aflame with energy and lightning. A finger pointed to the peak a few steps off and the heavens which lay beyond. He said simply, "Look."

She gazed at the endless darkness which lay overhead. The light was fading fast, now nothing more than a belt of orange around them, bordering life between the green fog below and infinity above. Dumbstruck, the pair walked the remaining distance in silence.

The crest was a flat plateau of grey rock; the only bland thing amongst the multitude of visions on offer. Father and daughter reached the top, sat down, and saw that they were not alone. In the distance they could make out similar scenes—other couples resting, talking or pointing upwards. The daughter lay down and looked up.

It were as if a jeweller had spread a black velvet cloth and cast their wares upon it. Twinkling gems sparkled in the sky. "What...what are they?" she asked hesitantly, watching some blink, seemingly in and out of existence.

Her father put his pack down and lay next to his daughter. "They're called stars."

The answer served only to fire more questions in her head, though only one mattered: the reason why they had made the pilgrimage, survived the six trials and climbed their designated rock spire. "Which one's mine?" she asked softly, scouring the sky for a sign.

Her father held her hand. "Patience, little one, for it is yet to be born."

DUNCAN P. BRADSHAW

"I have not come here for such reasons. I have come to take away their gold."

– Francisco Pizarro, Spanish Conquistador

174, 942 days until the end of the world
Cuzco, former Inca Empire
4 March 1538

DUNCAN P. BRADSHAW

1.

"Go home, Matías, you're drunk." The prostitute's words were as brief as the physical act which had ended abruptly with a shudder, a whimper, and, after a clumsy withdrawal, the man emptying his port-filled stomach onto the floor.

Wiping a sleeve across his acrid, tangy lips, he fumbled his wilting member back into his trousers. After a number of aborted efforts, it was finally docked in the harbour of his undergarments. "Guess you're right," Matías slurred. "I've shown you the lights of heaven, reckon I better go get some sleep."

He gyrated his groin at her provocatively. "If you're lucky, I'll be back round tomorrow for a repeat visit."

Palla let a smile break upon her usually reserved demeanour. "Of course, Matías, I *really* would be lucky. You bring the coin and we can do this again. Now, go home." With that, she twirled around, adjusted her gown so it covered what modesty remained, and sauntered off into the night.

Matías let the myriad images play across his vision; his shivering, brought on by the vomiting and fresh evening air, jolted him back to life. Successfully planting one foot in front of the other, he tottered off towards the plume of smoke in the distance, which signalled where his barracks were.

Showed her a good time, huh? Yeah, she loved it. Got all the moves, that's for sure.

Lost in a replay of the tryst, he failed to spot the man standing in his way, and the pair collided. "Sorry, I'm a little bit merry," Matías spluttered.

His eyes were locked on the floor and he saw a pair of filthy feet. *Bloody local.* He traced up the legs to the edge of a black gown; intricate lines of golden thread were woven into the hem. The lines cracked violently left and right, forming a right-angled map of interlocking roads and dead ends. As he finally made his way to the face, he saw that the features were covered by a black mask. A pair of stern eyes looked back, demanding an apology.

"Already said sorry, haven't I? Now why don't you fuck off back home, before I go and get my mates and we'll introduce you and your family to a bit of Spanish justice. Comprende amigo?" Matías said with as much conviction as he could muster whilst shaking.

Their eyes maintained contact. Matías could make out deep lines running from the corners. They gave the appearance of trenches which had been carved into the man's skin. He fought the impulse to touch them, but failed. Fingers, still flecked with ruby red port and stomach lining, ran over the cracks. As they reached the end, and a tract of smooth skin around the temples, Matías became acutely aware that he was not alone. He could sense movement behind him.

Dank breath washed over his neck like a frothy tide, and he pulled back from the man's face, only to bump into someone to his rear. "Sorry, mate. I'm a little tipsy" he mumbled. Matías turned around with the speed of a bogged down supply caravan. The figure he was greeted by was shorter than the man whose face he had just brushed, but was similarly dressed. Just as he was about to remark on this coincidence, he heard a whoosh of displaced air, followed abruptly by a firm connection to the back of his head.

As he sank to the floor, he noticed that he had got some splashback over his new boots. He managed a solitary thought: *Bugger, that'll soak in.*

Before unconsciousness claimed him.

2

Matías came to and stared into a familiar yet distorted face. His bruised features stared back, though imbued with a flaxen hue. Turning his head this way and that, he could make out a dingy cave, and a golden bowl polished to a mirrored sheen beneath him.

His appendages felt tight and, despite struggling, he was unable to move. "Help!" he shouted. His voice came out like a frog being squeezed, crackly and hoarse.

After his exclamation, a realisation flooded his addled brain; he could feel that he was naked. A gentle breeze, like a lover's whisper, played over his shoulder blades. He fought to stop himself from laughing.

Staring into the bowl he saw a pair of grimy calloused feet appear on the floor beyond it. "Help me," he beseeched, "whatever it is you want, I'm sure I can help you." The toes bent and gripped onto the stone floor. He felt a hot flash of pain run down his cheek. From the edge of his peripheral vision, dark beads of liquid ran to the corner of his eye, and then dropped into freefall.

Blood pitter-pattered against the hard metallic surface, each splatter echoing around the large chamber he was undoubtedly in, but as yet could not appreciate the dimensions of.

"Please," he begged, "you don't have to do this. I'm not anyone."

A symmetrical flash of fire slithered down his other cheek, and the gentle tapping of the bowl increased in tempo. The feet turned and disappeared from sight; the only sound to convince him they had existed was a scuffing against the dusty floor.

Matías flexed his fingers, trying to feel for the binding. The tips made it to the bottom of his palms, but were unable to move any further. Accepting the futility of his situation, he began to sob. Salty tears mixed with his blood, causing the rhythmic tapping against the bowl to increase in frequency.

Over the sound of his own breathing, a collection of bassy monotonal voices rumbled around him. It was an alien language, each voice muttering the same phrase over and over again. With each completed verse, the volume increased, as if the speakers were becoming consumed by an opiate. Soon the mutterings became a din, his senses assaulted by the words which bore through his skull and rapped against his brain.

Just as the cacophony threatened to consume his entire being, it ceased.

He listened to the shuffling of cloth and feet on the gritty floor. Along the length of his exposed flesh he felt cold fingers slide, plying his body with a greasy liquid. The little body hair he possessed stood on end, every nerve-ending alert. As the last patch of skin was covered, the digits withdrew and he was left shivering. The basting accentuated what little breeze there was. It were as if a cloak of pure cold had been draped over his back.

In the lull, he wondered if this was some kind of initiation test. His fellow conquistadors were quite the pranksters on occasion. Matías had heard countless stories of newcomers being subjected to weird and wonderful jokes.

A missing eyebrow here or there or a few drops of laxative slipped into a drink before guard duty. One story, he recalled, had cost a man the end of a finger.

"Guys?" he ventured.

"Okay guys, ha ha, very funny, you can let me go now," he huffed. He twisted his head from side to side, trying to see which of his so-called mates was involved. Matías still couldn't see much more than the stone plinth beneath his body and the small puddle of blood and tears, *his* blood and tears, in the bottom of the golden bowl.

As if in retort, he felt a stick of cold metal press into the base of his spine. Matías felt the pressure increase and his skin pucker and puff up over the initial incision. He howled in agony.

His anguish echoed around the room, clawing and mocking him, pushing his fragile spirit into the realms of madness. The skin invader bit through his skin and was slowly drawn up the length of his spine. Further waves of pain washed over him as nodules of bone were scored and clusters of dense nerve endings severed.

Matías clung to consciousness as if he were the sole survivor of a storm at sea. He was expended from the screaming. Endorphins flooded his body and the searing agony abated. Gagging on a thick wad of saliva and mucus, he spat into the bowl. "Ha ha ha, you guys," he bleated deliriously.

Amaru withdrew the tumi from the offerings back. The bronze crescent blade glistened with the sacrifice's blood. On the hilt, the stern face of Supay, the Death God, looked back blankly, his lolling tongue hungering for another taste of the heathen's flesh.

Ignoring the words he could not discern, Amaru looked at his handiwork. In his anger, he knew he had carved too deeply. The blade was chipped and pitted after being delved too far into the sacrifice's spine. Grooves in the ivory bone filled with spilled marrow and thick black blood.

Calming himself down with a mumbled prayer, he placed the blade head horizontally atop the incision he had made, just below the neck. With the man tied firmly to the stone block altar, the skin was pulled apart. The cavity was slowly growing in size; Amaru could make out the edges of the bottom most ribs.

He pressed the blade down, causing the captive to splutter and gurgle. Working from the centre to the left, he pulled the blade across the shoulder, and then, with care, continued his way down the arm, crossing the tricep, elbow, and ending at the wrist.

The gurgling continued. Amaru looked into the bowl and saw that it was filling more quickly now. Bubbly spit floated on top of the reservoir of congealing blood. Unsure whether he had made the cut correctly, he pried his rough fingers into the freshly made gash down the arm. Sharp fingernails curled under the skin and, with a gentle pull, Amaru was satisfied that he had made the right depth.

He circled to the other side of the altar. The sacrifice

was fading in and out of consciousness; he was mumbling barely coherent words. It could've been a name, but he didn't understand the language of the people who had ransacked the empire, plundered their riches and slaughtered his people.

Amaru repeated the incision on the other side, again testing that he had cut through beyond the skin and into the meat and sinew beneath. He walked to the foot of the altar, reverently bowing towards the other members of the cabal who stood as sombre guardians on each end of a six pointed star.

Once at the foot of the plinth, he placed one hand on the man's ankle. The legs were splayed and affixed to opposite corners of the altar.

The tumi blade rested at the base of the coccyx, just above the testicles. Amaru pushed the blade in, which brought the Spaniard back to life, albeit briefly. Mirroring birth, the man wailed and screamed as if being delivered into the world.

The priest again worked from the centre to the left. He sliced to the bottom of the buttock then straight down the middle of the back of the leg, stopping only when the blade hit the middle toe bone. Repeating the process on the other side, he held the bloodied weapon aloft, thanked Supay for the divine assistance, and placed the weapon on the altar between the man's legs.

Matías felt his tongue slap against his lips as if it were a fleshy bell clapper. He blinked rapidly, trying to flash away the sensations he was feeling. Failing, his eyelids grew heavy, his breathing became laboured and shallow. With his tremulous body slashed and the innards exposed to the air, he retched, closed his eyes and his soul fell away.

Amaru's fingers plunged beneath the ribs and worked their way up through the multitude of densely packed organs and muscle. Elbow deep, his hand clutched the sacrifice's heart. Digging his fingernails in, he pulled it free from now redundant arteries. He held it up to the flickering torch light, and turned to each point of the star, bidding his comrades to stir from their vigil. When all of their eyes were on him, he said firmly, "It is ready, we must work quickly."

"What are you doing?" a voice demanded from the gloom. Dressed in the same black and gold gowns, another group of six priests surged into the antechamber. Poma, resplendent with a headdress fashioned from harpy eagle feathers, stormed towards the altar and Amaru, who still clutched the Spaniard's heart.

One of the priests from a point of the star retrieved a deep, ridged gold bowl from beneath the altar, and placed it next to the tumi. The metal clanged against the thick stone. Amaru placed the clammy organ into the bowl and accepted a cloth from another of the priests. "Poma, we have spoken about this before, I—"

A raised hand signalled silence. Poma and his retinue stopped by the altar. He shook his head with dismay. "We have, Amaru, and I thought my views were clear. We use only the chosen, not *their* soldiers. Our intention is to raise Inti, and to do so we must stick to our tenets and collect only from true Inca." He pointed at the dead body; the edges of the skin were curling up. "Their kind will only sully our work."

Strands of claggy blood held firm to Amaru's hands,

15

despite the intensity of his effort to clean them. "Brother, when we studied the teachings and began this mission, our only adversaries were the fire mountains and the floods which plague us. These men..." he gestured towards the cooling corpse, "...came to us and have slaughtered our people. They are the real monsters now. We have to accelerate the collection process so that we can summon Inti and make our foes fear us."

Poma shook his head. "That is not the way. For thirty four seasons we have harvested the quyllur allpa from the righteous. We cannot abandon our ways now, just because *they* are here."

Amaru flung the cloth to the floor. "If we do not do this, our way will not survive. You are living in the other world too much these days. If you only saw what we do...they are wiping us out. I will not bend my knee to their kind any more, we must—"

"Enough," Poma commanded. "It is not your decision to make Amaru. Dispose of this, and hope that it does not impinge on our work. Tomorrow is the high moon. We will harvest then, as we always have."

Balled fists quivered with barely controlled rage. "Of course, Poma, it shall be done," Amaru grunted through gritted teeth. He signalled to his fellow acolytes, who bowed in deference. They approached the altar and began to untie the body. As the restraints fell slack, the skin chasm grew. Blood ran from ridges of skin; fingers twitched as the final synaptic pulses arrived at their destination.

"Amaru, I share your hatred of the Spaniards, but if we do not live by our principles, then our lives will be for nothing," Poma implored softly.

The priest shrugged. "It would appear our lives are already worth nought. Now, if you please."

3

Rodrigo Quintaro rubbed the end of his moustache and dared to look back at the table. "Where did you find him?"

"Hanging from the belfry at Santo Domingo," Alfonso replied, the words muffled through a handkerchief held tightly over his mouth and nose. "They found him hanging from his wrists. My lord, there is something else." He nodded at the two attendants, who stepped forward and turned the body over.

A dark line signalled the divide between the two halves of the man's back. The edges of the skin had been sewn together with a thick gold thread. The skin was a putrid mix of green and purple. At the base of the spine, the thread had been cut. One of the men pulled back the unwieldy flaps of skin to reveal a hollow cavity. From within came the smell of spoiled meat and damp stone. "My God," Rodrigo uttered involuntarily.

Alfonso nodded and the two men carefully turned Matías' corpse over onto his back. Like a spider wrapping a trapped insect, they cocooned the body within the shroud. "He's been hollowed out, my lord. A number of our men have been found this way. Our retribution must be—"

"Enough," Rodrigo implored. "No amount of blood will bring him back. It will only lead to more bodies like this. Their time is already marked. We did not come here to kill; we came for the gold."

"As you wish," Alfonso acceded. The two men had swaddled Matías' remains and, upon receiving a further nod, carried the tightly wound parcel through to the next room, to prepare for the funeral.

Rodrigo headed towards the door. "Alfonso, follow me."

The two men marched from the murky barracks into the morning air. The sun hid behind a mountain range bordering the valley below. Streaks of golden light rotated through the air, like a kaleidoscope from heaven itself. As they stalked through the city streets, the locals shuffled past, heads bowed.

"They expect reprisals," Rodrigo said absently. A child turned a corner blindly and collided with the men. His mother shouted at him and hurried away clutching the boy's hand. As he was castigated, he cast inquisitive glances over his shoulder at the strange men dressed in leather and silver.

"My lord, I appreciate the sensitivity of the situation. It has only been three months since we reclaimed this accursed place, but—"

"Enough," Rodrigo cut short Alfonso's diatribe. "You tell me what I already know. I do not think you listen to my words." The duo stopped by a market stall selling melon. The owner gulped and knelt down behind his pitch, busy with some forgotten menial task.

Rodrigo stood a foot taller than his aide, and each inch

now seemed to propel him to titanic proportions. "I take my instructions from King Charles, as do you. Tell me Alfonso, what were his last words before we boarded the Pinto?"

Alfonso mumbled a reply, invoking an exasperated sigh from his liege.

"His majesty told us that we are to come back from the new world, not with blood or slaves, but with gold. Everything that we hold dear is under threat these days, the English a constant thorn in our side. Without the gold, we cannot build a navy, nor train an army. His majesty does not care how many of these heathens we slaughter, as long as our boats are laden with riches upon our return. Those who came before us have pillaged much already, look." Rodrigo walked over to an Inca temple, reduced to a pile of rubble and broken prayers.

"Do you remember when we first saw this place? The buildings were lined with gold. In order to fulfil our levies, they pried it off the very buildings they live and worship in. All the while, we hoped they would lead us to the place we have heard of so many times."

"El Dorado," Alfonso said in a hushed tone, as if anything louder would destroy the myth like the building they stood next to.

Rodrigo nodded conspiratorially. "Exactly. Imagine what would be bestowed upon the men who find it and present its riches to the King?"

The aide swallowed uncomfortably; his mind boggled with images of nubile women and cooked meats, his imagination causing him to dribble. Rodrigo laughed. "I see that you too can picture the prize? I have found someone who claims to know the location. With your knowledge of the local tongue, we can learn its location and those dreams will become reality."

Alfonso's eyes lit up, matching the sun peeking out from the mountain range and suffusing the city with a coruscating glow.

Built on the foundations of a now destroyed stables, Rodrigo Quintaro's humble villa was a poor imitation of the one which sat on a hilltop overlooking his vineyards back home in La Horra. The hastily constructed walls let in frigid air during the colder months, whilst insects made it their home during the summer.

Despite numerous requests to the artisans, both local and Spanish, he knew that it was very much a case of make do. The knowledge that his time in the new world was coming to an end filled him with joy, but also with dismay. He knew that to return to the King empty handed would certainly mean the end of his life, and the destruction of everything his family had worked for over the generations.

Nodding a greeting to the two guards, Rodrigo and Alfonso crossed the threshold into the modest house. They headed to the dining room, the recent scene of the latest puppet governor's installation. At the head of the table sat one of the local priests, bedecked in a fine black gown with intricate gold stitching. Alfonso's breath was momentarily taken away by its splendour and the attention to detail.

The priest acknowledged the men's entrance with a languid blink. His features remained as stony as the idols found within their fey temples. His rough hands lay palm down on the cedar table. Thick fingers, with cracked sun-weathered divots carved into the knuckles, lay motionless on its surface. It was as if the two Spaniards had invaded his home, instead of he being the guest.

No sooner had the two men sat down than the priest began chuntering away. Rodrigo silenced him with a raised fist and a loud cough. "Alfonso, if you please," he said across the table, before indicating to the priest that he could begin.

"He says that he knows of a…cult? And that they are the guardians of the location of…gold," Alfonso said incredulously, asking the priest again to ensure he had heard correctly.

Rodrigo nodded. "It is as I had hoped. This priest volunteered himself to our men this morning. He said that he wants the killing to stop. On both sides."

Alfonso let out a chuckle. "Priests are the same the world over, eh? I guess he's sick of burying their dead."

The Inca priest babbled away again, his words crashing against Rodrigo's ears like a fierce tidal wave. It was as if they were trying to carve their way through his skull and infect his brain with their harsh and oblique melodies.

Alfonso began to scrawl down details of the discussion, making enquiries when his own linguistic understanding failed him.

Rodrigo sought refuge from the verbal barrage. He walked over to the drinks cabinet and poured out three measures of finest port. He passed a fine crystal glass to Alfonso, who took it gladly, and offered a scratched and pitted receptacle to the priest, who sniffed it and gazed into its amber depths. The priest wrinkled his nose, shook his head, and continued to impart instructions.

"We have the location, my lord," Alfonso said, knocking back the last of the alcohol. "He says that this cult are meeting this very evening, in the catacombs beneath Qurikancha."

"But that's…" Rodrigo spluttered.

"Yes, that is the temple upon which the cathedral of Santo Domingo was built. The same place we found the butchered remains of Señor Trello this morning," Alfonso replied gravely.

Rodrigo refilled his glass and knocked it back in one. "Then perhaps we will kill two birds with one stone tonight. Good news indeed."

Alfonso nodded in agreement, but the priest looked on impassively. "He says that the information is stored on a quipu which the leader carries around with him at all times. If we find it, I can translate it with ease."

Rodrigo smiled. "Excellent. Please convey my gratitude. Pray tell, what is his name?"

A brief exchange of the guttural tongue followed. Alfonso turned back. "He says his name is Amaru."

4

Chaska imparted curt instructions to the crypt guards and hurried to the centre of the dingy room. "We do not have much time. We must invoke the ritual immediately. I fear we are betrayed."

As one, the other five members of the sect, resplendent in their black gowns adorned with crooked lines stitched with golden thread, turned to the head priest. Panicked eyes looked from one to another, searching for courage to bolster their flagging reserves.

"It is not ready, Chaska. We do not have enough. If we begin the ritual now, we would lose all that we have gathered," Huk replied, gesturing to a plain clay pot sitting underneath a raised stone dais.

Upon the altar lay a drugged teenage girl. She writhed as if she was being rocked to sleep. Her eyes flickered beneath closed lids; her face was coated with sweat. Nestled within a narcotic fog, she murmured the words of the dead.

Standing at the head of a six-pointed star, Poma opened a leather knapsack and withdrew a length of cord with knotted string hanging from it. As his eyes struggled to acclimatise to the murk, he wiped bobbles of perspiration from his brow. "Am I destined to forever repeat my words? We cannot profane the ritual, this sacred quipu states it clearly. Our journeys in this world and the other have shown us the way. We cannot give in to impatience and lose all that we have worked for."

Huk shook his head angrily. "We have ignored the Elder's wishes to offer the chosen in the traditional way. We have risked everything already. The threat from the lightning devils is more dire than any of us could've predicted. Even Chaska, our seer since her father was called back to the fire mountain. Even *she* was unable to see the evil before they invaded our lands, killed our people and desecrated our temples," he lectured. Eyes infused with desperation looked into the faces of each member of the cabal in turn.

Chaska's head sagged. "For my lack of vision, I am truly sorry, not just to you all, but also to my people, I—"

Poma held up a hand. "Your lack of foresight is irrelevant, Chaska. Can you all not see that this is a test? To forget our reasons now, even in this moment of potential oblivion, is to ignore *His* words and wishes. We cannot use him to slay our enemy. If we are unable to defeat them with spear and arrow, when Inti is summoned, he would be displeased with us. His wrath would be total if we were to ignore his teachings and debase ourselves this way."

Murmuring and anguish ran round the group. "This is not the time for weakness; it is the moment when we complete our task. I too have studied the teachings and I believe that if we can offer ourselves along with the quyllur allpa, we will fulfil our tenet, and Inti will become one amongst us, as we live and breathe now," Chaska said softly.

"But—" Poma began to speak.

"Our light is soon to be extinguished from this world, of that I am sure," Chaska said solemnly, gesturing towards extravagant and vibrant paintings on the wall behind her. "I have seen our end. It is in a swirling sapphire light, with smoke and fire. The old ways will come to an end. If we do not take this chance now, time will never know of us and the path we walk between this world and the other."

The flames from the torches affixed to the walls danced and flickered in time with her words. The light cast long shadows across the hand carved floor. Every nick and chip formed small abyssal pits, devoid of light. Insects took their chance and scuttled across the floor, using the gloom as a cowl of invisibility.

The seer's speech was greeted with nods and deference, except for one. "I do not wish to mourn our culture and our knowledge, Chaska. But this is not the way. If your visions are true, then we have already failed. Nothing we do this night will stop that," Poma said forcefully.

"Not now," the altar sacrifice whimpered, her face a knot of wonder and fear, lost in some ethereal plain. Her fragile body squirmed like a trapped guanaco. The cabal looked from her to the ground.

"Regardless of your impatience, we must sacrifice the offering, for she has been prepared for Inti. To deny her to him would be a grave insult," Poma said. They each nodded in approval. From a small alpaca-skinned scabbard, wrapped with human tendon, he withdrew a keen-edged bronze tumi.

The others began to chant the words of the offering, imploring the Sun God to accept the girl.

From birth, Ocllo had been chosen. Her entire life had been spent in preparation for this moment. Her parents willingly gave her to the temple priests, their hearts swollen with pride that their daughter had been selected. Through months of fasting and learning, Ocllo accepted the mantle of being a gift to the gods.

Huk had already ensured that the girl had been plied with enough coca leaves to numb the sensation of reality. Though she was being sacrificed, pain and suffering would not be bestowed upon her. As the knife pierced her heart, her near skeletal frame quivered and fell slack.

Poma slid the curved blade from the base of her throat down to her naval. Replacing the tumi in its pouch, his strong hands pulled open the skin, baring bone, flesh and sinew to the world. As fingers pulled free organs from meaty pipes, the girl sat bolt upright and screamed, "THEY'RE HERE."

Like a torch being cast into a lake, she melted back onto the dais. The group looked around frantically. "Guards, prepare yourself, buy us the time we need to complete the harvest," Poma shouted. He turned the girl onto her side and, forsaking the usual sanctity of the ceremony, hauled the steaming flesh and offal into the stone sink beneath Ocllo's slender frame. The smoothed stone bowl was now awash with thickening blood and stringy bile.

Chaska and the others picked up their spears and

27

circled the cramped room. Scraping sounds were barely audible, their direction impossible to discern.

Poma paid nothing except his task any heed. Having removed the viscera, he pulled the carcass off the altar and rested it against one of the stone supports. From within his knapsack, he pulled out a stone club, as long as his own forearm and as thick as his balled fist. The end was warped and twisted as if it were a petrified tornado.

With a speed and surety honed from years of extracting the quyllur allpa from sacrifices, he began to grind the meat with the stone implement. As he worked, he spat onto the paste, ensuring it did not become too claggy and unworkable.

The bowl within the centre of the altar was ridged with half inch lips, carved into the bottom half of the vessel. Poma pushed the mush into the middle and then smeared and dragged it up against the ridges with the stone tool. Each scrape deposited small shimmery particles into the crevices of the ridges.

Within a few hundred heartbeats, the paste had been dragged up to the very top of the altar bowl, and a sprinkling of dust was scattered on each rocky plateau. "I can hear something," Huk warned. The scraping sound had grown quiet and there was a slight hissing, as if a nest of snakes was searching for the now hidden floor insects.

Poma placed the blood-stained stone tool into the middle of the altar bowl and, using both palms, twisted the shaft. He removed the device, which took a stone plug with it. Plucking two of the harpy eagle feathers from his headpiece, he brushed the powder from each level into the created hole. The dust floated down into the clay pot beneath the altar.

The plug was screwed back into place. Poma picked up the collection pot and placed it on the floor. "We must hide the quyllur allpa. Our work must continue—"

An explosion punctuated the sentence; chunks of masonry were flung around the interior of the room. Huk screamed as a shard of rock sliced his midriff. Blood poured from the wound and soaked into his gown. The antechamber was bathed in a sickly glow. Clouds of smoke and cordite wafted through, transported on a gentle breeze.

Chaska was disorientated from the commotion and lurched this way and that, seeking some grounding in reality. Her hands touched the wall and, in an attempt to seek solace from the noise, she slumped against the floor. As her eyes cracked open, rebelling against the beams of pale light blown through the wall, she saw the last picture she had daubed whilst experiencing 'the sight'.

She gasped, a tear running down her cheek, barging through the fine film of dust which now covered her face. Bony fingers ran over the image of a woman dressed in black, kneeling in the ruins of a destroyed temple. A trio of silver-horned monsters stood in front of her, their evil fire staffs raised. "No," she sobbed, seeking out the light. She turned, knowing what awaited her.

Voices dripping with the devil's tongue ran around the destroyed room. A man wearing a shiny breastplate and helmet stood before Chaska. Either side of him were similarly dressed men; the invaders, the malaise on their lands. As her sight returned in full, she smiled up at them. With arms outstretched, she closed her eyes and offered a silent prayer.

"No one gets out alive," Rodrigo growled. His cohorts pointed their harquebuses at Chaska.

"NO," screamed Huk. Forcing back the pain, he ran towards the seer. The chamber echoed with more explosions, slighter of sound but no less devastating. The woman slumped to the floor, and a pool of blood began to form under her body. Rodrigo prodded the body with his boot, ensuring she was dead. The light from outside grew pale as more Conquistadors stormed into the basement of the ziggurat.

Huk held the spear in one hand. The other was clamped to his torso, trying to stem the blood loss long enough for him to vanquish the seer's murderer. As he staggered towards the fallen lady, Rodrigo pulled his sword from its sheath. He swatted the puny wooden weapon to one side and headbutted the wounded man in the face. The blow from the steel helm caught Huk on the bridge of the nose and he dropped to the floor, blood squirting from his nostrils.

"You people die easy enough," Rodrigo grunted. He placed the tip of the sword against the back of the man's neck. With little effort, he shoved the blade through the vertebrae, severing the spinal column in one strike. Huk's body fell to the floor in stages. His head dropped to one side and, as it did so, the weight pulled on the skin and it tore off. It bounced once and then rolled across the stone floor.

Poma had ducked behind the altar when the assault began. As the dust settled, he regained his bearings and saw that the other exit was unguarded. Amongst the screams of the injured and dying, he scurried along to the doorway.

Rodrigo flicked the blood and bone shards from the edge of his sword. "Release the mastiffs," he shouted. From outside came rabid growls and fierce snarling; two savage dogs bounded over the destroyed wall and scampered across the dusty floor.

A flash of movement to one side caught the attention of one of the dogs. It leapt at a priest, catching him on the throat. As the pair landed, the mastiff bit down harder and shook as if it were playing with a length of anchor rope.

Gargled screams emanated from Kanak. He slapped the animal's snout, trying to loosen its deadly grip. This infuriated the dog further, and it entered a frenzy, thrashing violently. Kanak's fight disappeared as the jugular was severed and his life force was pumped into the air and over the animal.

The exit was in sight. Still clutching the pot to his chest, the weight of no consequence, Poma could almost smell the drying meat from the next room. As he bounded for freedom, he felt something wrap itself around his ankle. His momentum ceased instantly, and he crashed to the floor. The pot flew through the air before shattering against the ground. A cloud of glistening dust was cast into the air. Poma howled inconsolably as his life's work fluttered to the floor, mingling with chunks of stone and dust.

Rodrigo removed his helmet, placed it on the altar, and marched over to the man who had been trying to escape. The dog held onto Poma's leg as if it were the most precious of treats. "Release him," Rodrigo commanded.

Reluctantly the mastiff's jaw opened and it sat on its hind legs, licking the blood from its teeth.

Poma held his wounded leg. The euphoria of being so close to escape had evaporated, and only pain remained. Silhouetted by the evening sky through the breached walls, a tall figure loomed over him. "You and your kind are nothing but the Devil. You know only of fire and death," he shouted at the shadow.

The words crashed against Rodrigo's skull, and he held a hand to his ear to try and block out the sound. "Shut up!" he shouted and placed his thick boot onto the man's ragged wound.

Poma screamed in agony. Three of his fingers were also trapped between his own leg and the man's foot. Drawing from a reserve of strength, Poma vowed, "Inti will take our revenge on you and your people, of that you can be sure."

Rodrigo leant over the priest and struck him across the face. "Quri. Where is the quri?" he demanded.

Poma looked up into the man's eyes. "Gold? You have taken all of our gold."

"I tire of this. Perhaps in death you will be of some use." Rodrigo placed the sword's edge against the priest's neck. With a slow deliberate motion, he drew it across, opening the throat up like a ripe guanábana. Stepping off the man's leg, he watched as the life drained from him, his throat gushing like a waterfall, blood soaking into the ground, mingling with the glittery dust from the broken pot.

Rodrigo knelt down and frisked the priest, even as he floundered against his mortal wounds. Finding nothing secreted within the gown, he opened the knapsack and smiled. "Looks like I was right, *priest*. This will be most useful."

Spanish soldiers prowled the interior, rounding up any survivors who were still unharmed. Those who had been injured were killed on the spot. Alfonso stood guard over one warrior and two priests. Rodrigo marched past them all, heading towards the chasm formed in the wall. "My lord, what do we do with them?" he asked, pointing at the captives.

With an irked huff, Rodrigo stopped in the freshly formed entrance and cast a withering look at his aide. "I told you already, Alfonso, none live. Kill them immediately. Then form their bodies into a pile and burn this unholy site until nothing remains. When you are finished, come to my villa. I have a job for you." Rodrigo slapped the bag which was slung around his shoulder and left.

5

"I will be glad to be home and taste proper food once more," Rodrigo mused as he idly cut another slice of roasted llama and forced it into his reluctant mouth. The four men invited to dinner for their part in the temple raid laughed at his words, eager to worm their way into his favour.

Alfonso rushed into the dining room, bloodshot lines stretching from the iris across the grey of his eyeballs. "My lord, I have translated the quipu. It is—"

Rodrigo held up a weary hand, stopping Alfonso in his tracks. "Alfonso, my brain is ill-equipped to deal with the speed of your words. Please, take your time. Drink?"

"No, thank you," Alfonso replied and hurried over to the head of the table. "It took some time, and although I haven't managed to decipher everything, I have the gist. It's not about gold at all. This cult, this *group*, they—"

"What?" Rodrigo interrupted. "Not about gold? Then what the hell is it about? That damn priest sent us on some fool's errand. When I see him again, he will taste Toledo steel." This garnered a slurred round of applause.

Alfonso stood firm. "My lord, no, but from what I've managed to discern, it may still be of use."

Rodrigo dabbed the corners of his mouth with a cloth napkin and stood up, looking down at his adjutant. "My concern is solely for the gold, nothing else. It could hold the sacred instructions on how to amply satisfy a woman, I would care not one jot. Leave, we shall speak on this later, after I have let this meal settle under a bottle or three of Tempranillo."

Defeated, Alfonso bowed and left the room. Rodrigo walked across to the drinks cabinet and poured himself another glass of port. Allowing first a mouthful of tough meat to be passed to his gut, he took a sip and sighed, *What will it take to find El Dorado? What pact must I make?*

As he replaced the crystal stopper in the decanter, he heard a clatter of cutlery from behind him. "I did not invite you here to destroy my finest plates, gentlemen. If you cannot—"

Turning back to his guests, the scene which greeted him was far less convivial than he envisaged, and a lot more on the blood-soaked side of things.

A group of six Inca men, dressed in black and gold gowns, the same variety he was now becoming familiar with, were arranged around the dining room. Four of the group were wholeheartedly engaged in the act of slashing throats open with knives, which ended in a bloodied glistening crescent moon.

As Carlos patted the previously virginal white tablecloth with bloody hands—his neck a chasm of exposed meat, bone, and ripped vein—his mouth flapped open as if he were a fish. No words came out, just a wet 'gah gah gah', which ended when his attacker stuck two fingers into the ruin of his Adam's apple and pulled back, the way one might remove the top to a pot containing salted beef. With a revolting slurp, the head separated from the neck, allowing a geyser of blood to further ruin the previously pristine white and terracotta room.

Whilst one of the men covered the back door through which they had entered, the one remaining Inca not engaged in murder strode purposefully towards Rodrigo. Standing at arm's-length, the man pulled down a black scarf covering the bottom of his face, exposing a set of gums where teeth were in the minority. As he smiled back, his lips struggled to form into a shape. He managed to crackle out, "Quipu?"

"It's you. Damnable priest. I should've known that you had an ulterior motive for your apparent altruism. I'll run you through, you bastard." Rodrigo launched the bottle of wine at Amaru's smirking face. Despite moving quicker than his craggy face and general appearance hinted, it still caught him on his ear, and he grunted in pain.

Rodrigo drew his sword and smacked the priest in the face with the pommel, causing him to sink to the floor clutching his bloodied nose. Having bought himself some room, he pulled the sword back, ready to administer some Spanish vengeance.

Icy tendrils of pain ran from the bottom of his ribs up to his shoulder. To his left one of the priests leered at him, fists clenched around a knife buried up to its hilt in his guts.

The priest had struck too firmly, though, and try as he might, could not retrieve the weapon to strike again. Rodrigo fought back the pain and backhanded the man with his free hand. The Inca priest clattered into a chair, reducing the backrest to a pile of kindling. Holding the sword in both hands, he swung downwards and cleaved the man from under his armpit through to his hip.

Steel sliced through skin and bone as if it were soft cheese. Rodrigo placed a boot on the man's face and dragged the weapon free. The priest spat out chips of broken tooth and tried desperately to place his insides back into his body.

Sensing movement from his other side, Rodrigo recalled his dreaded Salsa lessons as a child, and executed a near flawless cross body lead. His assailant was left stationary as Rodrigo sailed past him, pulling the blade across the priest's torso. The knife fell to the floor, quickly followed by its bearer, who held steaming ropes of intestines. Rodrigo followed this up quickly with a thrust to the neck and severed the priest's spinal column with ease.

The coup de grace and flashy move came at a price, though, as another priest, fresh from exsanguinating Pedro Hivello, stabbed Rodrigo in the back. Heeding his cohort's earlier folly, he opted for speed over power. The wide end of the blade pulled out of the skin with a little difficulty, but left a sizeable gash which quickly pooled with blood. The man lashed out again and again. Rodrigo howled in pain and brought his sword arm across at a clip, catching the man on the temple.

Caught with the blade still embedded in the infidel's back, the priest spun backwards. Cold-cocked by the blow, he landed face down on the floor. As dazed hands sought to gain purchase on the floor slick with Inca and Spanish blood, he slipped, and butted his chin against the tiled ground.

Rodrigo placed a leaden boot on the man's back. The power had gone from his backhand, so Rodrigo rested the point of the sword onto the base of the fallen priest's skull. Using his own body weight he leaned forward and the sword tip plunged through the bone and out of the man's eye socket.

Rodrigo slapped at his own back, seeking to remove the foreign object which was still interred within his flesh. As feeble fingers started to curl around the hilt, another jolt of pain ran up from his kidneys. A bolt of lightning ran across Rodrigo's vision and his legs buckled and gave away.

He could feel that his waist was cold and wet, but there was no sensation beyond that. For all he knew his pelvis and legs were still dancing on his aunt's bone dry garden, trying to not step on Conchita's feet for the hundredth time.

Using his one remaining good hand, Rodrigo struggled to drag himself across the floor and to the front door. His fingernails strained and cracked from the exertion. They fought to find purchase within congealing puddles of blood and clumps of flesh. Agony-encased seconds were spent trying to traverse the floor. As he reached out again, a filthy foot came down on the back of his hand and pinned him to the floor. "Ha," he mumbled.

Rodrigo felt the blade twist within his body, before it was yanked free. He felt the bones in his hand crack and splinter as the foot pressed down harder. Another foot pressed against his shoulder and forced him onto his back. He thought it was impossible to experience further pain, but the transition from looking at the floor to resting with his back on it, was a journey of excruciating agony.

Rodrigo blinked away the spots and swarming lines of translucent writhing maggots in his vision and stared into the face of the bastard priest. "Quipu," the priest said, as if by repeating it the object would manifest itself. Rodrigo coughed up a thick paste of black blood and bile. Unable to eject it, he swallowed it down, coughing on the metallic taste.

"QUIPU," the priest said again, this time pushing down on Rodrigo's chest with his foot. The Spaniard laughed and yelped in equal measure. With a weak finger, he beckoned Amaru closer.

"Go. To. Hell."

Amaru's grin disappeared like a deer upwind from a hunter. He tutted, leant in further, and stabbed the Spaniard again. The priest withdrew the crescent blade and held it to his victim's face. Rodrigo's vision cleared. He felt all the air in his lungs escape through the side of his ribcage. As he gasped for breath, unable to suck in anything which would sustain him, the priest looked on impassively.

Rodrigo could feel the end. His vision wavered as if he were underwater. He saw the priest's head look up quickly. He could've sworn, in those final seconds of life, that his name was called out, as if he had been discovered in a game of hide and seek.

6

"Heathen, you have been found guilty of heresy, murder and treason. The only punishment worthy of such heinous acts is *death*. The sentence to be carried out immediately. Señor Albero, if you please."

Amaru shifted uncomfortably in his restraints. Panic flooded his eyes, and he implored the judge with unintelligible words. Señor Albero, Captain of the guard, sparked the torch into life and teased the flames to grow higher, mastering the meagre breeze.

Gerald, a young Conquistador who had recently arrived on the Santa Maria, turned to Alfonso, who looked on impassively. "Why does he bellow so? He has not spoken a single word since his capture, yet now he chatters like a chaffinch in spring seeking a mate."

Alfonso watched as Albero knelt down and drove the fiery collection of sticks into the pile of dry wood which engulfed the bottom half of the Inca priest. "The Inca say that the soul cannot travel to the afterlife if the body is burned. Amaru is asking for forgiveness."

"Ha, good, let him. He'll receive no such mercy from us," Gerald scoffed.

Alfonso looked down on the young man, whose face

had not yet felt the caress of a razor. "He is not asking for *our* forgiveness boy. He is asking for the God's forgiveness. If you'll excuse me."

Leaving the young man to his spectating, Alfonso turned on his heels and headed away from the square. It was awash with people, mainly Spanish soldiers. They cheered and cursed as the flames caught and grew in size. The vitriol and hatred seemed to act as an accelerant, the fire flared violently, lapping over the Inca priest.

Even as the flames washed the skin from his bones, boiled the blood in his veins, and chargrilled his flesh, he screamed to the heavens. A pall of smoke rose from the pyre and bathed the square in a sickly sweet smell of willow tree and cooked meat.

The route to the villa was a sombre solo procession. Any locals he chanced upon hurried out of his way, regardless of his attempts at acquiescence.

He was sick of this place, of the things he'd seen and done. His anger was mainly reserved for himself. He thought himself better than his peers, a man of morals and courage, yet so often in this new world he had stood by and done nothing. Whilst he did not participate in the brutality exhibited by so many of his kin, he knew, in his heart, that he had done little to stop it.

Alfonso wondered if he would ever see his home again. A modest two-roomed house at the base of the Serranía de Cuenca. The wife he had barely gotten to know before his service began would probably be done with another day of her life. Tilling the fields, or worse, garnering attention from the men who stayed behind. He cast those thoughts aside, for now was not the time to wallow in self-pity.

The door to the villa hung from one hinge; the other had been sheared off upon his entry. The rooms were still painted with dried blood and ribbons of dead skin and sinew. Vinegary wine mingled with death and wrapped itself around him with no care or grace.

Kneeling by the place he had found Rodrigo, he recalled that he had arrived too late. The man had already been sent to God. No chance for valediction or rousing last words, just his insistence on the acquisition of gold over that of knowledge. Picking the folded piece of paper from his jerkin, Alfonso studied the text again.

It still didn't make sense, not wholly. References to a God and the retrieval of…dust from the deceased. It all sounded suspiciously like the word of Baphomet. Perhaps this was a test? He discarded the idea no sooner had it formed.

These men, this cult, they had clearly been working on this task for some time. The debris in the temple's basement was testament to that. How many had been stripped down to their essence this way? And the end purpose was as vague. The quipu made reference to Inti, the Inca Sun God, but little else. Were they to raise him? Form him in some way? It made his head hurt, and offended his personal beliefs.

The end result, regardless of what it was, could not be allowed to pass. Yet, he felt as though he owed these people something. The Inca had welcomed them with open arms, and they had taken this acceptance and met them with steel and fire. He had no doubt that soon their ways would not be their own. What would remain?

Tracing his fingers over the ridged channels of baked

on blood, he stumbled upon a solution. One that would ease his own mental struggle and counter the relentless materialistic acquisition of the late Rodrigo Quintaro.

Alfonso stood up and walked through to Rodrigo's bedroom. In front of the large window, which afforded breath-taking views of the valley below, stood a mannequin's torso adorned with his breastplate.

The crest of the Quintaro family had been formed on the front, and the craftsmanship was astounding. Alfonso removed the armour and rested it on the bed. Looking at the interior, he placed his dagger between two bonding plates and pried them open, exposing a cavity within.

Gently placing the parchment to his lips, he mumbled his own prayer of forgiveness and slid the paper into the gap. With it stowed away, he pressed the plates together again to forge the seal anew.

"Father, may the sins of these people and this man be forgiven." Alfonso heaved the armour back onto the wooden torso. "May you guard this knowledge and ensure that my lack of conviction does not damn us all."

Casting one last look at the breastplate, which caught the midday sun and reflected it back through the window, Alfonso closed the door and headed back outside.

The priest's screaming and yelling had given way to birdsong and hatred.

DUNCAN P· BRADSHAW

heXAgRAM

"Then rose from sea to sky the wild farewell!
Then shrieked the timid, and stood still the brave;
Then some leaped overboard with dreadful yell,
As eager to anticipate their grave;
And the sea yawned around her like a hell,
And down she sucked with her the whirling wave,
Like one who grapples with his enemy,
And strives to strangle him before he die."
— Lord Byron, 'Don Juan'

109,786 DAYS UNTIL THE END OF THE WORLD
PRESIDIO SANTA MARIA DE GALVE,
PENSACOLA, FLORIDA, USA
23 JULY 1716

DUNCAN P· BRADSHAW

CoNFESSIoN

Padre, thank you, I hoped you would reach here in time. I wanted to make sure that I spoke to a conduit of God, especially after everything that happened.

I expect that *they* have told you of the things that transpired, of the bodies they found and the...other allegations against me.

Did you know that it was exactly a year ago today since we were all in Cuba? Have you ever been?

No?

There is no place I'd rather be than Havana in summertime. Especially after being at sea for so long; the solace and calm is breathtaking. Truly, it was a harbour of respite. The demons were crawling over me by then, and why would they not be? For two years we had been sailing aimlessly around the Caribbean, trying to stay one step ahead of the English and those damned privateers.

We were supposed to be gone a matter of months. Catarina was waiting for me. I think of her, even now, wondering...hoping, that she still checks at Cartagena for my return.

Alas, that is not to be. We both know that I will never return home, not even my...

No. Not yet. I HAVE SO MUCH TO SAY. Where do

I begin Padre? The things I've seen, the veil has been ripped away and the hidden design revealed to me.

Is this truly the work of God?

Or something else?

These questions have plagued me night and day since the discovery of those words.

WHAT MUST I DO PADRE?

"Begin at the beginning my son. Tell me of the storm."

WRECK

Of course, a thousand apologies, your grace. My mind and wits have been through the wringer since we left Cuba. So much has passed. My ship, El Señor San Miguel, was one of a dozen. What was a simple charge, to collect his majesty's treasure from the new world, became a constant game of thrust and parry.

We were harried as soon as we arrived here. The Nuestra San Tinto was grievously damaged and boarded. We were only spared the same fate by the crew of the Nuestra putting up a stern fight. Those poor bastards bought us the time we needed to escape. Even now I pray for those men. Yet in some perverse way, had we been ruined, then at least I would not be here now. With this burden.

We departed Havana, and headed up the coast. A risky move for sure, but the weather was set fair. We encountered no ill omen or curse; the mood was joyous.

We were going home.

I had made Catarina a promise. Six months, no more. If she would only check the docks upon my return, I would marry her. Yet fate cast me upon the waves fourscore that tally. I still had hope though. Those nights in your bunk when all you have are your thoughts. They consume you from within. Talons of doubt and futility pry loose the floorboards of your sanity. Tugging and heaving on those strands of hope. For sure, I was at my lowest ebb before I got the news of our homecoming.

Our journey up the coastline was hazardous, but only if the weather turned sour. The first five days were near perfect. Meat was still edible. We even had shore parties forage for fresh supplies. The rum flowed freely and we had not a single care in the world.

On the sixth day…well, that was when Hell visited us.

The Griffon must have had some oracle bones to divine the future, for the previous night, the French headed out further east. We mocked them and left them to it; they were always the first to skirt peril or a fight.

By morning, the winds had picked up and were lashing over the starboard side. The sails fell slack one minute, the next, they were in danger of being ripped free. The mood had become sullen. Some even lamented Captain General Ubilla for not following the craven French.

As each hour dragged by, the wind grew and grew. Finally, by mid-afternoon, Ubilla at last ordered us to sail into the wind. One by one, the fleet turned and fought to free itself of the invisible shackles.

Night fell early, tentacles of lightning crackled in the heavens, the wind turned savage, howling into our skulls as if the devil himself was lambasting us.

I remember Filipe Garcia simply cast himself into the ocean, having shouted at some invisible spectre for nigh on three hours. Despite many attempts, no man could stir him from his internal fight. He hit the surface and disappeared within the frothy brine.

Throughout the night we fought to wrest control from nature. We lurched this way and that, desperately groping for the edge of the storm and sanctuary. Yet all we found was despair and anguish. Hector and Roberto were swept overboard as they fought with the rudder.

Jonas was garrotted as he sparred with the rigging. His still thrashing body was borne aloft. Even through the black night, you could see his eyes bulging from his skull. Cold fingers clawed at the rope, trying to extricate himself. The wind swung him from side to side as if he were a child's mistreated ragdoll. His body was dashed time and again against the masts. Arms and legs became misshapen, bent into unholy ways. His screaming finally stopped as the rope snapped, and he was flung into the deadly swirling storm.

Everyone was spent, fingers slipped as they tried to quell ropes and cling to life. Splinters found their way through the skin and itched beneath. The deck was awash with foam and blood. As the ship listed from side to side, I thought of Catarina, and how I would soon die, and it would be my turn to wait.

For her.

As I prepared for God to take me unto His holy kingdom, I heard an almighty rapturous crash. As I flew forward, I remarked to myself of my weightless form, before the darkness consumed me whole.

I awoke not to His holy choir singing, but to the sound of gulls braying and fighting. Through weary eyes I looked up and saw the sun hanging low in the sky. The warmth caressed me like my mother used to. Its rays stroked my face and I could taste the salt on my lips.

Sitting up, I saw that I had been discarded onto a beach like a piece of flotsam or seaweed. Strewn around me were barrels of provisions and items of clothing. I could see mounds formed into the sand. Crawling towards the nearest one, on knees rent open from my ejection, I came upon a hand jutting from beneath the sand.

Such a peculiar thing.

Fingers arranged as if they were a creature's ribcage pointed skywards. The fingernails had been plucked off and the meat underneath had been picked clean. Nubs of pristine bone glinted back at me. It was then I realised that the mound before me was not some kind of jettisoned cargo, but poor Umberto Gallasi.

We had fought once. In a bar in Port au Prince. The reason as to why I can no longer recall. We were both quite drunk and scrapped on the floor until the Captain separated us. Since then we had uttered nothing more than primal grunts or snorts. Yet, to see him so was quite repellent. I scraped the beach from him and it revealed a back shorn of clothing. Lacerations and deep grooves had been visited upon his form. Some were so deep that they exposed the internal framework of the poor fellow.

Ha, if I knew then what I know now, would I have left him so? Probably not. I did become quite preoccupied in my task, to the point where it did, I believe, strip me bare and consume me whole.

Much like poor Umberto's fingers.

Looking out to sea, I saw vast sections of the ship arranged on jagged rocks. The poor girl's belly had been ripped to shreds. Her innards slopped out through brutal gashes in her side. I remember the rocks sparkled from the sun.

As I waded out to her, I strode past more of the crew. Floating upside down as if they were the bait in a macabre fishing contest. The rocks were slippery and sharp, and made short work of my boots, but I deduced that I could easily find some more from the poor wretches I had seen. The sparkling had me in its thrall, and I was unable to do anything except discover the source.

Crawling over the rocks like a crab, I saw that I had finally arrived. As I thrust my hand through the surface, the water mixed with my blood, giving it the appearance of liquid amber.

Pulling the sparkles free, I looked down upon a fistful of silver reales. I laughed, for I knew that we would be saved. Our lives may be forfeit, but no man would leave this treasure. With my senses returned and a semblance of hope restored, I vowed to search the ship.

SCAVENGE

Do you know the true nature of man, Padre?

I guess someone like you would say that man possesses potential, goodness, and virtue.

I would then ask you another question. What is man's nature when they are in a situation where they believe they should be dead?

As I searched the ship, twice I was accosted by men I knew. They had been driven mad by the incalculable thought that they were dead and already living in Hell. In their eyes I saw something so utterly base and primal that I would suggest it is easier to resort to those emotions than it is to convince ourselves that we are anything other than animals.

They saw me as denizens of that accursed place, convinced utterly that I was there to lay claim to their soul.

Twice I was attacked.

Twice I had to kill.

The first was Enrique Polazzo, the cook. His arms had been gouged so badly that the muscle bulged with no skin to burden it. Were it not for his desperate swing, I would have been like the others I found after I strangled him with my bare hands. They had been clubbed to death and there were teeth marks running up and down their necks.

The second was more of a mercy killing, but only when poor David had launched himself at me with murderous intent. I snapped his leg as he went past me, and he howled like a lame horse. His cries tore at my sensibilities and I could stand it no more. I crushed his skull with a bronze orb, plundered from some bedevilled temple.

I remember looking at the object in my hand after his head had been breached, and watched as pink worms of brain wriggled through the cracks. Some idol from a far off land looked back. David's blood pooled in the recesses of the false God's face. I remarked to myself how it looked as though it was crying crimson tears. As I discarded it to the broken mid-deck, I swear a voice from within begged me to kill again.

There were survivors scattered inside the wreck. I consoled those entrenched in sorrow, and counselled those who struggled with the quirk of fate. To each I made mention of the beach, that they should gather as many provisions as their current form would allow and make for safety. Who knows how long the beached vessel would remain intact? Another bout of hurricane or titanic waves would find any who sheltered within and they would live no more.

Before I knew it I was by the Captain's door. It was as if I had been spirited there by mysterious suggestion. I rapped upon the door and admit I was glad when I had no reply. The door was partially braced from within, but my emaciated body managed to easily gain entry to his chambers. My aching ribs grazed against the sodden frame and tore further at my sallow skin.

The pistol shot rang around my head, shaking my

fearless endeavour to the core. I heard the wooden frame splinter behind me as the ball struck it vehemently. Captain Rino cursed and made to reload his weapon. As my panic-filled eyes searched the room, I saw that he was trapped beneath an oak desk. The edge was buried deep within his groin and the bottom half of his legs were arranged as if he were preparing for birth.

Instinct kicked in, and not a moment too soon. I charged the stricken man and struck him across the face with my balled fist. It caught him atop a recently formed welt and must have pained him dearly as he yelped like a wounded deer.

The pistol skittered across the floor and came to rest beneath a pile of soiled laundry. I made to strike him again, but his battered face and deflated appearance robbed me of any ability to inflict further pain.

The room itself was in a terrible state. The distant horizon, met by both water and sky, looked back at me through a vast hole where the starboard windows used to be.

I had only been in his cabin once before, and it was the reason for my return. Ignoring both his pleas for assistance and the oddly placed vista, I walked across to the turned over wardrobe and prayed it would still be there.

My heart leapt with joy when I discovered it.

Hidden beneath dress shirts and long johns, there it was: the cuirass which had caught my eye, back when I supped upon coconut rum and tore at meat jerky all those months ago. Using a pair of starched trousers I buffed the surface to a mirror sheen. The crest, formed by expert hands, appeared to come to life before me. The lion's head growled at the gazelle beneath, their infinite chase resumed, despite the years of their display.

It felt weighty, as though the previous owner's respect and might had somehow seeped into the metal. As the light danced upon its surface, I detected faint nicks and scratches, no doubt from a fight of suitable majesty.

I remember the captain laughing then. His words mocked me, saying that I was nothing more than a common criminal. That I was not worthy to have such an item bestowed upon me through noble means.

I must confess to you, Padre, I was no saint when I enlisted into his majesty's navy. That my decision to leave Spanish shores was an enforced exile rather than a voluntary pursuit. Yes, I knew of thieves and of criminal ways, but I was reformed.

In this matter, too, I had no choice. I *had* to have that cuirass. As I affixed it to my meagre frame, his mocking increased. For the briefest of moments, when it was finally in place, everything shrunk from view.

The sun waxed, then waned, and the captain's words fell silent; the world itself stuttered to a pause.

Just for the briefest of moments.

When I stirred from my reverie, the captain was beneath me. His neck had been snapped to one side. The brittle bones beneath his skin were jutting out as if they were the wooden frame to a cathedral. His fat purple tongue hung to one side and his eyes, previously full of disdain, now contained only fear of the void beyond.

I retrieved his pistol and made to leave. As I removed the debris prohibiting the exit, I knew what must be done. I would rally the men, we would scavenge. We would hunt.

We would hold out until greed summoned our salvation.
Alas, fate had something else in store for us all.

SAVAGES

I'm sure you are aware of the people of this land? The ones who were here before us? The primitives? Though that word does them a great disservice. Yes, they lack our industry and skill at fabricating items, but they make up for it with something else entirely.

Pure…unbridled…faith.

This is their land, Padre. We are but guests upon it, and unwelcome ones at that. I had heard the stories from my father, of the glorious conquests of the Americas centuries before. As we washed over them like a tide forged of fire and steel. Nothing they had, and nothing they could do, could stop us.

We crushed them utterly, yet their ways endured.

The ship remained stricken upon the rocks for six days. Slowly, but inexorably, the wash and our desperation caused it to split in two. By now, we had plundered most of the hold. Chests laden with gold, silver, and all manner of equity was piled into a nearby cave. This was also our home. Thirty seven of us remained, from a crew of one hundred and twelve. Upon our beaching, some had taken the opportunity to forge life anew, to start again in a land which knew not of their name or their sins.

It was the day after the last of the ship had cracked and

splintered upon the sea that we found the first of them.

Fabio was foraging for food, as there was little to sustain us. We had encountered some feral animals: cats, dogs, rats. Some took more coaxing than others, but each was easily despatched and prepared. As our bellies grumbled, we heard frantic shouting. I had appointed myself leader of the group, as no one else had the stomach for such a burden. What fool would lead the broken?

He came running out of the scrub brandishing a neatly formed pole. Impossible he could have claimed it from a tree in such a state. The end was fat like a club, but as he got closer, we realised what was making him shriek so. The bloated head of one of the crew was jammed on top. The wood ably replaced the structure of his neck and spine. Dead eyes looked up as if a joke had been made in poor taste. Fabio stuck the grisly totem into the beach to display his find to us.

The poor devil's hair and scalp had been removed. The bone itself was cracked where an implement of some kind had crudely stamped a shape approximate to the poor man's hairline. The skin by his forehead was ragged as if, after slicing the skin, it was ripped off as some kind of distasteful trophy.

We spent a good hour trying to discern the identity of the man. His face was slick with dried blood and fluids I know not the name of. His ears had been removed. From the marks around the base of where they once resided, it looked like this was the mark of a hungry animal, not man.

The tongue too had been removed. Again, the jagged ridges of flesh suggested that it had been pulled out with some force. Though none said it aloud, heads were bowed in hope that this had not befallen him while he was still alive.

In the end, it was Fabio, the most imbalanced of us at the time, who managed to identify him as Alessandro Henrique, one of the tiller men. Finding a patch of land with soil as its base, we buried what little remained of him.

The mood in the cave grew dark. Hushed whispers were abound. Rumours of cloven-hoofed beasts bearing axes crackling with flame, seeking the souls of the damned, were rife. Many swore blind that they had seen these monsters prowling around at night. Shimmering eyes, like moonlight on a still lake, watching our every move, waiting for a chance to pick us off, one by one.

The truth, as is usual, was far less fanciful. Four days later we were awoken to a wall of hooting and jabbering. Stirred from my fitful slumber, I staggered to the cave entrance and was greeted by five riders on horseback.

Each wore a solemn face, devoid of emotion or haste. Painted on their bodies were large birds with claws that scratched the sky. Fire danced behind the animals and human skulls were intricately inked onto their shoulders.

The one at the front pointed at me, and spat forth words of impossible construction. His sermon was delivered at a loud but steady tone and proceeded for a good minute or two. When he was done, the others beat their fists against their chests, echoing his final unintelligible phrase.

As I struggled to comprehend the noise, the leader brought forth a coarsely-woven bag which straddled his horse's back. Reaching within, he withdrew strips of skin and hair and cast them onto the sand before me. I recoiled from the ghastly sight. Bile burned the back of my throat as I fought to keep it within. The savage pointed at the curling scraps of flesh, then to my men, and finally to me, before drawing a blood-stained finger across his throat.

With a grunt, he rallied his steed and they took off, down the beach and into the forest which bordered our vision.

I kneeled by the vile offering and picked through it with a dagger. Each patch bore similarities to the decapitated head of Señor Henrique, which Fabio had discovered previously. As night fell, we huddled around a fire which struggled with the sea air and discussed what we should do.

We had few weapons: a small number of pistols, some muskets, yet little to no ammunition that had not been spoiled by the ravages of our disastrous arrival upon this land.

Of other armaments, each man had some kind of hand weapon; mainly daggers or crudely-formed spears which we had used to catch the animals that ventured near our camp.

The debate lurched from desperation to anger, as each took a turn to venture their opinion. By the time everyone had been canvassed, it was evenly split between fleeing in smaller groups deep into the mainland, or to stand and fight.

The deciding vote was mine to make, and I made it without question.

'To acquiesce to these people would be to deny our Spanish heritage, to desecrate our noble history and spirit. Our ancestors set forth upon the world to discover new lands and enjoy their bounty. The cargo we had spent the past two years, collecting and hiding from the English, belongs to his majesty. To abandon it would not only be an act of treason, it would damn us all to uncertainty.

No man, especially of noble blood, would allow this treasure to be stolen by our enemies, whether known or unknown.

Our only hope of salvation, and of certain return to Spain, would be to remain by the cargo we had so diligently retrieved from the razor-sharp rock and the shallow ocean lapping against our weary legs.

To die for one's country is an honour. But to die to protect your brothers and their dignity is one which few could countenance.

We stay.
We fight.
For Spain!'

B∧TTLE

Such honeyed words, your Grace. I must confess that it did stir even the most reluctant of the crew, and though a handful left in the night, we still numbered thirty two by the break of dawn.

We were to use the terrain to our advantage. The ocean to one side, coated with its hide of jagged rock, and a steep hill from our cove which led to a forest on the other, meant there was only one way we could be assaulted.

The best marksmen were tasked with getting to the high ground above the cave entrance, and to secrete themselves there. Even with a handful of shot available, I hoped that the shock of such weaponry upon the primitives would shake their fighting spirit. The men hurried to their positions and ensconced themselves within the bushes atop our home.

Victory or defeat rested on negating their one main advantage. Those infernal horses. If we were able to funnel them towards the cave entrance, we could fight them one on one, and our odds would increase significantly.

I knew of two methods to deal with cavalry, and both were from the scattered teachings of my father. Besides drinking, he cared a great deal about war and the art of killing. From memory, the first was fire; the second,

64

wooden stakes, driven into the ground.

From the poor efforts at making the evening campfires, I discarded the idea of fire immediately. We were seaborne men, apparently incapable of surviving on firm ground. This left stakes. A forest bordered the beach and I despatched a number of the more burly men to fetch as many sturdy branches as possible.

By midday, we had enough for our purposes, though the heat was taking its toll. Whilst the foraging crew rested, myself and the others prepared the logs by forming fiendish points at one end and thrusting them into the firmer ground around the cave entrance. Luckily we could work in the shade of our sanctuary, and whilst others slept or organised our meagre provisions, we slaved away on our preparations.

We were ready with not a moment to spare. A lookout we had posted announced the arrival of the locals. Their numbers had swollen since the previous day and my heart missed several beats before finding resolve within. If we stuck to the plan, we would prevail, of that I was certain. As we scurried behind our rushed fortifications, we waited to see what they would do.

Just under a dozen men had managed to salvage some armour from the ship before it fell apart. It was not as magnificent as the one I had procured, but it did at least provide some protection. Or so we thought.

The armoured men took to the fore, brandishing the few swords we had. They yelled curses learned from the mouths of dockyard workers, and some which even I had never heard uttered. Building in bravado, they clattered the hilts against their breastplates. With the cave acting as a conch, it built to a crushing crescendo.

Yet still they stood. Proud warriors looked down at our pitiful efforts with disdain. Their leader, resplendent in a plumed head dress and armour fashioned from nature, raised some kind of stick to the heavens.

The men girded themselves for a charge of primal ferocity. Yet from them came only silence. The mood changed and the men ceased their baiting as one. From behind the host came forth a swarm of elongated flies, whistling and streaking through the air like a celestial body.

It was only when the first arrow pierced Julio's armour, and he called for his mother, that I, and the rest of the survivors, realised that we had sorely underestimated these people.

For years, they have fought the invaders from Europe. Unlike us, with our arrogance and hubris, they had learned how to overcome the challenges that we presented them. They discovered quickly that fire-tempered arrows rendered our plate-mail completely ineffectual. Within the first salvo, seven of the eleven men bedecked in steel clutched their mortal wounds.

I ordered the men to seek cover behind the rocks. Their volleys could not then penetrate. The arrows clattered harmlessly against stone. Some that were fired short, however, peppered those who had been stricken initially and sealed them against the ground yet further.

Where once the cavern resonated with the clash of metal and defiance, it now rang with the screaming of the dying and the weak. Seeing our defence would nullify their horses; the riders dismounted and readied spears and tomahawks.

As they sallied forth, I saw that they were about to cross the line my mind had drawn where our firepower would come into its own. I allowed a smile to break my stoic features and strode forth, trying to encourage the savages to engage us faster.

As I neared the cave entrance, in line with the rows of spiked wood, I heard no crack of musket nor discharge of gunpowder. Fearing that the weapons had jammed, I looked upwards, seeking out the picket line placed above.

Instead of fire and iron raining down on the enemy, hacked appendages and torn offal cascaded from above, landing at my feet. A rope of intestine snaked silently from the ridge and slid down my cheek.

Hands removed at obtuse angles slapped against the ground. Heads, misshapen and cracked, hit the rocks surrounding me and rolled to my feet. Accusing eyes looked at me, certain that I had caused their doom.

From above, savages drenched in Spanish blood swung down on the entrails of the dead. Bloodied handprints covered their bodies as if they had been passed up from Hell itself. We were undone, and in that moment any notion I had of victory evaporated.

We had one option left to us: with the discovery of our abode, there were several passages to the rear which snaked this way and that. Of the many we discovered, we knew of two that did not end abruptly in a wall of stone. Neither were fully explored.

I shouted to the men to break and make for these channels, and hoped to God that we would be delivered from this place. As we ran past the piles of gold and riches, shots rang out from behind us. The primitives were using our own weapons against us.

Luck saved us as they were poor shots, and only a couple of our number fell. Though as we divided down the rocky avenues, their screams as our attackers fell on them reminded us that fortune was a fickle mistress.

I was the last to enter the left passageway, and could hear frantic yells ahead of me. I prayed that we would not hit a dead end.

For what seemed like an eternity, foot was planted in front of foot, light faded and we had to make our way through whispers and fumbling in the dark. From time to time, someone would fall or strike their head on a low hanging stone lintel.

Eventually I heard a ripple of excitement from ahead of me. Sure enough we made it to the outside world again. The night was a deep blue. The swollen moon welcomed us back to reality. I counted a dozen men sprawled upon the sand, and not one was unharmed.

I ordered them to search where we had exited for another passage, to try and help those who had taken the other route. As they reluctantly explored for such a way, I heard a guttural roar from behind me. One of the savages had made his way through.

As I turned to face him, I saw the captain's loaded pistol in his hand. As he bore down on me, I saw a flash of light. My chest buckled and I fell to the floor. Feeling the icy tendrils of the other world paw at me, I closed my eyes and gave in to them.

REVELATION

I awoke not with a mild rousing, but with a vast intake of breath. 'Twas as if my lungs had ceased to operate whilst I was in the cradle of limbo. I remember little of my time there; no familiar face or recognisable figure did I witness. Just the certainty of nothingness and an itching behind my eyes.

A few of the men, whose faces swam in front of me, pulled me up gently. I took in the scene and saw a number of my brothers blockading our escape route with logs and boulders, desperate to halt those murderous bastards. A short distance away lay the man I recalled instantly—the savage who had shot me.

Thoughts tumbled down my brain and I patted my body numbly. Feeling that I still had the cuirass on, I laughed when I plucked the pistol ball from the crater created within the plate. Thanking God, I forced myself to my feet, though regretted my folly immediately. I staggered as if I was inebriated, lurching from foot to foot.

As I steadied my senses, I looked around and saw that our numbers were the same as before. I asked the men if any sign of the others had been detected. Their glum faces and mumbled words told me that we were now on our own.

My survival instinct kicked in. To stay here would be our downfall. We had not gone through disaster and battle to stand here idly whilst death stalked us. I admit that I had to suppress the pain in my ribs whilst I did so, but I climbed on top of the dead native and commanded the men to follow me. We would forge a path through the forest and find civilisation. I commented that with our numbers reduced we would require less sustenance and make a smaller din.

Though they were weary and not fully pliable, the men agreed that to stay would be suicide. After gathering up what we could from the beach, I cast a final glance at the sealed cavern, uttered a private valediction, and led the men away from the site.

The day grew long and endless. We stumbled over root and clattered into branch. Insects, drawn to our melancholy, ran over our sweaty necks and jabbed us with needle-like snouts. Within hours our spirit, already dangerously slack, was a yoke around all of our necks. As night fell, we chanced upon a small clearing.

We all knew that to camp there would be foolish, but logic had deserted us. After tasking a few of the more alert crew to sentry duty, I leant back against the trunk of a hollowed out tree and fell into a sorrowful introspection.

As I wallowed in our misfortune, I saw that one of the metal plates within the cuirass had buckled from the shot. I chuckled to myself, realising that I had located the source of my shortness of breath. After a brief remonstration, I unbuckled my armour and set about investigating how I could repair the damage.

My cold fingers fumbled at the crevice, and though I

grazed my clumsy digits against the metal, I felt something within. At once, my mind raced with questions; was this some form of indigenous animal that had burrowed inside, ready to ambush me when I was at rest? Perhaps it was mere padding, and the reason why I still breathed? These, and more fanciful notions, were dismissed as I retrieved a folded piece of paper from the vacuum.

For the first time since I had…*acquired* the armour, it vanished from my thoughts. Even the trees, the distant water splashing against the shore, the buzzing and clicking insects, all of it, melted away, as if a cleansing fire had been applied to them.

It was brittle, and I dearly wanted to not sully the one thing that was fresh and vibrant in my world at that moment. Peeling it open with the touch of a tender lover, I saw an elegant and refined hand had made this note. I had to stifle a chuckle as I noted that it was written in Spanish. I was awash with even more questions. Who was this person? What seditious words could they have possibly birthed which warranted it being hidden so?

Age and condition had robbed some of the message, but enough was there for more questions to swim around my mind. It was as though someone had written down a recipe and list of instructions.

It made mention of something which was inside all of creation. A residue, or powder, which was formed from the birth of the world and each star in the sky. It seemed fantastical. Preposterous even. Thereafter followed suggestions on how it could be removed. Some of the passages were missing, but enough was legible to make out '…dead…', '…divine from within…', '…sacrifice…' and the word which stood out the most, '…Inti…'

My father, the consummate drunk, was equally fascinated by cultures. Our family, though not well off, has formed the backbone of Imperial conquest over the centuries. Tales have been passed down from father to child for time immemorial. Of savages killing the young. Drinking the blood of the innocent, and removing still-beating hearts from the chests of the willing.

Also, the stories of Gods.

The primitives had many. Some were guardians or harbingers of death. Others, when offered a tribute, would make crops grow or fatten animals. Amongst them there was one who was master above all others. Inti, the Sun God, the most sacred of their false idols.

My mind ran free with this notion. Whilst I had no faith in the deities of people who could not even master our crafting and language, I knew one thing we could do with on our side right now was the one thing the recent events had shaken my belief in.

God.

What if…it is madness to utter these words aloud, Padre, and for that I apologise. You must remember my state at the time. My limits and internal borders were encroached upon. I needed something, a foothold in the world.

What if it were *true*?

What if God and the very dust of our creation resided in us all along?

Reading on, the sentences suggested that by harvesting enough of this dust, one could invoke God to come to this realm. He would be born in flesh and blood, yet still magnificent and apart from us.

He could right the wrong and truly deliver us from this place.

He could take me home. To Catarina. He could make her *love* me.

But to do this, I needed to see…inside…I had to prove these words to be true.

I had to know.

INSIDE

Though it pressed against my mind night and day, the focus in those early days was evasion. I am sure now, with hindsight, that our attackers ceased their pursuit as soon as we had vacated their land. But fear is an all-consuming habit, and so it was with us.

Murderous shadows loomed tall and lurched at us within the forest. Sounds of animals were misjudged to be growling or clumsy assailants. Our wits were at a frayed end, and we were glad when we finally reached the plains.

With a river to one side, we trekked overland for weeks. We survived off the land and were beginning to adapt to the conditions. In time, our pace slowed and we allowed ourselves a release of tension.

All the while, the words played around in my head. When I was certain that I was alone, I would read them again, although I knew each character and inflection off by heart. What dismayed me the most was details of the method. If this dust was inside us, how was it fathomed?

I envisaged the acquisition of enough dust to summon God would be vast. Though dimensions of the receptacle were present, what if only a small amount was present in each person? In time, I managed to deal with it in a more pragmatic way. Until I was able to discover the answers to these questions myself, I would bide my time in other ways.

It is fair to say that my obsession with the parchment managed to assuage my guilt over Catarina. It was only when I saw *her* that I realised I had forsaken my distant lover.

By then, we dozen spoke of creating a camp, a place to call home. We knew that to strike out for the coast again would most likely result in death or disillusionment. Over a fire one night we spoke excitedly of how we could fabricate simple huts and allocate tasks. It was strange to speak of such things. The time we had spent wandering the countryside after the wreck was sombre and sullen. Whether it was our collective guilt, or the realisation that we would never see our beloved Spain again, I know not.

But we now had purpose. We had something to live for again.

And then, like that, everything changed. We awoke the next morning and decided that we would form our new settlement right where we were. We had everything that we required to hand. Stout trees nestled along the base of hills, water was a short carrying distance away, yet far enough that, if it should flood, we would be safe.

I was foraging the riverbank to see if I could make clay. Ha, we had such grandiose ideas. I had no idea what I was doing, but believed that with some application, anything was possible. I pottered idly along the shore, stopping at points to scoop handfuls of mud, testing its viscosity. I'd mix it with dry reeds and moss to see if it held together and offered any promise.

As I cast aside the latest effort, which squished

between my sodden fingers at the slightest increase in pressure, I heard a lilting voice. Ducking down into the tall reeds, I listened again to try and discern where it was coming from.

I listened intently, and heard it once more. I recognised the guttural tongue from the natives that had routed us so thoroughly. But whilst his voice was harsh and obtuse, this one was like a breeze. The same words were melodic and enchanting. I crept towards it, enraptured by the siren's soft call.

Before me, a primitive woman was washing what looked like rags in the river. Her back was to me, and I could see a swathe of cloth across her back. It was pulled tightly and cut into her otherwise pleasing form. Droplets of water glistened on her exposed arms and neck. The sun, trapped within, winked, rolled down her soft skin, and plinked back into the water.

My fascination was my undoing. Unable to contain myself and take in the lady's song, I stood upon a stick, snapping it in twain. Instantly, the song fell silent. The native stopped stock-still. Hands, in the process of wringing out water from a thick rug, stopped.

She turned around, and her beauty matched her voice. Her eyes blazed like stoked embers, her lips trembled ever so slightly, full of trepidation. Black hair was plaited and draped across one shoulder. The end looked like a shaving brush waiting to be used.

Enamoured, I stood up. I must have been quite the sight. Hands covered in drying mud, unshaven and insect bitten, a battered and scratched metal cuirass still clinging to my skeletal frame.

The next two things happened so quickly that even now I am unsure as to the exact order they occurred in.

There most certainly was a scream, a complete contrast to the dulcet tones emerging from her body moments before. And there was also blood. When time started again, the space she existed previously was bereft of her presence.

As I looked to the ground, I saw my filth-covered hands holding my dagger, now running freely with blood that was not my own. The thickening crimson liquid mixed with the dried earth, forming a crusting paste. Beyond my disgusting hands, the woman was lying down on the floor, her fingers pressed to a wound in her neck.

Instead of water, the sun was now trapped within bloody red orbs that flecked her hands. No singing now from her pale lips, just a gurgling as if she were blowing air into a goblet of tar.

I knelt down next to her trembling body. As I went to staunch the flow of blood, she shot me a look of pure venom. Her hands batted mine away. Though I tried again, she scratched at my face, jagged nails scraping through my beard and gouging my cheeks. Her strength faded, and soon she fell slack. Her head dropped to her shoulder and finally the grisly gasping ceased.

As her final breath was expelled, I heard another sound. Muffled, yet close. My heart sunk, and that good man within shook his fist at me. Knowing what I would find, yet pleading within that it was not true, I turned the woman over onto her back. Tied to her chest in a hide pouch was a squinting child, orphaned by my hand.

The signals which would normally control my body

stopped and I wilted to the floor as if my bones had been removed by witchcraft. As I fell, the child awoke and started to call for its mother. I am ashamed to say what I did next, Padre. For as much as the woman's death was instinctual, the murder of the child was wholly known to me.

'Tis an awful thing to look into innocent eyes, those who have yet to find their level, and to watch that life become extinguished.

I came to, and the horror was still there. No dream was this; it was a nightmare made real. At once, the voice in my head, which had been patiently waiting, spoke.

No.

I do not think the word *speak* is adequate for what came out, for I said it aloud.

It was a command.

It demanded I look inside.

I still clutched the knife. By now it felt as though it was a part of my hand, such was the mix of matter which had combined to form this grisly mortar. I ran the knife across the hide strap and severed the maternal bond with her child. I did at least offer a prayer for their souls, no doubt hell-bent on my end, perhaps slowly and under torturous means. Laying the baby's body in the grass, I paused, hovering over the woman's form.

Something took over me, as if my limbs were guided by an expert puppeteer. I was a spectator the first time, though I would not stay in that role for long.

The knife cut through her clothing with ease. Flakes of her dried blood came loose as the blade glided through the deer hide. Her naked body was revealed, yet no carnal yearnings did it create.

I plunged the knife into her chest and worked my way towards her pelvis. As the skin parted, revealing the viscera beneath, a wave of warm air washed over me.

I scratched at the bloody cement rooting the weapon into my hand and, unburdened, started to haul her meat from the cavity I'd created. For a moment my addled mind was lost. Now that I had removed the slippery organs from within, slick with her blood, I realised how infinitesimally small we all are.

Yet that thought, though it threatened to dwarf me and engulf me like the kraken, reaffirmed my desire to know.

I took a sack of meat in my hands. No surgeon am I, but it was one of a pair. I tore at a meaty tube and separated one from the other. With ravenous thirst, I ripped at the fibrous membrane, gouging at the avenues of nature contained within. Yet after a few moments, and having rent it apart so utterly that it was laid bare, I could find nothing. No dust. No divinity. *Nothing.*

Anger lapped at my consciousness. I had let this foolish notion drive me to such barbarism, and for what? To trust in a piece of paper which had plainly been hidden as some form of jest.

With balled fists, I pounded the remnants of the organ. As it turned to a lumpy paste, a twinkling caught my eye. I took my knife and gingerly scraped away at the vile concoction. As I spread the pulp, I saw tiny specks of glittery powder within.

I broke down and cried. This was not meant to be seen by human eyes. We're not meant to discern the workings of a power so great; that although made in His image, we fall foul of repellent wants and desires.

Daring to touch it, it felt as plain as a grain of sand. Yet somehow, it was imbued with something comforting, and sinister at the same time.

Having seen these sights, I knew there was no going back. I would continue. I would harvest the woman and her child. Storing the handful of precious dust in a small pouch I found tied to the dead native, I worked as fast as I could. The men could not know of this. No one could know of this. I washed my hands in the stream, placed the baby's skin and bones inside his mother once more. I then filled the hollow carcass with rocks, and pitched the reunited pair into the water.

I knew that their disappearance would be noted, so upon my return I made some excuse as to the unsuitability of the site. We gathered the items procured during the day and made our way further upstream.

The harvesting had begun. Without the container created, I did not know how much I required. But I knew that God was on my side.

VALEDICTION

"So where is this parchment, my son? A great deal of good could come from—"

Padre, please, I have yet to complete my tale. I doubt even a man as virtuous as you would want to possess something which drove me to such extremes.

May I continue?

Our camp was set up with ease. Within a few weeks each man knew their tasks and duties to act as a necessary member of our little community. We spoke less of home and more of our plans for our new lives. Perhaps we could gather enough supplies to strike out for a town? Though, at heart, the freedom we experienced on the sea, or at least the perception of liberty, always told us to stay where we were.

Sure, we encountered hardships, and fights were commonplace. But that is to be expected amongst men. Our habitat was also only a few miles from a native camp. And that allowed me to continue with my charge. Aside from women, I was able to kill a few men. They were too preoccupied with the hunt, blissfully unaware that I was hunting them.

I had started to hone my craft. I ensured that they

suffered little, for the eyes of the mother and child still plagued my dreams. They bore within my soul and poked and prodded at the coward hiding within. The one who abhorred their demise, though instead of fighting the monster I had become, that coward chose to shy away.

A stiletto blade I managed to procure from one of my fellows made the perfect tool. With one hand clamped over their mouth, I would drive the pointed blade through the temple and into the brain. Though I yearned to get my hands on the squishy mass within, it would be an undertaking which would cost much time. I did not have the implements to quickly crack open the skull. The one time I used the hilt of my dagger, my hands were bruised for days, and the face of the native bore too many marks which pointed to the violence of man.

The blade to the brain worked quickly and, after a brief struggle, I would disrobe them. I made sure I searched their garments as they often had many useful items within. After the search, I would fold the items together, ready to dispose of in the fire late at night.

Sheathing the stiletto, I would use my dagger to slice open the belly of the harvested. I made sure to skirt around the navel, for it is a tough piece of flesh and can ruin the efficiency of the task. With my hands, I would then pull open the flaps of skin. It felt so warm and sticky within the interior of the body, as if a gentle furnace was cooling.

Reaching up the inside of the ribcage, with fingers touching the shoulder-blades, I would pull the meat and organs free from the bone. This task was messy and. after being covered in blood the first few times, I started to do this part shorn of my own clothing. It was easier to wash my body or conceal the splashes than to explain again how I grazed my body fulfilling my menial tasks.

Once it was removed from the carcass, I would drag the shell of the person to a nearby tree and bind them to low branches. Using my knife once more, I would carve angular symbols and marks upon the profaned flesh. The final act would be to cut the tendrils holding the eyes in place and pull them from their skull caverns so they looked at the ground. I then pulled the tongue out of the mouth and hacked it off as if it had offended me. I discarded this into the grass as an offering to some passing animal.

My aim was to prey on these people, their sense of faith and affinity with nature. I knew that they relayed stories of monsters dwelling in the world, and I sought to make these come to life. By the time I was done, it looked like no sane man could've mutilated this person in such a way.

Honestly, Padre?

I was beginning to *enjoy* it.

I was only able to go out for a few hours, every week or so. As time went on, I hungered for the next body as soon as I had returned to camp, laden with my haul of mundane items.

Once the body was displayed, I took the meat and sought refuge. I discovered a shallow trench, which I was able to cover with branches and weeds. In time, nature snaked its vines over my roof and flowers grew from the puddles of blood and tissue dotting the area.

I became concerned that the parchment, already fragile with age and my handling, would be irreparably damaged and that should I descend further into madness, I would forget the words. So from a victim, I removed the skin completely from their back.

Remembering a trick from a week in the brig—after I was accused, falsely, of stealing bread—I began to tattoo the words onto the cured skin. Whilst slow-going, I found it settled my nerves and allowed me to uncover sections of the text I had either ignored, or deemed lost to the ravages of time. I stored this within a skull I kept from a rather large native, whom I managed to kill with remarkable ease, given his size.

This study allowed me to discern some more of the instructions. I managed to obtain a wooden bowl from one of the local women who had been collecting fruit. After I claimed her insides, I carved ridges into the bowl. Taking handfuls of the meat, I pushed it into the centre of the bowl and kneaded it with my knuckles. Years of seasoning from the sun and salt had formed them into two orbs of granite.

Once the paste had formed, I used the back of a spoon to smear the pulp up the ridges inside the bowl. This deposited the dust into its grooves. I repeated the process until I gathered all that I could. I had by now fashioned a pot from the riverbank's clay and stored the sacred powder in there, within the burrow. This had been made to the exacting measurements contained within the text.

I then collected the paste and scattered it through the forest on my way back with the firewood that I had gone out to gather.

Within a few months, though, the voices grew more demanding. Adding to the heap of dust every few weeks was not enough. I needed more. I needed it *now*.

I hatched a plan that would free me from my constraints. Upon my travails of the land, I happened upon a great many of the flora and fauna. One day I stumbled upon a dead dog, lying not five yards from a plant which had upturned trumpets hanging from its head. I found the same plant heads lodged within the dog's teeth.

I collected as many as my pockets would allow and headed back to camp. That evening I cooked a sumptuous stew containing fish, leaves, roots, and this plant. Making my apologies, I headed for my ramshackle abode and waited.

Within minutes I heard convulsing and retching. It was as if we were caught in our first storm and our stomachs had not adjusted for the tilting and lurching. I counted to one hundred and then made my way back to the men, my bowl tipped clean, as if I was going back for more.

They were scattered around the fire like seed pods in autumn. A thick white froth flecked with red had burst forth from their mouths. Eyes open wide with agony looked skywards, searching for forgotten family or a more pleasant memory.

I got to work immediately. Needing to not maim them as I did with the locals, I arranged them into a row. It was only when this was complete that I realised I was one short.

Sure enough, Jorge Wiles returned from his call of nature to discover his friends dead and me the sole survivor. At first I reasoned with him, that I too had wandered off and returned to find them in this state. He grew wary quickly. No story could I create that would allay his fears.

Jorge walked away quickly to his bed, and I knew that my ruse had failed. I followed a few paces behind, unable to catch him. He disappeared into his hovel and came out clutching that infernal pistol. Jorge warned me to stay away, said that he would fire if I attempted to stop him leaving. By now I had decided upon this course of action. Like our boat caught in the hurricane, I could not turn back.

Taking my chance with his aim, I rushed at him. The weapon discharged as my shoulder met his and I felt a thud connect with my collarbone. I realised immediately that I had been shot, though the damage was not severe. I seized the initiative. I stabbed him in the groin, into the blood carrying vessel there. Jorge released his hold on the weapon and it fell to the ground.

Looking deep into his eyes, I drew the blade up slowly, savouring his anguish, willing him to scream, to mirror the noise that echoed deep within me. I did not stop when I reached the bottom of his ribcage, and though I could feel his entrails emptying against my legs and feet, the blade continued its vertical path.

It finally ended when I hit his jawbone. His screams became a feeble collection of gasping, and his fingers scraped against my metal cuirass. As his throat opened up, the last of the fight went out of him, and I was alone. I realised then that I had something I had not possessed when I snared the locals.

Time.

This was also my undoing.

The soldiers arrived early the next morning. I was in

the process of smashing in the skull of Julio Campos with the stone hammer he used to build our shacks.

The look on their faces as they walked into the clearing, thinking that they were rushing to assist someone in peril, only to find a butcher's yard instead, is something forever engrained.

The shot which had cracked my collarbone—a fortuitous one, I might like to add, as it had struck me through the leather strap—had summoned them from a few miles away. They arrived to eleven dead bodies, five of which had been flayed and decapitated. The meat, sinew and head workings of each lay in a pile to one side, ready for harvesting.

Their captain strode amongst his men, still stricken by terror and shock at the sight that befell them. He took one look at me, then the bodies, before ordering his men to seize me. I tried to fight, but was no match for them.

So now, Padre, I am here. My trial was quick. I think there was little I could say or do to offer an alternative to my guilt. I asked but one thing of them: to confess my sins to a man of the cloth.

I thank you for that.

I go to my death now unfulfilled in my divine task, but unburdened by what I did.

Do I regret their deaths?

No.

I only regret that I allowed Jorge the time to get his weapon and bring these men unto me.

I am only sorry that I did not get to see the face of the God I was going to create.

"Tell me where this parchment is, I implore you."

No, Padre...Rodriguez, is it?

I can and will not. Though they seized the armour the parchment was originally stored within, neither you, nor they, will find it there. It is destroyed as my work in copying the text is complete. As for the location of the barrow with the skull, I will not divulge this either, even under the most terrible of torture.

If I cannot fulfil this mission, then no one can. I would advise you to purge everything that I have imparted to you. Only madness and catastrophe lie down that path. You serve a higher purpose, not one which relies on vulgar actions.

I realise now that we were not meant to create God, for He *is* the creator. To do so would be to blaspheme severely. Now if you'll excuse me, Padre, I do believe it is time for me to atone for my actions.

If you are to pray for me, pray that the rope snaps my neck as the trapdoor is opened and I am cast into the void, for I would not like to suffer.

Good day.

"The soul shall mightily rule in all hidden secrets:
but it must not let in the devil."
— Jakob Bohme

55,772 DAYS UNTIL THE END OF THE WORLD
MT. ZION CHURCH,
KOLB'S FARM, COBB COUNTY, GEORGIA, USA
22 JUNE 1864

DUNCAN P. BRADSHAW

1

Time slowed to a crawl as the artillery shell exploded in the midst of D Company. Chunks of molten shrapnel snaked their way through the displaced air, lacerating the men who were still in the act of reloading after their initial volley.

George was the first to die. Occupying the same spot as the explosion, his body was shredded into chunks of meat and sprayed over his comrades. Thick clumps of viscera splattered against the side of the wooden church and slid inexorably downwards. Another five men were incapacitated as limbs were slashed with bent metal hurtling out from the epicentre.

Rusty was at the end of the picket line, and whilst spared from the worst of the impact, he still shrieked in pain as a shower of razor-sharp metal raked his left shoulder. He dropped the rifle as the muscle in his arm was rendered useless. His agony-wracked body hit the floor moments after his weapon.

As his ears popped, time resumed its regular speed and the sound of the dying and lame lapped over the long grass. Rusty stared up at the evening sky. The stars were stirring from their slumber and a few brave ones winked down at him, blooming like a fine paintbrush dipped into a glass jar.

Memories of summer days spent painting the Chattahoochee river, with the picturesque hills lying behind it, played across his mind. Dragonflies danced in front of the canvas as he fought to capture the wonder of nature, to truly do it justice.

Truth was, he had grown irritated late in the day and, convinced that his work was not befitting such a vista, he had broken it over his knee and used it as the base for the evening's campfire. Though how he had managed to make this while inebriated on his papa's potent moonshine was quite the mystery.

War had taken everything from him. His brother had died the previous year at Gettysburg. Ever since then, it had been one setback after another. He could feel that the noose was closing round the south's neck; it was just a matter of time now, of that he was sure.

A trickle of liquid running down his own neck, interrupted his melancholy. Patting it with his hand, he knew it was blood. He was intimately familiar with its consistency, having tried, and on so many occasions, failed, to staunch the flow from wounded men. He shuddered unwittingly as he felt its tacky surface.

The river and countryside faded away and was replaced by the gully he had discovered his brother Ike in. A Yankee officer had run him through with a sabre. He was all but gone by the time Rusty had found him. His face as ashen as clean bed linen, crimson hands clutching at his midriff, fighting to hold in his guts. Lumps of shiny pink flesh bulged between his fingers. Rusty had laughed at first, thinking it some prank his elder brother was playing on him.

Always the joker. But then, and in the minutes before he passed, no joke or brotherly ribbing did he utter. Washed out eyes struggled to recall the face looking down on him, chapped lips mouthed a name, yet Rusty was unable to hear Ike's familiar lilting voice one last time.

Rusty held him close, until the end came. Since then, he'd been going through the motions. Something had also died inside him in that ditch. He was now the first to volunteer for the rear-guard, trying to buy others time to escape, usually with their lives.

Though the Reaper had not cashed in his chit, he felt that it would not be long now. Soon he'd be with his kin. Ike, his mama and papa, even his dog, Scraps; they were all waiting for him at the farm in heaven. Just thinking of this made him smile, and he let out a chuckle, which he silenced as he heard voices pierce the muggy evening air.

Rusty pinched his shoulder to try and stem the bleeding and to find out if he had any sensation left below the impact. He winced in pain as his fingers pried into the wound, but managed to not let any sound leak out. Lying on his back, he tilted his head towards the voices. His eyes met the blood speckled face of Tom Turner, a farm boy from a small town just south of where Rusty grew up.

Tom's mouth was agape as if he had been caught on the latrine. A stream of blood ran down his face from where his ear used to be. Ragged feathers of flesh were singed from the array of hot metal peppering the side of his head. The blood met the corner of his open mouth and gathered there, as if dammed. After a moment, droplets pitter-pattered onto Tom's arm, which lay useless beneath him.

"Ha ha, jeez Louise, look at these folks. Don't look like they took too kindly to our cannon, eh, Frank?"

The words pinned Rusty to the floor as if he were a butterfly in an entomology display. Even the white hot filaments of pain within his shoulder fluttered and dissipated. Rusty heard the sound of boots clumping through the grass around him. Thick soles thudded against the baked earth. From behind him he heard a whimpering and a pleading.

"Well, well, what do we have here, Frank? Say, mister, does this hurt?"

Whatever enquiry was made to the begging man, the screaming increased tenfold.

"It does appear as though that hurts, Jake. I say now, perhaps if I just put this in here…" Another round of blood curdling screaming filled the night air. "…yep, it would seem as though that does indeed smart a little, huh?"

Another voice then squashed the other two. "Will you two stop fucking about and get on with it. Make sure there are no survivors and push up through the streets. We ain't got time for prisoners or torture, you hear me?"

Rusty's desperate breathing and the sound of his heart pounding in his head washed out the mumbled replies. Craning his neck, he could make out the silhouettes of two men. They saluted a figure unseen and then one knelt down and pulled something from his belt.

What followed was a flurry of stabbing and the muffled sound of metal chipping away at bone. Rusty lost count of how many times the knife was brought down into the victim. The attacker finally relented, panting with exertion. "Go on, git, I can't be doing all these on my own," he shouted at the other man.

The shape affixed a bayonet to the end of his rifle and stalked through the assortment of bodies. As he crunched through the dry grass, he stopped and then lanced prone shapes on the ground. Hands reached up to the man, before falling slack and melting into the horizon.

Shit, shit, I can't be going like this. I'd rather bleed out than this.

The footsteps got closer. Occasionally they stopped and a sound like a bag of maize being stabbed could be heard. Rusty lay still, trying to quell the rise and fall of his chest, willing his breathing to fall shallow.

A pair of black boots appeared between him and Tom. The heels were so close to his face, he could make out scuff marks and smell the horse shit flecked up the sides. The rifle and bayonet was thrust down into Tom's skull. The trickle of blood turned into a brief torrent, giving the dead man sideburns made from his own gore.

The soldier fought to retrieve the blade from Tom's head. "Goddammit," he muttered. Placing one boot on the side of the breached skull, he heaved once more and pulled the bayonet free. The momentum nearly sent him toppling over onto Rusty. Time again guttered like he was freefalling in a nightmare. The soldier placed one foot onto Rusty's injured arm, and it took all of his willpower and strength to not cry out or react.

As the weapon was raised, Rusty summoned the image of the family farm in good times, before war had taken everyone he loved. "C'mon, Frank, let's get going. I can hear a hollering down the road. Sounds like they're finally putting up a fight."

Frank stood immobile, like a rattlesnake, coiled, ready to snap and strike. A cruel smile cracked over his face and he spat onto Rusty's face. The thick paste slid down his cheek and into his mouth. Frank, looking pleased with his shot, turned on his heels and headed off, shouting, "I'm coming, don't go killing all of them greybacks before I get there."

Once he was sure that the men weren't coming back, Rusty remembered to breathe, and gasped in lungfuls of air. With oxygen coursing around his body again, the pain in his shoulder flared. He gritted his teeth and rode the wave of agony out.

He looked up to the sky, not wishing to stare into the eyes of dead Mister Turner any more. Rusty raised his one good hand towards the North Star and pinched it between thumb and forefinger, the way he and Ike used to do when they were kids.

"Hey, mister."

The words sent a shiver down Rusty's spine. He dropped his hand to his side, but knew it was too late. He gulped and braced himself for a steel kiss to his forehead.

From his right, he heard a shuffling as someone made their way across the ground to him. Rusty lay there and wondered which of his injured friends had also been spared, and how they could get out of there in one piece. "Over here," he mustered feebly.

The bustling sound stopped, and from above, a face, the features of which were shrouded within a cloth hood, peered down at him. "Hey, mister, don't you worry about

a thing. Me and my buddies. We'll take good care of you."
He felt hands slip underneath his armpits, and was then
dragged slowly backwards.

2

Though it looked about as comfortable as a stone slab, the bed Rusty was placed on was surprisingly pleasant. No sooner had he been set down than his hosts bowed and skittered back whence they came.

The journey was a brief, but puzzling, one. He knew that he was somewhere within the church, as he remembered seeing the side of George's face stuck to the wall as he was carried past. At a guess he was in some kind of crypt or basement, but it was buried deep. Chunky stone blocks formed the outer wall; green fuzzy moss and stalks of red lichen stuck to its surface.

Whatever the room's purpose, it was dimly lit. Rusty could make out other beds, lined up in rows, each with a small pine box stowed underneath with all the hallmarks of the fastidious. His saviours were equally mysterious. They each wore brown robes. The material was a coarse fabric, almost like burlap sacks, repurposed from storing grain to containing the human form. Although polite and civil, they spoke only when required.

"Erm…excuse me?"

Rusty thought the fragile voice at first to be an internal one until he felt breath on his cheek. Turning his head, his eyes locked onto a beautiful pair of green orbs, flecked with orange and grey. Unlike her associates, the woman had her hood pulled down. Her black hair was plaited and tied at the back; her skin was as smooth and wan as alabaster. For a moment Rusty forgot even the most basic of functions.

"Hewwo…" he mumbled. Clearing his throat at least helped him regain his poise, and he finally managed a much more masculine, "Hi, I'm Rusty, pleased to meet ya."

His fumbled introduction eased the tension within the woman. The corners of her thin lips dimpled and her demeanour softened. "Do you mind?" she enquired, nodding towards his wounded shoulder, which was still bereft of sensation.

"No, no, of course not." Rusty picked up his slack limb and rested it on his chest, doing his best not to wince at the pain which rippled through his collarbone. The woman produced a pair of shiny silver scissors and proceeded to snip away at the torn and bloodied cloth covering the puckered and ragged wound.

"Ow," Rusty whinged, as the woman peeled off a piece of fabric that had been pushed into the wound, wrapping itself around vandalised tendon. She offered an apologetic head tilt before resuming her work.

"This is going to sting a little, mister," she warned. Rusty barely had chance to prepare before a healthy slug of whiskey was poured over the mangled skin. It took all of his restraint, and the thickness of his bottom lip which he chomped down on, not to scream blue murder. The woman ignored his reaction and pushed a cloth into the exposed flesh. "Hold," she commanded, and he did so, fearing another dousing in alcohol.

His arm below the impact site began to tingle. Rusty fought, and won, to wiggle his fingers, smiling like an imbecile as the tips tickled the air. "Much obliged to you, miss. Say, what's your name? I'm Charles, but everyone calls me Rusty."

She looked him dead in the eyes again. "Molly. Pleased to make your acquaintance. Now be sure to keep pressing that against the wound. With some luck, you might get to keep your arm."

Rusty gulped. "Really? It's that bad?" Molly looked to the bag which contained her medical supplies. She pushed the stopper back in the bottle of whiskey and placed it back in her bag. Once complete, she nodded and stood up. "Molly, say, I'm mighty pleased you and your kin saved me an' all, but what is this place? Where am I?"

Molly sighed and straightened out her robes. As the folds fell away, Rusty saw a symbol sewn into the front in golden thread. "We are members of the Church of the Saviour's Star, and this is our home. Least it was until those damn Yankees came here and started killing folk." Seeing that the man was staring at the insignia on her clothing, she leant forward so he could see better.

"It's a hexagram. Our teachings are simple. We follow the word of God and seek to work towards his resurrection. He—"

"Molly, if you please, there are more brave young patriots in need of your assistance. Would you kindly?" a hooded man interrupted. He stood impressively tall, back as straight as a gallows support. Embarrassed, she bowed her head and trotted through to the next room. As she passed the man, he whispered into her ear.

"I didn't mean—" Rusty began to say.

"No muss, no fuss brother. Now, if you please," the man drawled, he nodded and left.

3

They began to bring in the bodies an hour or so later. Rusty had just given in to his tiredness and was in the midst of chasing Scraps through a cornfield where tombstones grew, when a loud thud and cursing woke him up.

At first he thought they were more wounded, gravely so, judging by their lack of mobility. It was only when Tom Turner's cauterised, maimed face looked at him accusingly, he realised that he was amongst the lucky ones.

Rusty sat up, clutching his arm to his chest. Sensation was returning to the lower extremities, and he curled his fingers into a ball, though the action was painful to complete. "What ya doin' with 'em?" he asked of a robed man. His question was ignored as the figure hurried to catch up to his accomplices, who were heading through a low stone archway behind him.

Rusty huffed and swivelled on the firm mattress, planting his feet on the floor. Looking around the room, he counted out eleven bodies. All were laid on beds as if they were resting, though some were in such a state of dismemberment that he wondered if this was part of his dream.

Molly trudged into the room, her face one of dejection. "You alright, ma'am?" Rusty asked sincerely.

At first, she looked as though she was lost in a trance, honeysuckle scent adrift on a breeze. She reached the foot of Rusty's bed before she stirred. "I'm okay, thank you. It has just been one of those nights."

Rusty patted a space next to him. "Why don't you take a break and sit down for a moment? Catch your breath."

She looked at him, and those eyes—which had initially captivated him—were now sullen and filled with intangible knowledge. Nodding grudgingly, she sat down, her blood-caked hands resting palms up on her equally sullied garment.

They sat in silence for a while. The only sounds were her laboured breathing. The noise reminded Rusty of Scraps' final few hours, gasping for air, too weak to scrabble around on the floor, barely able to lift his head to look at his master.

When she eventually spoke, the words rang louder than they were, shattering the memory. "Just never seen anyone like that before."

Rusty shifted on his behind and turned to face her, waiting for her to continue.

"Sure, I've seen people die. Sometimes not in very pleasant ways, but the things we…the things we…" She coughed, holding her hands to her mouth, trying to build up the strength to finish. "…The things we do to each other. It don't make much sense, huh?"

Rusty looked to the floor and shook his head. "No, ma'am, it don't. I sure have seen enough killing and death to last me several lifetimes over, that's for sure. I wake up most days wondering if today will be the day that I breathe my last, or whether I'll get the chance to see tomorrow in. Though, to be honest, for a while now I've been hoping it was the former. Life ain't too kind, you see, not to anyone. Especially these days."

The words rebounded off Molly as if an invisible barrier had been raised. "We haven't had the war come to us. Sure we heard about it an' all, but it almost don't seem real, you know? Not much happens round here. We keep ourselves to ourselves, and that's the way it's been since Father Rodriguez set up this here mission. We like it that way. We don't want no soldiers coming in to our town and messing everything up."

Rusty sighed. "Well, not that it helps, Molly, but I don't think they'll be here long. Ol' one legged Hood sure messed this one up. We've lost a lot of good men today. Ha, and *bad* ones."

Molly looked across at him, shrugged and stood up. She fussed with her hair, pulling it tight again. "I'm sorry to have bothered you, mister. Please, get some rest," she said stoically.

"Whoa there, I didn't mean no insult, ma'am," Rusty said defensively.

She looked back at him. "None taken," she replied curtly and headed through the stone archway, into the murk beyond.

He sat there for a while, replaying their exchange over in his head, wondering what he could have possibly said to have annoyed her. Picking up the tattered sleeve she had removed, he tied the ends together, looped it over his head, and placed his hand into the crude sling.

Rusty shuffled across the room. At the foot of each bed, he looked down at the body and tried to recall the names of those he saw.

Most he recognised. Hank Uttley from Marietta looked as though he genuinely was sleeping. It was only when Rusty knelt down by the headboard that he saw a spike of jagged metal sticking lengthways through his neck.

Rusty chuckled. Hank had told him once that he and his sister had been caught out in a storm as children. With claps of thunder and lashes of lightning cracking up in the heavens, they cowered under the bough of an old oak tree.

Shivering, they jumped every time they saw a fork of lightning fizz across the grey sky, fearing that they would be struck next. The metal embedded in Hank's neck looked like a tongue of lightning had taken care of him at last, some fifteen years later.

Almost as an apology, Rusty pulled the edge of the blanket over Hank's face, remarking to himself how utterly tranquil he looked. Most of the other bodies gawped back open eyed, petrified in contorted gargoyle stares. The act of violence that caused their demise carved upon their skin and bone.

Some, though, were so utterly ruined, it was impossible to ascertain who they were. He prayed for them in particular, hoping that God would recognise them at the gates and welcome them in, forgiving each in turn for their sins.

Finally, he reached Tom. Pieces of grass were stuck to the side of his head, which had taken the brunt of the blast. Rusty smoothed down Tom's hair and hooked the eyelids closed with his fingernails, not bearing to look into the pits of oblivion for one second more. He spent an extra few moments watching over him.

"That one sure does look messed up. Should make it easier eh, Mister?"

The voice was thick with a Georgian accent. Rusty opened his eyes and turned to look at the source. Before him stood a man, at a guess in his early twenties, who looked instantly out of place. The only people he'd seen so far in this basement were dead or wounded soldiers and the religious folk walking around in their identical robes. This man was resplendent in a fine suit, elegant glasses and a timepiece nuzzled in a waistcoat pocket. A thick braided gold chain wormed its way from it to a clip tucked behind a button.

"Oh don't mind me. I'm just leaving. Got me a boat to catch. Just admiring this here view. Won't be seeing this for a while, I guess," the man ventured, peering down at Tom's broken body. Rusty swore for the briefest of moments that the man licked his lips, as if anticipating a date or an evening in a bar with a good friend.

"Yep, sure are the lucky ones if you ask me." The man ran a hand through his pomaded hair and placed a hat which matched his suit on his head. He doffed it towards Rusty.

"What do you mean: lucky ones? I'm the one who survived," Rusty retorted, bristling with anger.

The corner of the man's lip curled, as if a fishing hook was tugging at it, pulling it to shore. "Of course you did, son. You survived that there battle outside, though it looks like you took a bit of a pasting. 'Cept not all fights are the obvious ones, I guess."

Rusty looked at him dumbfounded, as if asked the answer to an impossible arithmetic question.

"No matter. I think I'll make my exit now, son. I've got places to go and things to do." The stranger patted a thick suitcase before tipping his hat once more and heading towards the archway.

"Well he's an odd one," Rusty mumbled to himself. Making sure Tom was no longer facing him, he headed back to his bed.

No sooner was he perched than two of the robed men entered through the stone archway. They walked to the nearest body, Hank, and took an end each. Rusty stood up as if his bed were ablaze. "What ya doin' there, fellas?" he asked brusquely.

The pair exchanged glances before the one holding Hank's feet looked across at Rusty. A sparsely hair-fletched chin poked out from the hood's shadow. "We is burying him." His voice was one of irritation, as if annoyed that his actions were being questioned. "Now, if you don't mind, we done got work to do."

4

The dream world held on unusually tightly to Rusty. Instead of situations and encounters, his head was a multi-coloured kaleidoscope with him at its centre. Shapes and patterns of no fixed creation swirled and looped around him as he floated free. He felt as if he were awake, hyper-aware of his surroundings, yet utterly powerless to mould the visions to his whim.

After a struggle with a fluorescent worm with distended mandibles and tentacles—which suckled on his shoulder and then withered away—he came to.

The basement seemed lighter. He could make out cracks coursing through the mortar in the ceiling. Small bugs scurried across its surface, looking down on him with a wary eye. He felt the way he did in his dream: lighter, malleable, as if dissolved in water and swilled around.

Rusty placed a hand beneath him and pushed up. His body rejected the notion of how he felt and resisted. To close the deal he went to put his other hand underneath him to help his ascent.

Nothing.

He looked to his left and saw that the bodies were gone. Only cadaver-like ditches remained in the stained and crumpled sheets. Feeling a bead of sweat run down his head, he tried to mop his brow.

Nothing.

"What in the name of heck is—?"

Words dried up as he looked down at his shoulder, which was wrapped in dirty bandages; a mix of brown watermarks and blood spots formed an odd collage. Below the bandages was nothing but thin air, synaptic messages sent to a missing limb.

Rusty screamed and then blacked out.

5

"...sty?"

The lilting voice was carried to him on the wings of a seraphim, shimmering with light. As the holy creature neared, it hovered in front of him, just out of reach.

Hands, soft and tender, reached for Rusty. They were perfect, not a single blemish, mark or callous. Its face was hidden behind a white mask. It hung over the head like a silk cloth. Eyeholes were cut out and an exalted pale blue light hummed from beyond.

Rusty went to speak, but was utterly devoid of speech. The mere thought of the beauty before him had rendered him mute.

He reached out to the figure, noticing that he now had both hands again. The seraphim recoiled at the movement and began to shake. Its body became a volcano. From its neck and shoulders, it trembled.

"...usty, co—"

Veins popped to the surface of the creature's skin, becoming as thick as snakes. They writhed in syncopation with the tremors. Muscles bulged and ballooned, becoming grotesque and unnatural in appearance. Its chest rippled with innate energy and popped and cracked. Ribs burst through the white skin. They were blackened embers of filth, rotten and putrescent smelling. The charred bones pushed their way free and groped for Rusty, waving in front of him like devilish branches.

Once they had achieved freedom, they whipped back against the seraphim's chest, forming a bodice of tar-covered ebony. As they struck the body, acrid smoke rose from the contact points. The smell of burnt meat filled Rusty's nostrils. The ribs clacked into place and then contracted, forcing the muscle and organs within to bulge through the fetid scorched cage.

Lines of flame ran down from the neck to the shoulders, pooling in the shallow divot of flesh between clavicle and rib like a lake of fire. Using the pronounced veins like lines of ether, the fire ran down the length of the arms, ending beneath the fingernails. The heat made them crack and flake off. From underneath, the finger bones flexed and pushed outwards, rending the skin open. The palms of each hand hung like sails becalmed at sea. The flame which still burned along the arms caught the hanging flesh and they went up like parchment in a firestorm.

Fingers formed into claws and tore at the air in front of Rusty, who was now stricken with fear. An ear-piercing shriek came out of the mouth behind the face cloth. The eyes now glowed a baleful red, flickering with hatred and loathing. Wracked with agony the seraphim screamed once more before clawing at its face with its own talons. It peeled the cloth away with ease, unveiling meat and bone beneath, laden with burrowing insects and their wriggling bulbous larvae.

The screaming stopped and the monster dug its claws

between the newly formed exterior ribs. Fighting against its own creation, it gouged and tore away, until it snapped off pieces of charcoal bone. With the covering removed, one solitary claw traced a six point star upon its beating breast. When the star was complete, a golden light shone from the wound.

All the fear, the terror, the excruciating feeling that his very existence was being crushed, fell away. The monster still hovered in front of him. Its six angelic wings a contrast to the corrupted twisted mass its body and face now displayed.

"...ack…"

Tips of its claws rested around the shimmering star. The peace was short-lived as the beast applied pressure and, uttering a guttural roar, slashed at its own body. Having rent the skin open, it pushed its fingers inside its chest, desperately searching for something.

Dread pumped around Rusty's body again, flooding his central nervous system with a big dose of flight, not fight.

"..come—"

The defiled seraphim panted. Its knuckles were visible through its own skin. With one final act of exertion it pulled its fist free, showering Rusty in thick black ichor. He slammed his eyes shut out of instinct.

When he dared to look again, he and the debased creature were sat opposite each other in a dingy room. The creature was dead, its immolated arms ending in elongated fingers of jagged bone, which lay slack at its side. There was a gaping black crater in its chest where the star had once resided.

As Rusty stared at the sight before him, the distant

swinging light from above caught on tiny specks of light within the rank spoiled meat. Without contemplating the consequences, he ran his fingers over the spongy black flesh. It felt warm to the touch, and surprisingly was not wholly unpleasant.

The air still stank of sulphur, but he was not troubled by it. Rusty picked off a chunk of flesh the size of an orange and brought it closer to inspect.

It had the same consistency as dung, but he was compelled to touch it, to break it open. His thumb rubbed it against his fingers. As it fell to pieces in his hands, small flecks of golden dust broke off too. His brain could not reconcile the two, how something so beautiful could live within something so utterly abhorrent.

"…to …"

6

Just before the war had started, Rusty had taken a spill into a lake. Too much moonshine and not enough attention had led to him slipping on the slick bank and nosediving into the inky blue depths. It had sobered him up instantly. He had floundered within the stygian darkness of that lake, unable to work out which way was up and out. His lungs burned as oxygen disappeared, his body spasmed, demanding that he open his mouth and take in fresh supplies.

He did so, and though the burning sensation was extinguished, it was replaced by a claustrophobic bear hug which made his eyes bulge from their sockets. Flashes of his life were scratched onto the inside of his retina, showing him the mistakes he'd made and the triumphs he had snatched. At the zenith, with his body on the cusp of death, he had felt a hand grab him by the scruff of his shirt and haul him back to life.

Rusty was reminded of this as he sat bolt upright, gasping for air and life, a mirror of the time Stuckey had pulled him out of the frigid water. His eyes felt like they were going to burst from their housing. The muscles ached at the tension and only when his silent scream ended did they recede back into his skull.

"...sty, are you okay?"

His ears popped and he looked to his side to see those green eyes once more. Her lips, thin stems of skin, were pursed with worry and concern. Molly smiled. "Rusty, it's alright, you're okay. We thought we lost you, but you're back. With us."

Rusty looked around and saw that his bed was surrounded by five other hooded figures. None of their expressions conveyed any sense of worry about his fight back to life. "Wh...what happened?" he struggled to say. A sickly-sweet taste lingered at the back of his throat.

Molly nodded and the others bowed and peeled away, disappearing into the recesses of the basement. "Your arm...it went bad, so we had to take it off. If it got infected, you would've gone downhill fast," she said calmly, smoothing down his shirt collar and rubbing strands of hair behind his ears. "We had to knock you out, but Brother Fabio used too much chloroform. When we tried to wake you, we couldn't. How do you feel now?"

He searched her face for any hint at falsehood. She was either telling the truth or was one hell of a card player. Rusty shook his head to rid himself of the pressure building up within, and gestured towards a jug of water. Molly released her hold on him and poured him a mug, letting him sip it slowly. "We...I was mighty worried about you Cha...I mean Rusty. I'm glad you're okay."

Recollection hit him like an angry mule, and he looked over her shoulder into the room. The beds were still empty. "What did you do with the bodies?"

Molly placed the mug down and wrung her hands.

"They…er, got taken out back, ready to get buried. Don't fuss over 'em, worry about yourself. I hope we got to the arm in time."

"*All* of them?" he asked angrily. "You folk sure work quick. I couldn't have been out that long. Now why don't y—"

She bowed and turned quickly, looking to make her escape. Rusty grabbed her arm with his one remaining hand. "Wait a minute," he growled. Her slight frame was ill-equipped to deal with his brute force and she was reeled towards him.

"Now look here missy, I just want some answers from you. None of this is making much sense to me. Why don't we…" Rusty trailed off, eyes fixed on the front of her gown, where his fingers had a firm hold.

"Let go of me," Molly protested, struggling in his grip. She dug her fingernails into the back of his hand and he released her.

Rusty pointed at her chest. "I've seen that…that star, in my dream. What is it?" he demanded.

The woman smoothed down her crumpled robe and ran her fingers over the embroidered symbol. "I told you earlier. It's a hexagram, the symbol of our church."

"Church of *what*, though? I don't see no crosses around here, or figures of our saviour, Jesus Christ. Just that damned star. What the heck do you people believe in?" he asked through gritted teeth, rubbing the back of his hand on his bedsheets.

Molly stood in the doorway. "God, Rusty. We believe in God. Our faith in the lord is unshakeable, of that I can assure you. The things we've seen…"

"What do you mean?" Rusty pressed further.

"Nothing. Get some rest, Rusty. You've been through a lot." With that, Molly ducked through the archway and left him to his endless questions.

7

"Bullshit," Rusty grunted to himself. After testing that his legs were able to support him, he stood up, placing a hand on the wooden headboard to steady himself. There were two exits. A wooden doorway hinted at burrowing further into the underground lair, but it was the stone archway that caught his attention the most.

He worked his way into the passageway and slumped against the cold stone wall. The sensation on his back began to wake him. From up ahead, he heard hushed voices and a scraping sound of metal on stone.

Working his way along the corridor, he saw a pair of openings opposite one other. Beyond that, and at the end of the tunnel, was a closed thick wooden door. Metal bolts and handles glinted from the sparse torches lining the walls.

The voices rippled out from both rooms, Rusty knew that he had to escape. Whatever was out there was infinitely better than the nagging uncertainty, telling him that he should not be in this basement any longer than was absolutely necessary.

Staggering to the lip of one of the openings, he chanced a quick look into the room. There were a number of robed figures within, hunched over a raised dais. The scraping sound was definitely coming from this gathering of people. With his mind consumed by thoughts of escape, he ducked and scuttled to the other side of the opening, the exit in sight.

Curiosity, though, is one mean mistress, and it pulled at him, cooing and telling him to look again. What harm could it do? Surely it would be better to know for certain what he was running away from? What if he was wrong? What if these people were honest God-fearing folk, with nothing but altruism in their hearts?

Rusty nearly coughed at the sheer preposterousness of that last thought. No, these people were *wrong*. He couldn't put his finger on why, just that they were out of step with how things should be.

Steadying himself against the wall, he looked into the room once more. The figures crowded out what they were working on. He could see that one of the robed men had a stone bowl in his hand, and some kind of metal spatula in the other.

Is he making a cake?

The man swilled the implement inside the bowl and then scraped the metal trowel up from the bottom to the very edge of the receptacle. He must've been a master baker, as he looked well versed in his task. He chatted away to one of his cohorts as he worked. With each completed scrape, he turned the bowl in his grip, then began the process again.

Rusty sighed. Perhaps he was wrong about these people? They had saved him from almost certain death, either at the hands of the Yankees, or his wounds. What had he done in return? Hurt the woman who had shown him kindness and compassion. Perhaps it was the chloroform. Maybe it had given him those hellish hallucinations. Perhaps this was another side-effect of that?

As the realisation dawned on him that maybe he was being a tad hasty, his eyes fell to the floor. Summoning the energy to return to the sanctuary of his bed, he noticed something in a bucket by the entrance.

Huh.

Something familiar.

Really familiar.

Kneeling down, he fumbled around for the item he'd seen, willing it to be another hallucination, although an altogether more sickening one. As he wrapped his fingers around it, he brought it round the corner to look upon it.

Sure as night followed day, there it was.

His arm.

He placed it in his lap and turned it over. It was definitely his. Aside from the ravages of the shrapnel just below where it had been hacked off, he ran his fingers over the chicken pox scars he had had since he was a child.

"Don't pick them," his mama had warned him, but the itching was *too* much for him to bear. He promised himself that he'd go around the spots and sores, and stick to the skin.

Having dealt with the worst patch, he had idly continued. The relief had turned to white hot agony as he looked under his fingernails to see three white crusty scabs. The wounds had bubbled with clear pus and he went crying to his mother, who clouted him around the head for ignoring her.

Those same three scars, arranged in a triangle below a mole, now looked back at him. Rusty stood up, and his arm rolled off his legs, slapping against the floor at his feet. Casting a forlorn look into the room, he saw Tom Turner's face staring back at him again. One of the robed figures had a large silver dessert spoon and was scooping out ribbed scraps of brain and heaping them in an adjacent stone bowl. After a few more spoonfuls, the man picked the bowl up and began the scraping again.

For the second time since he'd been in the basement, flight kicked in. He rubbed his hand on his shirt, convinced that he had some gunk or death on his fingers. Rusty, with new found determination, spun on his heels. He took one step forward and bumped into a robed woman. "Going somewhere, Rusty?" Molly asked. Before he had a chance to answer, he felt a sharp pain above his pelvis.

Daring himself to look down, he tore his gaze away from her emerald orbs and located the cause of his consternation. A knife was embedded up to the hilt in his stomach. Her hand was white with the force of the grip. Blood pumped from the wound over the blade, fouling her fingers.

"Gah…" Rusty managed, his mind unable to deal with so much in such a short space of time. He lurched forwards as Molly pulled the blade out. Respite was only temporary, though, as she thrust the knife into his midriff again. This time she placed her free hand on his good shoulder, pulling him in closer and forcing the weapon in deeper.

121

"Don't fight it," she murmured into his ear. "We were glad to get so many all at once. It'll help replenish what Brother Diego took earlier. With all the commotion, Father Umberto thought it best someone left this place."

Spots and strobes of light danced across his vision.

No.

Not today.

Not like this.

With the woman so close to him, he pulled his head back and butted her on the bridge of her dainty nose. It cracked like a whip. Blood gushed from her nostrils and splattered the pair of them, giving Rusty a red cravat on his shirt. The blow stunned her, and he took his chance, grabbed the side of her head with his hand and slammed it into the stone wall. It met with a muffled crunch and a confetti-sprinkling of teeth and tongue.

Rusty gripped Molly's hair with his fingers and repeated the action again and again. Each time her face was withdrawn from the wall, it was more ruined. Her eye-socket had come up in a nasty bruise already; vessels had burst and turned the white into a pink hue.

He did it again and again, zoning out until he felt his own fingers smacking against the wall. Coming to, he looked at his hand and saw that all he was holding was a strip of flesh and matted hair.

Molly's body had sunk to the floor, her head a mass of mush. Rusty dropped down and rubbed his hand against the woman's robe, trying to remove the grisly glove he had acquired. As the gore was smeared over her clothing, he felt something clunky beneath her garment.

He checked the doorway, and was relieved that no one

had become alerted to the fracas. They were all too preoccupied in their grisly harvesting, though of what he was not certain. Rusty pulled the knife from his stomach and, grimacing, tucked the blade into his belt.

He patted down Molly's body, trying not to look at the place her head used to be. Reaching into the folds of her gown, he retrieved a small red leather-bound book. As he turned it over, his guts tightened as he saw the damnable six-pointed golden star on the front.

Try as he might, he couldn't push it into his pocket. Resigned to carrying it, he stepped over the dead body and headed towards the exit.

It's going to be locked, you idiot. You're going to die here, if you don't bleed out first, and then one of them will find her and scoop your insides out like they did to Tom. What are they, some kind of cannibals?

Rusty didn't want to find out the answer to his question. Resting against the door, he reached for the handle. Pushing down, it gave way easily. The door popped out of the frame and fell loose in his hand.

Flushed with relief, he pulled the door open, and immediately felt the cold night air on his sweat-drenched skin. Stumbling outside, he pulled the door to and crawled up a set of stone stairs. He was still in a corridor of some kind, and aside from a pale strip of light from under the door behind him, there was only blackness ahead. Knowing that there must be something up there, he inched his way to freedom.

After painstaking minutes, his head hit something above him. His shirt was soaked with blood and perspiration. His hand still clutched the book, though he was growing faint and weary. Pushing out blindly with his hand, he levered open one half of a wooden trapdoor. After a few more agonising steps, he felt wet grass underneath him.

The dewy blanket comforted him. He had made it out; all he had to do now was find some help. He was going to make it, of that he was sure. Rusty chuckled gently to himself. "What a night…"

"Looky here, Henry. I found one of your missing stiffs."

8

A man with a wiry beard and beady eyes stood over Rusty's prone body. Even at night, Rusty could see that he was wearing the Union navy blue. He tried to sit up, but the man jabbed the butt of his rifle into the small of his shoulder and pinned him to the ground. "You should say thank you. I coulda spiked you with the bayonet," the soldier grunted.

"Please…help me. There are people in the church basement, and they—"

Rusty's words were silenced as the rifle butt was brought down onto his stomach, stretching the stab wound and tearing skin. He howled in pain before a clammy hand was clamped over his mouth. Another soldier loomed into focus and put a finger to his lips, signalling for quiet. "You were right, Frank, something funny *was* going on here. What do ya wanna do?"

Frank removed the rifle from Rusty's guts and tucked the weapon beneath the crook of his arm. He pulled out a pipe from a pouch on his belt and filled it with two pinches of tobacco. Striking a match, he applied it to the pipe and puffed out plumes of purple smoke. With the nicotine removing an ounce of menace, he watched the

125

flame dance around the matchstick, captivated by its movement.

"Well, Jake, we can't have anyone helping out the enemy now, huh? Why don't you go get that gunpowder from the artillery fellas. Church or not, we gotta make an example here," Frank commanded, never once blinking or taking his eyes off Rusty. Jake nodded and trotted off into the night.

"Please, mister, Frank is it? Those people in there, they ain't right. They done took off my arm for no reason. They are cutting up the bodies in there, doing unnatural things to 'em. You got to stop 'em, please?" Rusty begged.

Frank took another pull on the pipe and blew the smoke away. "I don't have to do anything. See, when Jake comes back, we'll blow them all sky high, doesn't matter what kind of shit they get up to, they won't be doing it too long."

Rusty went to speak again, but was met with a boot to the face. "Not a goddamn word from you," Frank warned. "Ah, here we go."

Jake laid a trail of powder from the top of the steps to the door at the bottom. Tipping the barrel to one side, he cautiously made his way back up into the night. He stood by Frank just as the man took his last intake of tobacco. "Well, any last words?" he chuckled, causing Jake to join him in a round of guffaws.

Frank struck another match and dropped it into the track of black powder, which fizzed and hissed before igniting and speeding down the stairs into the gloom. "We best take a step or two back now, Jake." The pair jogged backwards, leaving Rusty on the floor, his one arm aloft, begging them to take him with them.

An almighty explosion ripped through the basement. The wooden frame shook and pitched to one side. The church collapsed in on itself, the nave and altar now a burning pile of kindling and smashed wooden beams.

Frank picked himself up and dusted himself down. Refilling his pipe, he strutted over to the pile of rubble, blown clear from the stone staircase. Where he had left the injured man was a higgledy-piggledy mass of smouldering rubble and charred wood. Kneeling down, he flicked through the heap with his hands. Amongst the debris he found a dust-covered hand. Channels of blood ran down fingers still clutching onto something.

Shoving the pipe into his mouth, he fought with the cadaverous fingers to liberate the object. Winning the battle, he blew the dust off the item to reveal a cracked red leather book, with a worn gold six-pointed star on the cover.

Frank flicked through the pages, stopping here and there on macabre illustrations and in-depth instruction. Images of bodies carved open and hollowed out filled most pages. He could feel bile rising. Spitting out the acidic goo, he cast the book into the flames. "Goddamn savages," he muttered to himself, before relighting his pipe and heading back to his tent

DUNCAN P. BRADSHAW

"Grand work the last job was. I gave the lady no time to squeal. How can they catch me now. I love my work and want to start again. You will soon hear of me with my funny little games."

– 'Dear Boss' letter

46,907 days until the end of the world

The Clarence Pub, corner of Great Scotland Yard and

Whitehall, London, United Kingdom

29 September 1888

DUNCAN P. BRADSHAW

1

Having arranged to meet Swanson at one p.m. precisely, you can only imagine my irritation when I checked my watch and saw that it was already eight minutes past. With a heavy sigh and another pot of tea ordered, I resolved to wait. After all, I had information relating to the most heinous murderer of our time. I owed it not just to myself, but to the people of London, to ensure that I imparted this information to the Chief Inspector.

If he, like the others, chose to dismiss it, then so be it. I have found that with age, exuberance and indignation of youth is replaced by reticence and dispassion. One can only shout so many times without being listened to. Battles must be chosen, and if the generals in charge of them do not heed your words or advice, then your duty is complete and any consequences lie solely at their door.

Swanson finally made his entrance at twenty-three minutes past two. I was halfway through chewing on a particularly currant-laden rock cake, when his sullen face mustered a grumpy 'hello'.

With the cordial act of greeting out of the way, standard questions of the state of each other's family enquired to, and promises of how we 'really should've

131

done this earlier', I was finally able to get to the crux of the appointment.

"Donald, I, like most of the people in this city, are dually disgusted and intrigued with the recent spate of killings in Whitechapel. The sheer brutality and animalistic nature of the murders is beyond the pale of ordinary people's thoughts and comprehension.

I am sure that you have a list of suspects that both yourself, and your predecessor, have drawn up. I am here to add one to that tally, one which you will not be aware of.

I believe that the killer did not begin this rampage recently. Through the course of my investigation, it is my firm assertion that they have been doing this for over twenty years."

It was at this point that the pallor of his face took on the appearance of a waxy moon: pale and in need of sustenance. I took the liberty of ordering a plate of shortbread, which bolstered his constitution. After collecting himself, Donald asked, "Who is this man? This devil that preys on women and leaves them mutilated?"

Admittedly to add a dash of dramatic effect, I took a sip of tea. Though my cup was down to the dregs, I did not let on. Dabbing the napkin to my lips, I dropped the first of my many shocks. "Donald, this is not the work of any man, at least not now. The killings the media have seized upon this summer show that this murderer has gone far past their original task and purpose. They no longer kill to feed their original mission. They do it now because they know of nothing else."

Swanson, exasperated, implored me once more,

"Dammit Norton, tell me." His manner had become brusque, to be expected considering the stress and strain he was now under. Chief Inspector Donald Swanson had been assigned to the 'Ripper' case by the upper echelons of British government. His charge was a simple one: discover and apprehend this fiend, through whatever means necessary.

To calm him, I continued. "Let me tell you of my investigation, and I can divulge the identity of the offender. But please, indulge me."

2

The waitress returned to our table with a fresh pot of tea and two large gins, which were at my behest. Donald protested vehemently, stating that he wanted a clear head. I advised him that he would require a stiff drink at some point during my tale.

"After the Tower Hill street robberies, back in '79, I had had my fill of London and, as you are aware, relocated to Salisbury, Wiltshire, in the hope that a quieter pace of life would rekindle both my humours and my marriage."

Donald intervened at this point. "Really? The Tower Hill case *made* you, Norton. After that, you could've taken any number of lofty positions at the Yard."

"This may be true, Donald, but as we worked on it, dealing with the many twists and turns, I had become a man with whom I was not happy with. After the gambit worked and we managed to apprehend Yates and Tibbins, I was but an expended shotgun cartridge. Yes, the grouse were bagged and cooked thoroughly, but I was a spent force.

We took a house in Cathedral Close, and before too long, the mundanity of county policing had soothed away many of the ills. Miriam had taken up tennis once more, and I was enjoying the social life with my chums at the Haunch of Venison. All the stresses and strains that had made our lives practically unbearable here in London had vanished. Replaced by a slower pace of life, and a bottle of gin.

All that changed one day, though. On the morning of the twenty-ninth of April, 1885, I was handed a murder case; Roger Chatham, a labourer in Wilton, had been on his way to work, when he chanced upon an open stables in Crow Lane.

The morning mist had rendered visibility to no more than a few arm lengths away. As he investigated the open door, someone barged past him and fled down the street, in the direction of St Mary's church.

After picking himself up off the floor, he found that he had received a particularly nasty gash to his forearm. He searched the floor for what had injured him, and found a bloodied fillet knife. This perturbed him greatly, and despite trying to staunch the flow of blood from his wound, he was unable to do so.

Chatham made his way into the stables in search of something he might be able to use as a tourniquet or bandage. It was then he found the seven bodies. I say bodies, though a more adequate description would be 'husks'."

My choice of phrase had been carefully selected; it did indeed seem to pique Donald's interest. "Husks? Were organs removed?"

Having cast the bait, I now needed to reel him in, but gently, for too many fish had already been scared away from my over-eagerness. "Indeed, the bodies were relatively fresh. The Doctor surmised that all of them had been killed within the previous seven days. Each had had their hands, feet, and heads removed. These were lying between the legs of each body. It is at this point that things get a little on the grisly side, Donald. I trust your lunch is not easily stirred from within."

He nodded briefly and eyed up his untroubled gin.

"Having passed Chatham off onto Constable Channon for a statement, I began to investigate the corpses. The first, and most obvious, thing to note was that they were all naked. Of the seven bodies, three were female and four male. Beginning with the closest to me, I noted immediately that the hands and feet appeared odd.

Closer inspection revealed that they had been scraped clean of any muscle or tissue from within. Only morsels remained attached to the bone which wore the skin like an ill-fitting glove or sock. Turning my attention to the head, I discovered a similar situation. Severed at the base of the neck, the killer had made an incision from the middle of the throat up to the centre of the bottom lip. The skin had then been pulled open, so much so that I was able to peer directly up through the structure of the skull into the brain cavity. As per the appendages, all fleshy matter had been exhumed, though I could not see where this had been stored.

Curiosity got the better of me, I admit. I placed my thumbs on the closed eyelids and opened them up. Sure enough, two bloodied cavities stared back at me. Even the ligaments which would keep the eyeball in place had been sliced off and removed."

It was at this point Donald took his gin and swallowed

it in one. He caught the waitress' attention and asked her to bring another to our table. Not wishing to appear rude, I did likewise. Although it did break my cardinal rule of drinking before finishing my cup of tea, I thought it necessary to mirror his actions.

I continued: "With the state of the removed body parts, I predicted, correctly, that the bodies would be in a similar state. An incision had been made from a ragged neck wound down the front of the ribcage to the pelvis. From there, it ran to the middle of the ankle, and from the sternum down the arms to the middle of the wrist.

A skilled blade had removed all of the meat, tendon, and veins from within the bodies. Well, all except for one. Though seven were on show, each taking up a table and laid out as if they were a buffet, I saw a channel of blood running from a cupboard to the side of the stables. Upon opening the doors, I discovered the eighth victim. This was to be the key, as it was completely intact.

Doctor Young laid the body out, and was able to determine, rather easily, that the cause of death was the severing of the spinal column, between the fourth and fifth vertebrae. A small blade had been used, and when I mentioned the fillet knife to him, he concurred that it was, with a high degree of certainty, the very weapon that had been used.

This added a new dimension to the case. For one, to kill seven people around the same time and strip them so utterly of their internal workings is no mean feat, especially for one person, but to then go out and strike again, to what end?

It was then I made a leap of faith and judgement. That

the body I found crammed into the cupboard was, in fact, one of the perpetrators. With the bodies in their state, it would be nigh-on impossible to determine whether they were murdered in the same way, though Young could not find any contusions or wounds to any other part of their body. They were in too ravaged a condition to be sure, though.

But with this intact body, we had a lead. In order to kill this man, who was well-built and looked as though he could handle himself, the killer would've needed to have gotten in close. Which made me believe that they must've known each other. Chatham had by now recovered from his ordeal, and was able to say that he thought it was a woman that had pushed past him so forcibly.

So, I had the very real possibility that a couple had killed these people, and that something had happened which had led to the woman killing her accomplice. But to what end? What purpose did they have to do this? Despite a thorough search, we could find no piece of flesh or organ more than a strand here or a tidbit there. When we *did* find anything in quantity, it had been ground into a thick, coarse paste.

As I pondered on the scene, the morning sun had turned around and was now shining through the open doors into the stables. I noticed amongst the dirt and straw a sprinkling of shimmering grit. Ordering the men to stand out of the sun's rays, the full majesty of it became apparent. Littered around each body and table were glittering flecks. They looked like stars in the night sky."

3

Swanson had by now foregone any light refreshment, and had asked for the bottle of gin to remain on the table, along with an assortment of savoury snacks. Whilst he shoved handfuls of salted nuts into his maw, I picked at some pork scratchings. For a good eleven minutes he uttered not one single word. When he did break his silence, the question was an obtuse one: "Is a nut really a legume?"

I sighed disparagingly, and suggested that he slowed down on the gin intake, at least until I had finished my story. Grudgingly he agreed, though I could see that the taste had gripped him already. It was always a weakness of his. It was what had scuppered the Tower Hill robbery case, and why they were allowed to continue unhindered for so long.

His false assumptions and drunken finger-pointing had done little except give the pair more leeway. It was only when I concocted a plan and convinced him one morning that it was his own, that we were able to move on them and arrest them in the act.

I digress: "Doctor Young removed the man's body and conducted a full autopsy, which did nothing apart from confirm the cause of death, which he had already correctly identified. The only other clue he uncovered was a tattoo on his chest, between his pectoral muscles. It was of a six-pointed star, a hexagram, and had been done some time ago, judging by the condition of it.

Donald, this tattoo may allude to some cult or coven they were part of, but despite numerous searches, in some of the more inhospitable parts of our country, in particular Devon and Cornwall, I have not been able to fathom which crackpot faction it belongs to.

Even the usually relied upon deranged idyll of Marchwood, replete with heretic zealots and mentally imbalanced yokels, were unable to shed any light on it. Aside from one particular family mentioning some kind of hellish skybound jellyfish, I came away from there with no further information of use.

Whilst the medical examination yielded few clues, a search of his clothing gave me the first real break. Chatham had fortuitously disturbed the killer before she had had a chance to remove any items. Had she been granted another ten or fifteen minutes, say, I doubt I would have been able to begin my investigation in earnest, and would not, I believe, be sat in front of you here today.

A simple pocketbook. That was all it was. Written inside the first page, in rather pleasing handwriting, was a name, Diego Villa, and a series of dates. The earliest of which simply stated:

$$03/01/66, \quad \mathcal{PL}. \quad JJJ, \quad 12_9$$

It was evident that this Villa character was not born on this fair island, and 1866? That would mean that the pair had been at this for some considerable time. The series of dates and scrawls lend credence to this. Sometimes there was a number of months between entries, but each followed the same pattern.

So, the man and, possibly, the woman, were immigrants. With a name like that, Spain, Portugal or the New World were the most plausible. At first PL hinted that Portugal was the likeliest, but of course that made no sense. As luck would have it, when I was in Devon investigating the tattoo, I stumbled upon the answer.

PL was Plymouth. Of course! He must've come across from the Americas. Judging by the date, towards the end of the civil war over there."

I could tell at this juncture that Donald was glazing over, and so I ordered us a selection of sandwiches and made small talk about the recent Ashes test series against Australia, paying particular attention to the thrashing we had meted out in the third test at Old Trafford. Peel's eleven wicket match haul, in particular, was discussed at length.

The thick-cut sandwiches, with generous hunks of roasted boar and apricot jam, hit the spot and reinvigorated him quite miraculously. We chatted for a while on the merits of a solid forward defence shot before I continued.

"Plymouth was a raucous place, full of feisty sailor types and near feral children. I first made my way to the Harbourmasters office. Though I had convinced myself by now that any records, especially going back a few decades, would be long since consigned to cupping fish and chips down at the docks.

You can only imagine my shock and surprise when I met the punctilious and exacting Harbourmaster, a Mister Stuart Garnett. You will never meet a more particular person than he, and I for one am glad of that fact. Having been in charge of the many comings and goings for the last twenty seven years, his sheer bloody-mindedness and steadfast refusal for accepting anything even resembling slapdash, meant he was more than able to supply me with the details.

Though the one downside was that as I was 'from that there Wiltshire', I had to work in his rather cramped office. His distrust for anyone outside of Devon was complete. So much so that I had to wash my hands in a mix of fresh seawater and the guts of the first catch of the day each morning before I was allowed to handle the documents.

One does think, looking back, perhaps I was the subject of some kind of japery. For whenever the allotted time came around, there was quite the crowd of fishermen and other waifs and strays. Once my hands were doused in the liquid, they would whoop and holler, mumbling incoherent sentences and patting each other on the back. On occasion, money, lobsters and other crustaceans changed hands.

It took the best part of three weeks to go through the records. I operated on the premise that Señor Villa entered at some point during 1865, and whilst the logs were thorough, Garnett's filing system and handwriting posed a challenge.

Eventually I found a manifest for a ship called the 'Siren's Jaunt', a brig that had a colourful history under the care of privateers. After sustaining damage in 1861, she was repaired and used to ferry supplies to the Confederates from British sympathisers. In the main, she transported grain and weapons. A number of documents, however, showed that towards the end of the war, she was used to carry passengers.

On a voyage from Fort Fisher in September 1864, the passenger list was for five people:

Grant Thatcher (47), Teacher, Bristol, GB

Ursula Thatcher (42), Bristol, GB

Jessica Poirrot (18), St Brelade, Channel Islands

Diego Villa (21), Religious scholar, Marietta, GA,

Edward Bellhand (25), Tiler, Andover, GB

Whilst I am not naïve enough to assume that if someone has a gentleman's name, he must be so. I realised that I could quickly confirm if this Jessica Poirrot was the mysterious lady. Sure enough, a quick check at Bristol on the way back to Salisbury confirmed that the Thatcher's both succumbed to consumption three months after landing in Plymouth in early December 1864. Being the eternal cynic that I am, I checked their graves to make sure that the records matched, which they did.

After a brief break back home for a few days, mainly to rid myself of the wretched stink from the Harbourmaster's hand wash, I took the train to Andover to track down Mr Bellhand. I discovered that he was doing an emergency job re-roofing St Thomas' church in Charlton village, a few miles from Andover itself.

Despite the awful weather, Bellhand was in fine fettle, labouring through the ice and bracing wind. A devout Christian, he had refused payment for his services, save for two meals a day and lodging within the rectory, so he might make full use of the scarce daylight.

I quizzed him on the voyage, and I was satisfied that he was the person from the manifest. It was at this juncture that he said he would only answer the questions I had if I were to help him. I explained that my roofing credentials were non-existent, but he was insistent. Whilst I ferried tiles up and down a ladder, which, if I'm being truthful, was barely serviceable, I managed to enquire as to the other passengers.

Of the Thatcher's, he said that they were good God-fearing folk. They had gone to America to start anew, but with the war and their farm being taken, they decided that their old life was better than having no life at all. He expressed his sadness at their passing.

Diego, he recalled, was a gregarious man, seemingly always ready with a witty quip or scathing comment. He had with him, at all time, a red leather-bound book, about the size of a bible, but not the same thickness. Bellhand beseeched him to read a passage from it, but for all his pomp and bluster, any mention of the book was rebuked swiftly.

When I pressed him on the book—in-between nearly meeting my maker when I missed a rung and avoided plunging to my death by a last minute grab—he said that its only discernible feature was a worn gold-embossed, six-pointed star on the cover. No words, markings, or author name were visible on either the spine or the rear.

On the subject of Ms Poirrot, though, Edward became a little terse. Suffice to say that she had given him the come-on at the start of the voyage, only to then switch her affections to Señor Villa after the first week or so. They were reportedly inseparable until journey's end, going so far as to leave together when they docked at Plymouth.

Bellhand also stated that she was the only person who Villa allowed to look at the contents of the mysterious book, and that was only if he was present, and at the very end of the journey. After that, he said that they were 'conspiratorial'.

I would contend, though, that any such feelings were perhaps governed by his spurned loins than anything else.

Having thanked him for his candidness and powers of recall, I bid him farewell and struck out for home. The weather had worsened severely and my train home was cancelled due to a cracked rail. Finding solace at the Danebury Hotel, I decided to turn my sour mood into something of use, and went through the pocketbook in an attempt to decipher the other locations and the meaning of the other markings.

Though the latter was beyond me, with the use of a detailed map and of a number of the locals, who, with the help of several pints of ale, were most forthcoming, I was able to ascertain most of the locations.

The rest of the night was a blur, a cavalcade of drinking, eating and folk music. Numerous times I was asked to sing 'Old Brown's Daughter'. I believe purely so they could laugh at me stumble over the line, 'He's got

Jew's harps for the little boys, lollipops, and cheese', as frequently, 'cheese' would come out as 'cheeth'. A small thing I'm sure, but with the assistance of the rather splendid local ale, it was quite the hoot, I can assure you.

It was not until the morning, when, with a mug of steaming sweet tea, bacon and eggs—which I barely made inroads into—that I looked upon the map and was struck as to the audacity of the pair. For twenty odd years they had snaked their way through the southern counties of England. They appeared to stay in each town or city for exactly a year. Then whatever business they had, they concluded it, and moved on to the next place.

As my headache pummelled my senses, I tallied up the count next to the initials of the places. I was aghast. If they were what I thought, then Villa and Poirrot had taken care of approximately two hundred and thirty seven people."

Donald, now in control of his sensibilities, looked at the map I had produced, stroked his moustache, and looked at the route with a degree of detachment I was ill-prepared for. I knew that I was losing him. I had to move on and describe the findings of Chequers Yard, Chippenham.

The place that even now, when I close my eyes at night, still flashes before me.

"I spent months travelling along the trail which I, and the patrons of the Danebury, had deciphered. Every place, the same result. As expected, they must have used false names, and especially in the larger towns and cities, it was like trying to find the eye of a needle in several haystacks.

Even in the locations where the tally was high, such as Exeter and Yeovil, there were all manner of buildings that they could've done their wicked work in. And who is to say that they would've been as sloppy, or unfortunate, as they were in Wilton?

In addition, the time since elapsed would surely make any discovery remote to say the least. I did not let this discourage me.

I scoured empty warehouses, flophouses, opium dens and brothels, much to my wife's chagrin, I admit.

The closest I got was some more of that glittering powder in a few locations, but no bodies, nothing. Even the most fervent of judges would not prosecute someone on the basis of some shimmering grit.

Plus, for all my work, I had no picture of Miss Poirrot. For all I know, she could've been the lady I accidentally disturbed mid-coitus down the Corridor in Bath, or the doting wife I shared supper with at the Royal Hotel in Gillingham.

I had become quite morose. I had shunned all other cases except for this one, even going so far as to make my case to the Mayor of Salisbury. I knew that I was irritating the people who signed my pay dockets, but I had to find them.

Of course, no one believed a word of it. My superiors asked me the same question every time I reported back my findings: 'If this tally is truly a body count, where are the bodies, Norton?'.

I was beginning to believe them, until, by chance, I stumbled upon Chequers Yard."

At this juncture, I had to furnish a weary Swanson with the chronology. Chippenham had been the previous place they had been residents of, before heading for Salisbury, a mere thirty miles or so away.

"I had been canvassing the residents of a street called Lowden, a most peculiar part of town. Houses of multiple building methods ran up and down the street. It was impossible to tell what was original and what was new. Having received short shrift from number forty-four, I dusted my hat off and decided that now was a good time for luncheon.

The Audley Arms had been recommended to me, though with a warning as to some of the more… *aggressive* locals. My humours cared not for such things, and I must admit, albeit secretly, that I yearned for someone to take umbrage with me. True, I was far removed from the peak of my boxing days, but my left jab was still something I took immense pride in.

As I made my way down the road to the pub, I noticed a decrepit building to my left. Immediately, it struck me that there was something wrong with the place. I could hear a constant murmur from within, as if a chorus of mute monks were humming 'Jerusalem'.

Taking a swig of whiskey from my hip flask, my now constant companion on this fruitless task, I wandered over to the side of the building, which was down the bottom of a ramped dirt track. It was evident from the detritus and overgrown shrubbery that it had been some time since anyone had taken care of the property.

Peering through filthy windows yielded nothing but grubby hands, so with a well-placed shove to the rotten door—a trick I learned from the London bobbies, I might add—entrance had been effected. I removed my hat and patted the dust from it. As I did so, I noticed that a wad of paper had formed a crude doormat. Always an inquisitive soul, I picked it up and flicked through. Most were letters addressed to whom I presumed were the previous tenants. Others, though, were missing people posters. And not just for what you would say were ordinary people.

They were from the Diocese of Clifton, pertaining to a group of a dozen young clergy members who had gone missing after attending a scripture class at Salisbury cathedral. The number struck me immediately. Flicking through the pocket book, my fears were confirmed, as I saw CM IIIIIIIIIII scrawled in that lackadaisical script of a hand.

By now the murmuring had grown louder. The source appeared to be beyond another interior door. It had been securely fastened. The padlock, even after that period of time, was rust-free and in good condition. However, the frame to which it had been attached was of poor construction. Using a length of broken pipe I found on the floor, I was able to lever the lock free and the door lilted open lazily.

I was struck almost immediately by a hideous smell, of rancid meat and spilled blood, like an abandoned abattoir. Placing my handkerchief over my nose and mouth, I pushed the door open with the toe of my shoe and made my way inside.

I quickly discovered that it was not a gathering of mournful monks, but a swarm of thick-bodied black flies. They were so dense that I could feel them bounce off my hands and face as I made my way through them. Their bloated forms and incessant buzzing brought on a severe case of claustrophobia; not since my caving days in the Welsh mountains had I felt so constricted and terrified of being trapped.

I spun around, but was badly disorientated. In my state, I was unable to work out which way I had just come from, and to where I was heading. Were it not for my putting my foot into a fetid, rotting skull, I think I would've become one with those blighted insects and made my peace with the world.

At first I thought my foot had become trapped in a bucket, as I could feel liquid lap against my shin. It was only when I lifted my foot and placed it against the floor again that the sound did not marry with that notion.

Instead of a clanging sound, it was akin to a pestle tapping against the inside of a mortar bowl. I repeated the process, convinced that a number of the winged host had crawled in my ear canal and were burrowing into my skull, deafening me from within. The thud came again, this time with a cracking sound, like ice placed in warm cider.

My mind now was full of paradoxical thoughts, each vying for their own place and order. I made the mistake of removing my handkerchief to free my foot, and in taking a deep breath, ingested a number of the flies. As they slid down my gullet, their legs kicked out in desperation, they tickled my throat until they bubbled into nothingness in my stomach acid.

I managed to get a hand around the object my foot was embedded within, and again, a myriad of images swamped me. None of which made sense. I pulled one end down and slid my foot out, resolving to find the blasted main doors and escape from this den of droning bugs. Through the cloud, I could see cracks of light. As I paced briskly to it, my foot—slick from what I later discovered to be purge fluid—slipped on the stone floor.

Having finally reached the window, I worked my way along the wall to a set of large double doors. I lifted the wooden bar and, with immense joy, pushed the doors open, to freedom. The winged beasties, sensing an entire new world beyond their fiefdom, washed over me; a skittering mass of lacy wings and dangling legs. I collapsed to the floor and emptied my breakfast over the cobbled ground. It pooled in the cracks between uneven stone.

After a few moments respite, I managed to stir my resolve, and dabbing away the vomit-tasting saliva flecking my chin, I stood up and looked back into the building.

I thought no sight could ever have been worse than the mass of insects engulfing me, but I was sorely mistaken.

Hanging by butcher's hooks from the rafters, driven through the bottom of their hacked ankles, were a dozen bodies. Handless arms swung lazily as the swarm had made their escape. Heads, resting on their crowns beneath their bodies, were arranged neatly under each corpse, as if they were awaiting inspection by a sergeant major.

I examined one of the heads, which had a rather unsightly bulge in its cheek. As I prodded it with my fountain pen, the sallow skin burst, releasing a tide of fat, wriggling maggots over my fingers and onto the floor.

I retched once more, this time evacuating only a stringy pink goo from my stomach. In the strands which joined my mouth to the floor were disintegrating fragments of the flies. Legs still twitched in some macabre memory of movement.

Each body had been rent open from sternum to pelvis, but the way they were presented, so evenly spaced out and particular, implied to me that whoever did this wanted them to be found.

This was a message.

A memo from Hell to say that no one was safe, and that whatever the purpose was, it was borne out of pure, unadulterated evil."

5

"My apologies, Donald. I do fear that my recounting of that day tends to delve into details which are perhaps better left unsaid. Please, have another gin. I think you, and I, have earned it."

I spent the next half an hour reporting how each of the bodies had again been stripped of all internal fibre and sinew. How, again, no sizable remains were found. Even less so since the flies had used them as breeding grounds for a matter of time. I also told him about the strange glittering powder that we found, here and there, around each of the bodies.

I deduced that it must be linked to the bodies somehow, but I could not determine to what end. Were the bodies perhaps washed and prepared, and this was from the residue of the cleaning process? I made sure that this time I would collect a proper sample and send it to Doctor Young for examination. After an hour or two, I had managed to collect enough to lightly cover the palm of my hand, though a great deal of dust and flotsam were also mixed in.

However, the trail had now gone cold. With Chippenham my last stop before home, I had nowhere else to go. I had twenty bodies in total and, Señor Villa aside, the others were of no real use to me. I mused over this for a number of months. I was at a dead end, unable to make any progress.

Until one day, like the proverbial carriage, not one came by, but two.

It was now the summer of '87, and Doctor Young had finally been able to examine in detail, the material I had sent him. Miriam and I had just returned from a fortnight away in Cardiff, and were in need of alternate company. As she headed out to meet Pippa, a frightful battle-axe who had served as Miriam's bridesmaid, and who never took to me, I headed to the station to catch up on some paperwork.

Having reached an impasse, I was resigned to menial work and some light filing. However, no sooner had I walked through the door, I was accosted by Doctor Young. His grip was firm, far exceeding any expectations I had from his appearance. He shooed me into my office and appeared giddy with news.

Before he could utter one word, though, I asked Constable Coombes to furnish us with a pot of tea and some fig rolls. Tidings, good, bad, or indifferent, cannot be received unless tea is being consumed. This did appear to pain Young terribly, but a man's principles cannot be countenanced, based purely on someone's whimsical nature.

With a full cup of steaming tea—resting on a saucer at its usual place on my desk—I motioned for Young to at least be seated, and nodded to confirm that I was now a willing recipient to his news. He became highly animated almost immediately again, as though he were possessed.

Science had never been a strong point of mine, and I yawned profusely as he babbled on about the wondrous material I had provided him with. After several minutes of near nonsensical words, I held up my hand and said to him one thing: 'Tell me in plain English, my good man.' He sighed, and then told me that the powder I had given to him contained elements which were beyond categorisation, yet also shared many common elements found on earth, and inside people.

He quizzed me intensely, thinking that I had tampered with it somehow, or had not told the entire truth as to its origin. My dumbfounded face convinced him of the truth and he smiled again. Young was visibly shaking now, saying that this was a scientific breakthrough.

I asked him what could've caused it to appear, and he admitted that he was at a loss. He confirmed that no known compound could have created it. His original hypothesis was that it came from a meteorite. He had been a keen geologist and astronomer in his youth, and had studied a number of these extra-terrestrial rocks and noted similarities between them and the powder I had offered up for investigation.

Another whirlwind set of questions asked me how and where I found it, what form it took and its consistency. I told him all I knew. That I had found sprinklings of it at both the stables and the terrible Chequers Yard, never concentrated heavily and for some reason scattered around the maimed bodies that we had discovered. This did, for a time at least, quieten him, and he pondered my words.

He said that he would continue to investigate it, but

without determining where it came from, he would be unable to confirm too much more. Young implored me to contact him should I find any more of this powder. He shook my hand vigorously, and left.

It would be the last time I saw him. A few months later, he was killed on a hunt outside of Stockbridge. A beater startled him and, according to reports, Doctor Young made a sound like an irate pheasant and was fatally wounded by Lord Bartley's shotgun.

Terrible business.

I think his findings on the mysterious compound were filed and that, as they say, was that.

The second surprise came in the form of a mutilated body in Basingstoke. I would not ordinarily be told of every murder, bizarre or otherwise, in the land, but I had garnered quite a reputation with the Chatham case. So much so that when a body was found, decapitated, with portions of the skull scooped out and a number of organs removed, I caught the train once more and followed up on the tip.

There were many similarities between *my* bodies and the one in Basingstoke. It had been laid out on a butcher's block in a closed down shop. The head had indeed been completely removed, though unlike the others it was still relatively intact. As was the body. It was a male, and he had been opened up like the others, but instead of everything being removed, only portions of the intestine and lungs were missing.

I was on the verge of turning around and going back home when I noticed that there was a bowl beneath the table. Inside it was a section of gut, which had been mashed with a firm implement. On closer inspection, I could make out traces of the glittering compound, which had excited Doctor Young so. The amount there was so insignificant that I made no effort to extract it.

It did get me thinking, though. Perhaps the weapons and tools Ms Poirrot operated with had been imbued with some mysterious rock from outer space, and this was somehow linked to the killings. It was obvious that she was not of sound mind. But the pieces did not link together, and I was left, again, with a frightful headache and yet more questions.

Fortune favoured me as the medical attendants shifted the cadaver. They rolled it onto its front, spilling the innards onto the floor. Thoroughly embarrassed with their lack of professionalism, they attempted to correct their mistake. In doing so, they uncovered a crude message carved into the victims skin:

Dear Boss, the plan is undone
The end game now impossible.
All I have left is the blood to take
and the flesh to own. √

Something had happened to Ms Poirrot. Perhaps the killing of her partner had sent her over the edge, or her near discovery had reminded her that to dilly dally would be to risk capture. She must have known that we were onto her, though I think she overestimated our knowledge and understanding.

What we had now was not someone who was methodical and working to an end. What we had now was a monster.

I understand, Donald, that you have received a letter, which shares similarities?"

He looked at me as if I had just cut into his favourite pie and removed all the prime cuts of steak. He poured himself another gin, drank it whole, looked at me, and then said, "Thank you for bringing this to me, Norton, though it is not your concern. It is quite a fanciful story you have woven this day, and though I have no doubt that some elements are probably bathed in truth, you will forgive me if I insist that you do not contact me again on this or any other matter."

The pompous bastard stood up from the table, discarded some change onto its surface and made to leave.

"How dare you, Swanson. I came to you in good faith. No word have I uttered this day has been an example of my perfidy. The killings, the names and details, can all be checked and verified. What is it about this that you wish me to not pursue, I wonder? What do you know that I do not, and which would make me dig further into this than I would otherwise?

If I may speak frankly—and those words are a mere courtesy to you and your rank—you, sir, could not detect your thumb if it were not plainly evident on the end of your hand, and so distinct from the other digits.

I had to carry you and your ego through seven years of service together. Not once did I belittle you, or point out your deficits to our superiors.

I did not come here to score points or to rake over the past. I came here as I believed that you could put your shortcomings and guilt aside long enough to take on-board what I had to say. The fact that you are going to ignore this is a reflection of your facile nature, not mine.

Do not fear, dear Swanson. I shall not trouble you again. My service with the police force is soon at an end. Miriam and I plan to travel to India and sample some of the sub-continent before imbecility and infirmity consume us. Good day, sir."

I made to leave, and as I did so Donald grabbed my arm. He looked deep into my eyes. I could have sworn that I saw a flash of something dart across his pupils. As we stared into each other's eyes, like star-crossed lovers, he looked briskly from one side to the other, searching for some mysterious, unseen agent.

He pulled me in closer and whispered, "For the love of God, man, you have to let it go. There are forces at work here which are beyond the ken of man. You are not the only one who has come across this mysterious powder. Of the little I can say, it is not from a weapon, but from the very fabric of our being. I implore you to drop this."

His eye-sockets grew darker as the shadows consumed them. "We have known about this pair for a while now. Señor Villa was flagged to us from our sources in America. We thought his demise would give us the opportunity to study this further, but the damn woman went to ground before we could locate her and her stash."

My face, forever letting me down at cards, must have given away a tell. Donald quickly followed up with, "After she was disturbed by Chatham, she confessed all to a priest. All of their work, harvesting this...*powder*, it came to naught. She said that it was concealed from plain sight. When the priest pressed her on what this powder was for she just said 'to make us all whole again, to make us as one'."

I retrieved my pipe from my pocket and filled it to the brim. I shirked off Donald's grip and made for the exit. "Please," he shouted, "if you know anything about where it is, you must tell me."

I struck a match and applied it to the tobacco, puffing out plumes of smoke for effect. Waving the flame into submission, I threw the charred stick into an ashtray, turned to Swanson, and merely replied, "Good day, Donald. I wish you every success."

With that, I made my way home to pack for Calcutta and a life free of death and mystery.

"A man's gotta make at least one bet a day, else he could be walking around lucky and never know it"
— Jim Jones

12,870 DAYS UNTIL THE END OF THE WORLD
GIMBALTOWN
NEW PROVIDENCE, BAHAMAS
8 DECEMBER 1981

161

DUNCAN P· BRADSHAW

1

Samuel dropped the plastic-wrapped case on top of the others. It landed with a dull slap. "Man, this heat is too much," he grumbled as he mopped his brow with a damp cloth retrieved from the back of his jeans.

"What kind of horse shit is this?"

The booming voice from right behind him caused Samuel's heart rate to jump to near hummingbird levels of activity. Despite the abrupt interruption, he knew at once who it was and that he should mind his manners. "Pastor Gimbal," he mumbled into the sodden cloth as he turned around to face the squat, balding figure. "A fine day to you, sir," he finished.

A stern cough reminded him that his back-to-front baseball cap had not been removed. Not wishing to incur further ire, he took the hat off his head and held it behind his back. "Apologies, Pastor. I didn't hear you come in."

Jim Gimbal pulled the empty cigarette holder from his lips. It was evident that it had been held there for some time, as skin stuck to the slender black tube as he tried to remove it. Gimbal shoved another Lucky Strike cigarette into the holder and glared at Samuel. "I believe my instructions were crystal clear, Sam. Crystal. Were my words not explicit enough for you?"

Samuel, still looking at the ground, racked his brain for the cause of his castigation. Fighting the urge to remain docile, he looked around the wooden storage shed at the assortment of items, trying desperately to work out what he had missed or failed to adequately store. As the first possibility sprung to mind, Pastor Gimbal gestured towards the stack of canned drinks which Samuel had just brought in.

"You mean the Polka, Pastor? But, I just—"

"Silence, Sam," Gimbal commanded. His words slapped a restraining order over Samuel's ability to respond. "We all did the Pepsi Challenge, did we not? There was no other winner. One hundred and ninety four people out of the two hundred and twenty one people in this camp chose Pepsi as the winner."

"But I—"

"Not Coca-Cola."

"See the thing was—"

"Sure as shit wasn't that snake piss, Polka Cola. So, what in the name of fuckery do we have here, Samuel? Huh? Tell me. Tell me that someone in the Pepsi factory snuck into the Polka Cola factory one night and stole a consignment of empty Polka cans, just so they could take them all the way back to the Pepsi factory and fill it with a refreshing beverage," the pastor chided.

"Pastor Gim—"

"And then, having filled the Polka Cola cans with the mighty Pepsi Cola, they thought it would be highly amusing to sell it to some dumb fuck of a moron, just so he could have a good old laugh at his Pastor's expense."

164

Samuel tried to swallow but found his throat muscles, and indeed most of his body, in a state of paralysis.

"I can't hear you, boy," Gimbal mocked, cupping an ear on the off-chance that Samuel was speaking quietly. "Let me make this nice and simple for you, numbnuts. Where. Is. My. Motherfucking. Pepsi? Is this all a big joke? Behind that pile of forbidden books and LPs is the real thing, and you and whoever else is in on this are just having a big ole laugh at me. Tell me that's so."

Try as he might, the only thing his body allowed him to do was to make a strangled parping sound from his larynx. Samuel's hands wrung his cap, already laden with sweat. Misted beads of perspiration dripped from the brim onto the straw-covered floor.

"I can't hear you, Sam. I pray that some divine power is taking control of you right now, and that in a minute, you'll speak in tongues to reveal the truth behind all of this. Cos if not, then…well, I might very well have to shoot you in the head. Then, with your dumbass corpse still steaming on the floor of our wonderful pantry, I'd have to restrain myself from skull-fucking you before we make a start on the ol' ritual early," Pastor Gimbal continued to bate the dumbstruck man.

Finally, realising that he quite liked breathing unaided, and that he wished to consummate his relationship with Mary-Beth-Lou before the revelation, his brain fired out a stuttered response, "It was all Bert and me could get, Pastor. See, we went to Quantico-Mart and—"

Gimbal lit his cigarette with a rusting Zippo lighter, puffing out reams of purple smoke into the already humid and close air. "So now, not content with being a dumb

165

fuck, you're going to take poor Bert down with ya, huh? Poor old Bert, not even a whole year after his Lyndsey passed, the Almighty rest her soul. Not a full spin of this heinous planet around the fiery orb in the motherfucking sky since his wife died of the ass cancer, you are going to drag Bert, salt of the fucking earth, down with you. Is that what you're doing Samuel? I just wanna be *real* clear about your intentions right now."

Samuel squeezed his cap even more. The white beads of sweat mixed with the red dye from his cap splattered against the floor. "Pastor, I'm not meaning to say that Bert did this. It was *both* of us. *Equally*. Just we got to the store, and it was real late, and we knew how important it was you got the right amount, so we had to make a choice. There was only one crate of Pepsi left, but there was a ton of Polka, and it was on offer. We reckoned we could get all you needed and save a few bucks for the church."

Pastor Gimbal cradled his cigarette holder as his mouth opened up to blow squashed smoke rings from one side. The storeroom fell utterly silent, save for the dripping of dyed sweat against the floor.

Gimbal drained the cigarette in one last pull. Flicking the expended cigarette onto the floor, he looked at Samuel again. "Say, Sam. What need do we have of money? When the revelation comes in the next day or so, we will all join as one and merge with the Almighty himself. Pray tell, what use will the twenty seven bucks and eighty one cents you saved, be to me and our community? I wanted motherfucking Pepsi. These people deserve the best, you understand? When they relinquish their claim to their mortal coil, they should do so with the sweet taste of their chosen Cola swilling around their mouth, not with some piss-poor substitute."

Samuel clenched. "I'm sorry, Pastor. I didn't mean no offence, perhaps I—"

"Shhh, shhhh, shhh. It's okay, Sam. I mustn't have made myself clear before. It's okay. Say, here's Bert. How you doing Bert?"

Samuel turned towards the door, where he saw a man with a mean hunchback and a wild straggly ginger beard.

CLICK.

"Looks like you'll be going ahead of us now, Sam," the pastor said, and pulled the trigger of the .44 magnum which had been placed an inch behind Samuel's head.

Brain, skull chips and stringy segments of vein and artery showered the plastic-covered stack of Polka Cola which Samuel had spent the best part of fifteen sweat-drenched minutes piling up. He was allowed one last moment of existence as his eyes took in the viscera-covered cans before his light was extinguished and he landed on the floor in a heap, blood pumping from the large crater in the front of his face.

Pastor Gimbal grabbed his crotch, tutted, and refilled his cigarette holder. Through clenched teeth he said to Bert, "Drag this sorry sunnova bitch over to the retrieval room. Looks like Tony has got another to practice on before the big day."

Bert, nodding dumbly—as much as his deformity would allow—bent down and turned Samuel's body over. Chunks of brain slopped onto the floor. As he grabbed hold of Samuel's wrists and started to drag him to the entrance, Pastor Gimbal called out, "Oh, and Bert, tomorrow you and Marty are going back to Quantico-Mart, and this time, you do not come back unless you get some motherfucking Pepsi. Else Tony will get to hone his skills on your raggity ass. Am I clear?"

"Yes, Pastor," Bert mumbled, and dragged the corpse through the doorway.

2

"Least we know now how many are ascending at a time," Hank quipped. He stood in-between one pair of single beds, ten deep, liberated from an old US Naval port. The metal frames had been lovingly shorn of rust and hastily coated with thick black paint.

Hank folded the end of the pillowcase in on itself, plumped it up seven times from the side, five from the top and bottom, before three more times from the sides. Content with his handiwork and comfort incarnate, he carefully laid the plain white covered pillows atop a pristine white bedsheet, fitted to military specifications.

Sally whistled like a happy songbird. "Sure do, Hank. I wonder which batch we'll go up in? Imma hoping we get to go together."

Her words, laced with a southern drawl, caused the forty year old man to blush. "Shucks," he mumbled. "I sure hope so too, Sal, that would be swell. You've been awful kind to me since I found the light and arrived here."

She fluttered her long spider-leg-like eyelashes at him, and shoved one hand on a tight denim-clad hip, posing with her butt sticking out. "Well, you sure are easy on the eye, mister. While we may not get to be together now, we'll

169

get to spend all eternity with each other when we join with the Almighty."

Hank smoothed down the sheet, trying not to stare too long at Sally's provocative stance. *Gotta keep on keeping straight; only a few more days now and all this will be behind me.*

Sally turned around and got back to wrestling another pillow into its case. As she shoved the sleeve down, the door to the Nissen hut squeaked open, letting in a breeze of hot air. The ceiling fans kicked into high gear, trying to redress the temperature imbalance. "Hank, Sally, what fine work you are doing in here. My, my, this is a real oasis of calm," Pastor Gimbal said firmly.

The pair stopped working and stood together in the aisle, which ran from the door in the centre of the hut all the way to another at the back. By the rear doors, folded and pressed hessian rubble bags were stacked on the floor.

"I see you've even managed to get some of the scripture onto the walls, too. This is most impressive," Gimbal simpered, running one hand over the words written in Spanish as another dabbed sweat from his prominent forehead.

Hank nudged Sally playfully following the kind words and the pair exchanged a brief glance at each other. "Thank you, Pastor. That was all Sally, here. Said she wanted to make sure that folk were reminded of the reason they were here, you know. At the end," Hank winked at her after, and it was her turn to blush.

Pastor Gimbal shoved the handkerchief into his pocket and peeled his mirrored sunglasses from his face. The arms had created divots in his flesh as they dug into his chubby features. "This is my favourite passage. You know what it says in English?" he asked the pair.

Both of them nodded keenly and said, "Yes, Pastor," as one, before giggling together like lovelorn teenagers.

The pastor stood staring at them, twirling his sunglasses in one hand. The other reached for his handkerchief again as another rivulet of sweat ran down the side of his head and then along the channel carved into his skin. "Well," he said, "I'm waiting." A hint of devilry flashed across his face as he replaced his sunglasses back into their moulded position.

Hank's cheeky smile dropped off his face as if weights had been tied to the corners of his mouth. He gulped, and stammered, "We are all one. Each is our kin and our own maker are we."

Gimbal nodded and walked over to Hank. "What do you think it means, Hank? You've seen the divine material, pored over the design. What say you?"

"I don't know if I'm qualified to offer my—"

"I asked you a question, Hank. If I thought you unworthy to venture an opinion, do you think I would've asked it of you?" The pastor's face remained stripped of emotion. The only way you could tell he was alive was from another track of sweat running down his puffy face.

Hank shook his head vigorously. "Of course not, Pastor. I meant no disrespect. I have seen the divine material, and it is what convinced me of this path. To think that everyone is somehow connected, yet so different, is one that most are unable to comprehend."

Gimbal pulled the cigarette holder from his breast pocket, shoved a cigarette into the end and placed it in his mouth. "And could you?" he enquired through gritted teeth.

"Could I what, Pastor?"

A rasping sound foretold flame being applied to the cigarette. A pregnant pause as the pastor puffed on the Lucky Strike did nothing to ease the tension. "Could you comprehend it, Hank?" he finally asked.

Swallowing down another wad of endless saliva, Hank replied, "Only with your guidance, Pastor."

A timeless lull followed, before it was broken by a cackling from the squat, rotund Jim Gimbal. Hank and Sally looked at each other, unsure if they had missed the punchline. Nervously, they joined in. "Hank, how far up my ass did you crawl? I'm not here for you to give my ego a handjob. I asked you a serious question, and all I want is a serious answer. Not many people have seen the things I've shown you, not even purty little Sally Robbins here, eh?" When he finished speaking, the pastor licked his lips, leering at Sally's cleavage, before sucking on his cigarette holder.

"So tell me, Hank, what did you think?"

Like a fish floundering in the wake of a shark, Hank coughed and continued. "Honestly, Pastor, until I saw it I didn't know of my place in this world. I'd spent too many years killing in the jungle to know of anything which could possibly connect me to another human being. Yet seeing that dust back then, well…it changed my life, Pastor. Honest it did. I wouldn't have packed it all in and come out here to live with y'all otherwise." Hank hoped that he had said enough to pass this latest test.

Gimbal sucked on the cigarette holder. His teeth tapped against the thin plastic. "See, how hard was that,

Hank? That's all I wanted to hear, your thoughts, nothing else. Now, if you two don't mind, I best get g—"

The pastor stopped stock-still, staring at the bed before him, the sheet pulled so taut that it looked like a slab of ice. "What in the name of pissflaps is that?" he demanded, a fat cigar-like finger pointed at a pillow.

Sally and Hank looked at the pillow and then to each other, their faces a Rubik's cube of confusion. Unsure of what to say, Hank mustered a feeble, "It's a pillow, sir."

"I know that, Hank. I can see that it is quite clearly a shit-fearing pillow. As plain as the goddamn nose on your pretty boy face, I can see that it is a refuge for the weary and the fatigued. When one of us is tired after a day of working off our penance, what finer thing could await your heavy head but a pillow? Hmmm?"

Hank's mouth opened and closed like a goldfish shouting 'pick me' in a pet shop.

"But you see, Hank," Gimbal continued, "there is an ocean of difference in the world of pillows that perhaps y'all not familiar with. I believe my wishes were explicit, were they not?"

"But I—"

"Shhhhhh. I believe I said, quite plainly this morning, that you were to use only the finest goose-feather pillows in the chapel of transcendence. That no other would do, lest they fail to amply comfort the head and mind of the person who is travelling from this world to the next, as their vessels vacate, ready for transformation," Gimbal lectured.

"Tell me, Hank, Sally, did you search the village for the finest goose-feather pillows to fulfil my request?"

173

Sally went to take a step forward, but Hank held her back and took a step instead. "I'm sorry, Pastor, that was on me. In my haste this morning, I must've failed to notice that one of the pillows was of a synthetic nature. If you'll grant me this oversight, I will replace it immediately."

Pastor Gimbal eyed him up. Hank stared at his own double reflection in the mirrored sunglasses facing him. "I am nothing if not a tolerant man, Hank. I'm sure you know that. Just I have so much to do, and if I had the time to attend to all of these little details, then I have no doubt that it would be exactly as I have it pictured in my head."

"Yes, Pastor."

"Instead, though, given my limited time, I have to delegate certain tasks to members of this village, so that I am unburdened by triviality and may focus wholly on the preparation of the revelation instead."

"Yes, Pastor, I could j—"

"My papa, the Almighty bless his diseased soul, see, when I was young and he was drunk, used to come back home to me and my mama. After he beat me, he'd start on her. One day, though, he went a little too far, and my mama got pretty sick. A few days later, when she was still coughing up blood and wheezing as though she had a flute reed shoved up her nose, he got tanked again. He wanted her to shut up, but even he knew that he couldn't beat her anymore. The fun had gone out of it, you see. So he got a pillow from the bed and held it over her face till she left us. After he killed her, he picked her head up by her hair and put the pillow beneath. He kissed her on the cheek then went to the porch and, using his favourite shotgun, decorated the walls with essence of brain and three quarts

174

of whiskey. I went to check on my mama when I heard the shot. Guess what kind of pillow she was resting on when she went?"

Hank mustered, "A goose-feather, Pastor?"

"DING DING! Shit, Hank, I think maybe you are one smart motherfucker after all, huh?"

Mouth flapping was the reply.

"But then it makes it even more galling when I go check up on one of my flock, to see if they have been able to follow my instructions to the letter, and I am left disappointed. You don't want to disappoint me now, do you, Hank?" the pastor asked menacingly.

"No, Pastor. That's why if I could just head out, I can replace this one with a goose-feather pillow, just as you asked…" Hank managed to get out.

Sally clenched her jaw, yet still a solitary tear expanded in the corner of her eye. As it reached critical mass, it rolled slowly down her cheek, daring her to wipe it away.

"Ha, of course you can, Hank. Did the Almighty not show forgiveness when necessary? Go. Go on now. Go and get the motherfucking pillow I asked you to get in the first place. Go on. Fuck off. Best be quick now, before I figure out that the real person to fuck this all up was Sally here, and I go and break her fucking nose."

She wiped the tear away as it crested her chin. "Pastor, I—"

"SHUT THE FUCK UP, SALLY," Gimbal shouted. "I done gone think you've done enough damage for one day. Did I speak with a stammer, Sally? Hmmm?"

Sally looked back at him, utterly bemused. Her brain allowed her to pass a solitary letter from her lips. "B-b-b-

175

b-b…"

"I guess I don't, Sally. Sounds like that must be you with the speech impediment, huh? So in that case, is your head so full of that garbage from Tee Vee that you have forgotten all I taught you about the everlasting and the joining of us all together?"

"B-b-b-b-b…"

"That my words no longer soothe you like they used to. When I found you doing tricks in that Motel car park, that dumpster was so well utilised, it had your ass-cheeks embossed into the metal. Do you folk not realise that when y'all go, I want you to go with dignity and comfort, so that your souls are happy for when the joining commences?"

Sally managed to stop spluttering the second letter of the alphabet and instead fought back another raft of waterworks. "Pastor, it's fine, it's on me. I'll go get that pillow now, no problem," Hank said apologetically.

Gimbal turned his gaze to the man and stared. "Fine, best get going now, Hank. Make sure you don't crease the pillowcase as you take the old one out. Wouldn't want you to fuck that up, too."

Hank nodded and walked towards the bed marked by the pastor. He slid his hands between the pillow and the case and began to tease the pillow from the end.

CLICK.

"When you get to where we're going, Hank, I sure as shit hope that you've thought about what's happened here today, and how you got your brains blown out, covering for this dumb fuck," Pastor Gimbal said disappointedly. The revolver's barrel was brought up to the base of Hank's skull, who had just enough time to close his eyes and recall the time he had caught Sally naked in the shower room.

The bullet smashed through his spinal column and sent shards of bone out through Hank's open mouth. His lifeless body, still clutching the pillow, hit the mattress and bounced off, coming to a rest in a heap on the floor, the descent recorded by a stark red blood trail against the pristine white sheets.

Sally's grip on her emotions broke and she collapsed in sync with Hank's body and began wailing like a tripped household alarm. She pulled his corpse into her chest and together they rose and fell in time with her sobbing.

"Oh please, Sally, be quiet, else I'm gonna have to shoot you, too. Then poor Tony is going to get pissed at me for giving him so much to do on what should be his day off."

The bawling subsided, though it was replaced by jerky hiccups.

"Good girl. Now go put Hank in one of the bags over there and leave him out back. Then ring the bell and we'll see if those stoners, Drew and Poe, can remember what the fuck they are supposed to do. Honestly, you people are making this so hard, all I'm trying to do is help y'all."

3

"Hey dude, I think we should ask for more. I'm pooped, and we've only carried one body. On the day, there's gonna be like, what? Two hundred?" Poe moaned. He took a drag from the offered joint and held it in.

"Nah man, it's cool, Gimp-ball said he's got a gurney we can use. All we gotta do is chuck the body bags on and pull it on over here," Drew replied. "Hey, dude, if you ain't tokin' that, pass it on man. That's not cool."

Poe, still holding in the toke, topped up the minute amount of lung not doused in marijuana smoke and passed the spliff back. Dropping the bag handle, he banged on the door with a balled fist. A few seconds later, and unsure as to whether he had knocked in the first place, he repeated the door banging. "Yo, Tony," he bellowed.

Scuffing of leather on wood sounded from beyond the whitewashed door. Then came the sound of a bolt being pulled back, and the door opened into the building. It revealed a man with a goatee, a shaved head, and a plastic apron which appeared to have been dunked in blood and minced organ.

"Another?" Tony asked, exasperated. "Supposed to be my day off, dammit. Got better things to do than mash up more people."

Poe exhaled what little smoke had not been subsumed into his being, and looked up at Tony. "Dunno what you want me to tell ya, dude. The bell rung, we went, and there was the bag, complete with body. Why? Who else you got in there?"

Tony peered into the bag on the doorstep, but the mass of contorted limbs prevented him from ID'ing who the unfortunate bastard was. "Sam, Bert said that the pastor took offence to their choice of Cola, and offed him. Who is that?"

Drew's face dropped. "You're shitting me? Pastor killed him over that? Doesn't that strike either of you as a tad excessive?"

Tony shrugged. "C'mon you two. Let's get this poor S.O.B. inside so I can get started." Poe and Drew shared a stoned glance before they took a handle each and pigeon-walked the dead body into the building.

With the door shut behind them, Tony whispered to them conspiratorially. "Fellas, best not get too ornery. The pastor has a bit of a habit of this. We worked a camp together in Nicaragua a few months ago. Course, back then I wasn't on retrieval detail. Anyways, the final day, before, you know…*it*, well he must've capped a dozen or so people."

The trio trudged down a small corridor to a doorway which opened into another white-washed walled room. Extraction fans whirred at a steady drone, nestled either side of a large sodium lamp in the middle of the ceiling. Under the bright light was a metal workbench, with two metal-working clamps at the foot and one each on the long

179

sides. Tony nodded towards the bench. "Go put our mystery guest up there, will ya, fellas?"

Dumping the bag to one side of the work area, Drew and Poe fumbled around inside. After a number of failed attempts, they hauled the carcass out with one pair of hands under the poor sod's armpits, one around an ankle, and another hand firmly grabbing hold of the crotch area.

Tony sighed as the body was laid out. "Ahhhh, it's Hank. Damn, I liked him. His 'Nam war stories were pretty cool. Fucked up, but cool. Shit man, I wonder what he did to piss Pastor Screwball off?"

The two stoners started tittering. "Screwball? Why do ya call him that, dude?" Poe asked, still creased up with laughter.

Tony sighed, and started to unwind one of the clamps from the long side of the bench. "Well, in Nicaragua, there was this guy called Corey, and this dude was what? Fucking six foot eight, built like a brick shithouse, tattoos everywhere, including a dragon on his dong. He was the sweetest guy, though I think he was a bit slow. Ya know?"

Palm up, Tony slid Hank's hand underneath the clamp and began to tighten it until the pad pinched the hand to the desk. As he tightened it, the metal squeaked, causing them all to shield their ears. "Sorry fellas."

Tony walked round to the other side of the desk and repeated the process with the other hand. "Anyways, Corey is a fucking one-man lifting machine. The camp we were in then was only small-time; thirty people, I think, most of them from Jacksonville. The pastor gets a hard on when he picks them up from there. The place is in the middle of nowhere, so couldn't get any machinery in to move shit around. Doesn't matter, though, as Corey would fucking drag a forest to the end of the world, if the pastor had asked him to."

The clamp was wound down on the other hand. Tony took care to make sure it didn't elicit the same brain scraping sound as before. After checking to make sure it was secure, he walked to the foot of the table. Poe rested on the workbench by Hank's face, landscaped by a gaping hole from where the bullet had taken the jaw off, and began to skin up.

"So it's the day before retrieval. The pastor is wound tight, I mean tighter than Hank's wanking hand." This caused the trio to crack up again.

"Anyways, Gimbal has already smoked these two broads. One opened up the curtains the wrong way, left side first, so she ate a .44. Then this other one, Julietta I think, well, she made the cardinal sin of not rinsing the breakfast bowls with tepid water. So BOOM, she chews on a round, too." Tony wiped his hands on the side of his jeans and began to open both of the other clamps.

"People have heard the shots, but you know what they're like. By this point they'd believe that clouds are fucking cotton candy if the pastor said so. Corey had just taken the two bodies over to the chapel. Norm was the main man then for getting the stuff out. So Corey dumped them outside and lumbered off to the john," Tony continued. He pulled off Hank's boots and socks and threw them into the corner of the room, where Sam's shoes already lay.

Pulling the legs so that the feet hung off the bottom, he placed one clamp over an ankle and then proceeded to affix it to the workbench. "So I'm having a dump when Corey hits the head. I knew it was him. The dumb fuck would always whistle, errr...what was it? Fucking *Ride of the Valkyries*, y'know, from *Apocalypse Now?* He loved that film. He's whistling away, I'm reading about Charlie Brown an' some shit, when I hear someone else come in."

Tony moved to the other foot and clamped it to the bench. Poe sparked up the joint and, after a few pulls, passed it to Tony, who took it gladly. "I could hear them talking, fuck knows what about. Then I hear the sound of boots walking away. From the thudding, I guessed it was Corey. Next thing I know, the pastor is screaming at him, asking why he hadn't washed his hands, and if he knew how many germs were in urine. Corey ummed and ahhed for a bit before I heard Gimbal cock that hand-cannon of his and BOOM. Sounded like a fucking tree collapsed onto the floor."

With Hank secured to the bench, Tony passed the spliff to Drew and moved round to the side. He began to unbutton Hank's shirt, picking off dried-on pieces of face, blood, and bone in the process. "I don't know why I did, but I got up and left the cubicle, and there he is, the pastor. Standing there, with those fucking aviators on, magnum smoking, cigarette holder clamped between his teeth, looking down at Corey's body, which is still jerking like he's dry-humping the floor."

Tony picked up a scalpel from a blood-soaked tray and scored Hank's chest from what was left of his throat right down to the base of his penis. "Worse thing, though. The pastor hadn't even stopped pissing. Must've turned around as soon as he heard Corey walk past the sink. So he's there, holding the gun, with his dick sticking out of the fly, and he's urinating all over Corey. It was fucking disgusting, man."

Having sliced open the skin, he dug in his surgical glove-covered fingers and began to pry the flesh apart. Poe looked away the best he could and willed Drew to pass him the spliff.

"So what did you do, dude?" Drew asked, his face screwed up after a nasty toke.

Tony began to pull at the ribs with a claw-hammer. "What do you think I did? I washed my fucking hands and got the hell out of there."

The stoners began to laugh. "Man, that is fucked up. Hope we don't—"

BOOM!

All of their heads turned towards the main door. Tony sagged and resumed the rib removal. "Well, guys, sounds like the pastor is playing your song. Best go get the next one and drag them in here." He nodded towards the hollowed out corpse of Sam discarded against the far wall. "Gonna be a busy day."

Senator Boulder peeked out from underneath the trestle table, which was laden with wilting salad and fingerprint-smudged metal coffee pots. "Well?" he grunted. "That sure as hell sounded like a gunshot. What's going on out there?"

"It looks quiet, sir. There are people walking around with...*washing* by the looks of it. There's even a couple of guys over there with a rubble bag or something," Hunter reported, peering through the Venetian blind slats.

"Affirmative, sir. All quiet out back too. No one is spooked in the slightest; must've been something else," Baker confirmed. He slid his sunglasses back up the bridge of his nose and mumbled into his cuff intercom.

"I'm too old for this," Boulder grumbled, crawling out from his hiding place. As he stood up, he caught his tailbone on the lip of the table, causing the assortment of refreshments to judder. Hunter and Baker rushed over to the man, who spurned their help.

The senator dusted himself down and looked at his bodyguards; two identikit, square-jawed men, resplendent in black suits, white shirts, black ties and matching 'his and his' Beretta cufflinks. "Something doesn't smell right here, and I'm not talking about the salad dressing. Have you seen it?"

He gestured towards browning clam-shells of lettuce, limp batons of carrot, and curled up discs of cucumber. "Think the heat doesn't help, sir," Hunter ventured, incurring an icy stare from his employer.

"Well at least you two fellas have still got your guns, huh?"

Hunter and Baker shared a glance, and spoke into their cuff mics again. Their blank faces regarded Boulder. With an elbow to the ribs, Hunter nominated his friend to volunteer the information. "No, sir, we were asked to relinquish our weapons when we arrived. Pastor Gimbal told us that this is a pacifist colony, and the sight of weapons could spook 'em."

"You mean to tell me that, having hired you two for the sole purpose of making sure I make it back to Florida without resembling a human colander, you are now unarmed? Fellas, I gotta say, I'm mighty disappointed in you both." Boulder smoothed down his tie, fumbling with the pin. "What if things go south?"

Hunter nodded to his compatriot and knelt down. "Don't you worry, sir. I never hand over my Walther PPK." He pulled the pistol from an ankle holster and slipped it into his jacket pocket.

"Sir, I think you've got the measure of this place wrong. These people…they seem to have a purpose. Look at them," Baker interrupted, gesturing to a window.

Baker raised the blind, and the trio watched as the occupants of Gimbaltown milled around. Everyone strode around purposefully. Some helped carry provisions; a man

185

and woman worked to repair a generator on the blink. Boulder flitted from one person to the next, trying to find an exception to the rule, quickly realising that he couldn't find one. "Hmm, don't mean squat. Something's wrong here, I can just *feel* it. I wouldn't have been told to come here otherwise. would I?"

A pair of blank sunglass-covered faces looked back, devoid of any emotion. Losing his patience, Boulder tutted and headed over to the trestle table. Extricating a plastic cup from the bottom of a stack, he poured some coffee into it and rested on the edge of the table.

"I mean, look, I've been telling this Pastor Gimbal to go fuck himself for the past nine months now." Boulder put an arm across his chest. "And then *they* tell me I have to come. Well, I don't like it." He took a sip from the coffee and his face puckered. Boulder looked into the dark brown liquid for the cause of the offense. He took another cautious sip before spitting it onto the floor. "Dear lord, they can't even make good coffee. This tastes like someone has crapped in it."

"Did you know, sir, that there is a particular kind of coffee that uses beans which have passed through the digestive system of a bat?" Hunter said, matter of factly.

Boulder's face was still wrinkled in disgust. "Son, judging by this coffee, I think their beans have gone through everyone in this hellhole."

The front door creaked open, causing the three men to miss a heartbeat. "Gentlemen, I trust you are enjoying the hospitality of us humble folk here in Gimbaltown?"

"Pastor, you nearly gave me a heart attack," Boulder chided the intruder.

Gimbal put his hands out apologetically. "Why, I'm sorry, Senator, I was just checking up on one of the young ladies over yonder. Poor girl knocked over a cupboard, very nearly injured herself in the process."

Baker ahhed and spoke into his mic. The two bodyguards eased and resumed their duties. "Oh, well, I hope she's okay…" Boulder spluttered, mopping his brow.

"Say, would you gentlemen like some refreshments? I know it's mighty hot out here. Even more so than back home, huh? Huh?"

"What do you have, sir?" Hunter enquired, trying to muster enough saliva to swallow.

Pastor Gimbal strutted to the refreshments table and placed a tray down. Whisking a white cotton tea towel off, he revealed three glasses of fizzing Cola, ice cracked and split. "Taa-daa."

"Thank you, sir. That's appreciated," Baker said. "What Cola is it? It's not Polka, is it?"

Gimbal ground his teeth. "No. This here is Pepsi, the last cans we had. Apparently."

"I can't drink that stuff. Gives me gas. You fellas knock yourself out," Boulder huffed. The bodyguards walked over to the table, nodded thanks to the pastor, and glugged down the drinks. Baker finished his in one go, and emitted a loud belch. Boulder shook his head in disgust.

Baker clucked his tongue. "You sure that's Pepsi? Tastes kinda funny?"

Gimbal clenched his fists. "I can assure you that it is. Perhaps you just had a bad one? Why don't you try the other?"

Nodding dumbly, but still running his tongue around

his teeth, Baker picked up the other glass, and after another expulsion of wind, sipped on the fresh drink. "Mmm, better," he mumbled.

"Senator, indulge me if you will. I've invited you out here to discuss a proposal about expanding my operation stateside for a while now, and all I've had back are letters telling me, kindly, to fuck off," Gimbal said flatly.

Boulder sighed and picked at a flaccid stick of celery. "It's not that we don't think you aren't doing good work, just…we feel that it isn't right for our state. You're asking for a lot, and have yet to say what you offer in return."

Hunter crunched the ice in his mouth and put the glass back on the table. As he chewed on the shards, he walked back to the window to keep watch.

Pastor Gimbal checked his watch. "Well, Senator, if it's money you're after, then we have plenty of that. The lord does provide, eh? And if it's anything else you're after…then I'm sure we can come to an arrangement." He winked at the senator.

"Gimbal, are you trying to bribe me? I hope you know that it's a federal off—"

A sound of something hitting wood broke the senator's flow. He looked to the back window to see Baker fitting on the floor. "Good God, man, what's happening? Help him. You, help him," he shouted over to Hunter.

With one hand clutching his head, Hunter turned and looked back into the room, which was spinning around like a tombola. "Sir…I'm not feeling too good…think the heat must've got to me," he managed, before collapsing to the floor on his knees.

"Faster than I figured. Looks like Jonie was right after

all. Go figure," Pastor Gimbal said to himself, pressing a button on his watch.

Baker continued to make dust angels on the floor. A thick white paste covered his blue lips. Senator Boulder called out to Hunter, "Get your gun. Take him out before he—"

Before he could finish, Pastor Gimbal smacked the pistol grip of his magnum into Boulder's face, breaking his nose and sending blood spraying over the lifeless salad. "You fucking weasel," Gimbal growled. "Your kind are all the same. All high and mighty, thinking you're holier than fucking thou."

There was a click from behind him. Turning slowly, Gimbal saw one of the bodyguards trying to aim a gun at him. The pastor grinned and looked at his watch again. "You've got spirit, son, I'll give you that. You took experiment number three, which is equal parts Phenergan and potassium cyanide. I wager you have mere seconds to shoot one of the multitude of images you're seeing of me, and hope it's the real one, before you pass out and die."

The gun, held in a shaky hand, continued to waver. "I thought s—"

Hunter squeezed the trigger, settling upon the central version of Gimbal swimming in his vision.

"You son of a bitch," Gimbal moaned.

CLICK.

The magnum round slammed into Hunter's collarbone and exited through the back of his throat. He feebly attempted to push back inside the chunks of flesh and artery which had been blown clear of the impact. He slumped backwards and as a myriad of ceiling fans swirled and whirred in his eyesight, he gasped and died.

"You're mad, Gimbal," Boulder mumbled, all the while holding his face. Blood seeped between his fingers and dripped onto the floor. The Pastor smirked and pistol-whipped the wounded man around the side of the head, causing him to smack against the table.

Baker began to thrash wildly against the floor. "Excuse me one moment," Gimbal said softly and walked over to the one remaining bodyguard. The white paste had dissipated, leaving a chalky residue on the man's face. His eyes bulged from his skull; the veins in his face were pronounced and looked like thick plastic tubes beneath the surface of his skin.

"Unfortunately, mister, you took two of the seventy-thirty mixtures, so I don't think you can be included as a test subject. Any findings would be null and void," Pastor Gimbal said coolly. "Plus, your shaking is really beginning to fuck me off."

CLICK.

Baker's head exploded in a cloud of blood, brain and soot-covered bone. His pale face now flecked with blood and tissue. The shaking ceased and his legs fell slack against the floor. A pool of blood blossomed out from the impact site, soaking into the black suit.

Gimbal stalked back over to the senator, who had picked himself up off the table. "It's people like you that stifle creativity and the free market, you know that don't you? Every time someone tries to reach for the sun, you and your kind come along and trample all over 'em. I bet to fuck that you killed Elvis, too, you ungrateful piece of shit. My mama *loved* Elvis."

Senator Boulder held his face. Fingers traced over the smashed and buckled swatch of skin and bone that used to be his nose. Blood squirted from a single hole as the septum, which had borne the brunt of the assault, hung from a small patch of skin.

"I invited you here so we could build something beautiful, and now you're pissing blood all over the floor of my pool room."

Boulder looked around puzzled. "Where's the pool table?"

Gimbal began to lay into the man again, loosening a number of the senator's teeth in the process. "I had to move the fucking thing out of here, just to accommodate you and your men. When you fucked off, I was gonna get Poe and Drew to put it back. It's league night, you know? The conclusion of three months' worth of round robin games is this evening, before the revelation. And now, I guarantee you that when Kellie goes to pot the eight ball, with all eyes on her, the poor woman will slip on your blood or twist her ankle on a molar and BOOM, she'll flunk it."

The pastor went to strike the senator again, but pulled out of the blow. "You motherfucker. Anyways, least you'll be of some use I guess…wonder how much we'll get out of you. Once we've filtered out all the bullshit of course."

Boulder shot him another look of bemusement. "You'll never get away with this, you psycho."

"I think we'll have to agree to disagree, Senator. See, you and your two buddies here are gonna have a little plane trip once we're through with y'all. Only, I get the distinct impression that there will be a terrible accident."

CLICK.

"They ain't gonna find a scrap of you bigger than a postage stamp."

5

Poe rolled up another spliff and ran his tongue along the gummed edge. "Still can't quite believe that Darth Vader is Luke's father." He carefully stuck the paper together and smoothed down the edge.

"Sure makes you wonder where they're gonna take the next one, huh? So much bad stuff happened, you think they're gonna be able to sort it all out? I mean, fuck, man, Han Solo is all frozen and shit, off with that cool bounty hunter dude. Let me tell ya, there is no way that guy is gonna go out like a bitch, huh?" Drew replied, eager to get back to smoking.

Poe waved a fly away from his face and accidentally flung the joint to the floor. "For fuck's sake, man, it's like this one is cursed or something."

"Ha, just like Jonie. What do you think she did to piss off Gimp-ball, dude? I mean, she was the sweetest little thing. This one time—"

"Like I care, man. Thought we were having a fucking important conversation over here? We get to the med bay and she's missing her face; for all I know, dumb broad did it herself," Poe replied laconically. "Now, can we please get high and get back to the motherfucking conversation?"

193

Drew held his hands up in defence. "Fine. So, question for ya. How the fuck did Luke learn all that shit from the last film? That old timer, Benny Wang Kenobi, or whatever the fuck, he got chopped in half in the first one. Who taught him about the ol' 'pull my lazer sword up from the snow' thing?"

The flame lapped over the twisted end of the joint, at the tip, a gas blue flame licked around the edge. "It's a light*sabre* dude, not a fucking lazer sword. I don't know, old Kenobi was like a ghost or something, though, hey? Perhaps, he's been like training him and shit, as a ghost," Poe puffed until the cherry burned bright.

"That don't make much sense, man. The ghost only appeared when Luke was either unconscious or when he fucked off in his spaceship." Drew looked across expectantly. "Will you hurry the fuck up, man? I'm Jonesing over here. Been like twenty minutes, or something. Still got Jonie's brains under my fingernails."

Poe took a deep toke in and passed it to his friend. He looked into the empty bag they had used to ferry the dead woman's body to Tony's house of reclamation. "Anyways, that Darth Vader dude is going to be one tough sunnova bitch to break, huh? That Emperor don't look too tough though. His face looks all messed up like it's been melted, and what is with all the robes? Makes you wonder why Vader don't just pitch the old dude off a ledge or some shit and take over the whole Empire."

Drew's eyes had glazed over by now. "Yeah, man. Those Stormtrooper dudes are bad-motherfucking-ass too. Gonna take more than a few of those rebel soldiers to beat them, huh? I reckon it'll be *huge* robots, or perhaps giant dinosaurs or something. There's no way anything less could defeat them. Look at that armour. Pretty tough."

Poe idly kicked a stone from the top step and watched as it bounced twice on the dusty track leading away from the building, "Definitely, Luke and Leia are gonna have to pay top dollar for some decent people. Perhaps they can get loads more Chewbaccas? Plus…what is with those two? They kiss, then she goes off with Han, but then they're all like hugging and shit at the end when he's had his hand chopped off and Han is all frozen and shit. Man, this is making my head hurt."

"I dunno. That Yoga guy said something—"

"Yoda, dude."

"What the fuck?"

"It's Yo-*da*, not fucking yoga. Dude doesn't teach you to stretch and shit does he?"

"Whatever, man. Yogi or whatever the fuck his name is, looks like a green ballbag, he ain't anything. Plus, what the fuck was he on about? 'There is another'? Like another Luke? Perhaps there are clones or something. That would be cool," Drew replied utterly annoyed. He took one last pull and passed the spliff back to Poe.

"You're such a dumbass," Poe whined. "You need to pay attention to this shit. Remember when we went and saw *Raiders of the Ark*? You were asking how come Han Solo was out of carbonite, and asked if he was dreaming? If you're not careful, smoking this shit will make you, like, really retarded."

"Fuck you, bro," Drew answered. Smoke rippled out of his nose as he gave Poe the finger. "You need to open your mind up to shit, dude."

195

"The only thing my mind is open to right now is whether that dumb motherfucker Sam managed to get some Chee-toos when he brought the Cola back," Poe mumbled, lost in an intricate knot in the step he was sat on.

"Fucking-A, man. Shall we go and mosey on over?"

"Let's."

The pair wriggled around in the sitting position and, after several false starts, managed to stand up unsupported. As they tottered towards the store room, a voice boomed from the road behind them. "Boys! I need you two to go and take care of some more…problems."

"Fucking Gimp-ball," Poe muttered to Drew under his breath.

They turned around and saw the pastor waddle at speed towards them. One hand was dabbing the perspiration from his elongated dome, whilst the other was supporting his cigarette holder, complete with unlit Lucky Strike.

"Dude looks like the fucking Penguin," Drew mumbled back. The pair began to titter and exchanged bro hand slaps.

With his canvas slacks chaffing against his thighs, Gimbal huffed and puffed his way up to the two stoners. Coming to a standstill before them, he clamped his teeth on the plastic cigarette holder and wafted a lighter to the end. As the end crackled and smouldered, the pastor growled, "The senator and his men have had a bit of an accident, fellas—"

"What kind of accident, Mister Cobblepot?" Drew asked, eliciting more sniggering.

"Cobblepot?"

"Sorry, sir, I meant, what kind of accident missed the cob or pot?"

Pastor Gimbal blew a pall of smoke at the man. "I don't know what kind of bullshit you're pulling right now, son, but may I suggest you shut the fuck up before I pistol fuck you back up your mama's cooch?"

The laughter ceased.

Gimbal's mirrored sunglasses shot back their own reflections curtained by a wall of sweat. "Good. Now, as I was saying, get on over to the pool room. You're gonna need three—"

Poe looked to his friend and took another drag. "What's up, sir, you having some kind of embolism?"

"Why aren't you boys smoking that brown I gave ya? I got that in especially for you two. Are you even remotely fucking aware of the lengths I had to go to, to get hold of that fucking nine bar?" Gimbal said gruffly.

Drew took the joint from Poe and ran the butt under his nose. "Errr, sorry dude…I mean Mister Gimp-ball. *Gimbal.* We got this green from one of the kids selling rum in the street. Thought it would break up the brown binge, ya know? Plus, it's so fucking good, I me—"

Poe elbowed his mate in the ribs, garnering a grunt and a look of 'why man?'

"So let me just get this straight now. I, from the bottom of my motherfucking compassionate heart, go and get you both nine fucking ounces of finest Columbian brown squidgy, as a thank you. And to thank me, you go and see Tom fucking Thumb and smoke his weed? See, boys, where I come from, that's mighty rude. A lesser man

197

might seek to bring down furious vengeance upon those who try and fuck him. Are you trying to pull my pants down and fuck me boys? Cos I gotta warn ya, my ass hair is thick and matted. The only way you're getting something into my exit hole is if you've brought a motherfucking blowtorch with you."

Poe and Drew exchanged utterly bewildered looks. "You want us to burn your ass hair off?" Poe asked, his voice full of uncertainty.

Gimbal sighed. "No I do not. If I was going to get some man-sausage stuffed into my asshole, it most certainly would not be from either of you. Now, you two are making my patience grow awful small. How about you fuck off and get the senator, and the dumb shits that came in with him, over to Tony. Before the blood soaks into the wooden floor and completely ruins the ambience."

Drew looked at the man with a slack jaw. "Sir, can we use the gurney? It's an awful long way and it's mighty hot out here."

The pastor looked back at the young man with utter disdain. "Fuck me, son, tell you what. How about I go and ventilate your motherfucking head, so it stays nice and cool, then you can get a free ride on the gurney when Poe here uses it to drag your sorry dead ass back to Tony."

CLICK.

CLICK.

CLICK.

Drew's face was scrunched up in anticipation of the round rearranging his facial features from normal to mashed up. "Looks like it's your lucky day, boy," Gimbal wooted, "I done gone run out of bullets."

"Phew," Drew sighed with relief.

"Unless you want me to reload?"

"No, sir, please! It's cool, we can carry them over to Tony."

"If you want, I could hold the .44 by the barrel and use it like a club to beat your ugly fucking face to a bloody pulp? If you'd like? Tell you what, how about you two motherfuckers strip down to your panties and waddle over there with your jeans around your ankles? Would you like that?"

"I'm good, thank you, sir. We'll just be on our way now. The *pool* room you say? Good day to you, Pastor," Drew stammered. His mate wrapped an arm around him and dragged him towards the building. The door hung ajar.

Pastor Gimbal waited for the two to leave and let out a little chuckle. "Dumb bastards. Best get on and get this tape recorded. No rest for the wicked today, it would seem."

Tony tipped the last residual particles from the collecting pan into the large terracotta pot. The glittering powder now filled half of the inside. He did a rough calculation in his head, and guessed that the revelation tomorrow would elicit enough to perhaps even get it three quarters of the way to the top.

He'd been with the pastor for just under two years. Tony guessed that it was his no-BS attitude that had kept him from being minced up and added to the pile of dust that he looked down into. He figured that, once or twice, he'd come close. Gimbal had a fickle hold of his emotions in the run up to collection day. He'd seen the flicker play across his eyes, and had either got out of the room he was in, or been lucky enough to have someone else incur his wrath.

He looked behind him, making sure that he was truly alone. Aside from the stripped carcasses he had already worked on and discarded in the corner of the room, Senator Boulder and his two bodyguards were the only company he had. One of the men was missing most of his face. A crater ran from his bottom teeth to the tops of his eye-sockets. Everything in between was pulp and sundered flesh.

The other had a huge exit wound at the back of his neck and shoulder, but annoyingly his face was intact. Blood-flecked skin, agape shocked mouth, boggly eyes which looked at him accusingly. Boulder, though, was bordering on unrecognisable. His nose, or what existed in the middle of his face, was a welt of bruised and beaten flesh.

"It's rude to stare, fellas," he said to the corpses.

After he rechecked the door, he put his hand into the pot and closed a fist around the powder. Tony lifted it up carefully, so it was still above the yawning hole. Opening his fingers, the sparkly speckles flitted down into the bowels of the pot again.

He wondered how many different people he held in the palm of his hand, how many lives were now mixed together, collected for an unknown purpose. Or at least, unknown to anyone except the pastor. That was the one condition of the deal they made: no questions. Providing he stuck to that, he got a free pass.

The others, or the sheep as he referred to them, well, they got everything they deserved. Usually at the end of their mental tether, some literally snatched from the jaws of suicide or depression. Gimbal offered them something, atonement. Some were religious zealots, utterly convinced in the certainty of God, that the pastor's sermons and riddles were definitive proof of the existence of one true deity.

Thing is, Pastor Gimbal was about as religious as Ronald McDonald, but as he confided in Tony when they first met, 'If a man tells you that he is God, and offers you some form of proof, they'll put you on a pedestal and do anything you ask of them.'

He wasn't wrong. Gimbal did look after people. He provided shelter, the means to gather food and simple possessions. The desperate were given hope, the sick got better, the unfulfilled got new aspirations, and all of them, in the end, found peace.

It was a clumsy affair to begin with. The first batch Tony had to deal with turned out no better than an amateur slaughterhouse. A group of fifteen men, women and children. Gimbal had whispered his honeyed words and shown them the powder. After that, they had obeyed his every word.

So when one night, he told them that the end was nigh, and that the only way they could be saved was to relinquish their own divine material, so that they all could live, they said yes.

All except for one. Gerry Cullens, eight years old and the smartest of the lot. He knew something wasn't right, but he took the pastor at his word when he said that if he didn't want a part of it, he could leave.

Gerry got two streets down when one of Gimbal's men picked him up. Tony never saw the kid again, but it's safe to say that the kid didn't get to see his ninth birthday.

The pastor lined up the fourteen people outside a barn. One at a time they walked in and lay down on a pile of hay bales which formed an itchy bed. Tony then put the bolt pistol to their head and put them out.

Damnedest thing.

Every single one of them kept their eyes open as he did it. Some even said a thank you right before he pressed the trigger.

Once they were unconscious, he'd drag them out to the back, behind a sheet, where Corey would slit their throats and hang them upside down above a trough till they were drained. After that, Norm would take them down one at a time and start the harvest.

Tony wondered how many people were in the jar? How many lives have been ended? All for what?

Patting his hands together softly, the powder fell back into the pot. Tony picked the pot up and placed it in the cupboard beneath the workbench.

He eyed up the three bodies and opted for Boulder first. Anything to get rid of that face as quickly as possible. He dragged the corpse onto the table and worked his way around, clamping the hands and feet into place. A quick tug on the shoulders told Tony that the senator wasn't going to go and slip off the table and onto the floor.

He undid the tie and, after examining the crest that was stitched onto the bottom, tucked it into his pocket. Perhaps when they got back stateside, he might be able to take a nice girl out for some food and 'fun'. No harm in looking smart, once the blood had been washed out anyway.

As he looked at the shirt-covered torso, he noticed that down the middle of the chest ran a ridge of something. It was as if there was a snake concealed there, waiting for freedom so it could snap and bite him on the nose.

Irrational as it was, Tony ducked behind the senator's smashed up face and began to undo the shirt buttons from the top.

After managing to get three open, in the most awkward

way possible, Tony dared to get a better look. As his fingers pulled the crimson and pale blue shirt open, he realised that it wasn't a deadly king cobra ready to strike… it was something much, much worse.

NOTICE

THE BEST COPIES OBTAINABLE ARE INCLUDED IN THE REPRODUCTION OF THE FILE.

PAGES INCLUDED THAT ARE BLURRED, LIGHT OR OTHERWISE DIFFICULT TO READ ARE THE RESULT OF THE CONDITION AND OR COLOR OF THE ORIGINALS PROVIDED.

THESE ARE THE BEST COPIES AVAILABLE.

DUNCAN P. BRADSHAW

FBI EVIDENCE

TAPE: #13
SUBJECT: JIM DONALD GIMBAL
LOCATION: GIMBALTOWN. BAHAMAS
DATE OF RECORDING: 12/8/1981
LOG DATE: 12/9/1981
LEAD FIELD AGENT: GOFF, J.T.

JIM DONALD GIMBAL: When I found you, I was a sinner, a drunkard, thief, conman and swindler. There weren't many things I wouldn't have done in order to put a buck in my pocket or a drink in my hand. Nope, not too much at all. I guess you could say that, in a way, I had to go through all of that to become the man I am now, the man who you helped to shape.

Were it not for those good ol' boys taking me down to the bayou and beating me senseless, all

207

because I stole their mama's necklace, I doubt I would have ever found you. Heck, I'd probably be in rehab or resting in a shallow grave somewhere up state.

As I woke up in that ditch, my pounding head was the undercurrent to a multitude of aches and pains troubling me. A few broken ribs, a chipped tooth or three, and one eye closed up real good. Seemed to me I could've been in a far worse state, considering the look of hate in the eyes of those boys the previous night.

They'd accosted me outside of No Way Pedro. Part bar, part burrito shack, all shithole, on the edge of Jacksonville.

I sat in the back of their truck as they drove round the countryside, arguing over where would be best to kick my ass. An hour or so later, I got hauled outta the back and that's when they started. Would like to have said I put up a helluva fight, but I'd be lying. Don't think it lasted too long anyways, and when I did come to, it was morning.

After checking my injuries, I tried to stand up and put my hands behind me. I could feel jagged rocks and pebbles beneath. After a great degree of effort I finally managed to stand. I had this long rock in my hand. When I looked at it, though, I saw it was a bone. It was all dirty, but picked clean.

Well, I think I got a bigger fright then than I had the night before.

I scurried out of the trench, but something made me look back. My mind ran over the pile that was there, and I could see that it was at least two people. Spines of different sizes, and poking out from a patch of grass were two skulls, leering at me, for disturbing their grave, I reckon. Amongst the bones were thick pieces of a broken pot, or something. Don't reckon the bones were inside it, anyways.

Was never a God-fearing man, but I knew that it weren't right them bones just laying there. They deserved a burial at least. I figured it would be penance, as that could well have been me down there, waiting for the maggots to add my bones to the collection, joining them forever in that pit.

I got to digging and, as my hands pulled away the side of the bank, I broke into a hollow. First off I took it for a snake den, and nearly messed my pants. When I looked again, I could see something within, like a face.

I couldn't tell you why I took it out of there, even less why I put my hands around it.

Guess I must've been concussed or some such. The bone had been polished real good; been there a while I guess. Whoever put it there, well, they looked after it. Was one big sunnova bitch, too. Had this perfect hole stamped through the temple. There was a leather hinge on the jaw to stop it from falling off, and after I untied a little bit of tendon, the mouth dropped open. That's when this folded bit of something fell out.

I opened it real careful, and saw words etched in the surface. I didn't know what language they were in. Regardless, I knew it had to be pretty important for someone to have squirreled it away like that. It was written on material with the strangest texture. It was thicker than paper, and the back was a different colour to the front. The smell was something else, though. I guessed it was some kind of animal hide.

I shoved it in my pocket and heaped the bones into the hollow along with the weird-ass skull.

After a few words, I scrabbled out of the ditch and started walking south, following the river. Figured sooner or later I'd run into people, get a ride to a town, and take things from there.

That evening, sipping on a cold beer in a bar in Brunswick, I managed to finally get a look at the words. Didn't make any sense to me, but I worked out that it was Spanish. So reckoned I'd find someone who could translate it for me. Who knows, might even lead to treasure. Didn't matter too much what it was; I could just feel that I had to do something with it.

Like it was my destiny.

A week later, and I ran into this hombre

called Juan. He worked in the fields, doing twelve hour days for the owner who repaid him by not telling the authorities. Over a few beers, I got a good feeling about him, and asked if he would do me a favor.

I gave him the hide and, after he read a few lines, it looked like he wasn't gonna say anything, then he got real excited and started telling me what was on it.

I'll be honest, it didn't make much sense to me first off. Something about the design of the universe existing within us all, that every living thing is connected in some way, and how if you collect enough of this essence, you could create something. Juan was pretty excited by this point and was speaking so fast I didn't catch much of it. Needless to say, it sounded pretty important, albeit a little far-fetched.

We went and got good and drunk.

I woke up and my head was pounding real fierce, and I was cold. I opened my eyes and saw I'd been stripped down to my underwear and tied to a chair. Juan was looking down at me, in this shitpit of a motel room, jabbering away in Spanish again. Fuck knows what he was saying.

After a few minutes of me asking him what the fuck he was doing, hollering real loud, trying to get someone, *anyone's,* attention, he stopped talking and started laughing. Prick went to the front door and opened it up. After my eyes got used to the light, I saw that the outside world was one abandoned motherfucker. Wherever he had taken me, it was well and truly off the grid.

So he closed the door and walked up to me. Using this curved dagger he cut off my vest, and I'm pretty sure I pissed myself at this point.

I got a look at the knife and it was like nothing I'd ever seen in Wal-Mart. Motherfucker looked old, *real* old. This laughing skull was on top of the hilt, all decorative, like.

Juan started to laugh again and moved in real close, so much so that I could make out every one of his nose hairs. He pulled his arm back and I shouted WAIT. I'm pretty surprised to see that he actually does. I asked him what the hell it was I did that led to me being tied to a chair, sitting in a pair of piss-stained underpants.

He stood up and began to unbutton his fly. Great, I thought, all I've done is gone from being gutted to being sexually violated. Was on the verge of telling him to just stab me with the knife and get it over with, when he pointed to this tattoo he'd got above his manicured man bush.

I peered in closer. Well, as close as I could stomach whilst being so near to another man's dick, and I saw that it was a six-pointed star.

I looked back up at him and shrugged. This beaming, all-knowing, fucking smile he had on drops like a whore's drawers. As he's doing himself up again, he starts shouting about how I've fucked his people over for the last time, and that all we've done is steal shit from his kind.

He's proper pissed now, tucks his tee shirt into his chinos and leans in. Real slow like, he digs the tip of the blade into the middle of my chest. Not too deep, just through a few layers of skin. Smiling like a motherfucker, he then goes all Picasso on me, starts drawing something.

How I don't pass out is a complete fucking mystery. I look down when he's done and there it

216

is: the same six-pointed star etched on my chest.
Juan starts laughing. You can tell, now, that
all I've done is piss him off. What was going to
be over in a flash is now going to take as long
as my will-power can hold out for.

I know there's only one thing I can do. The
dumb fuck has tied my hands to the rickety
chair, but my legs are still free. I mumble
something under my breath, and he asks me what I
said. I play possum and let my chin hit my chest.
I mumble again.

See, curiosity is a motherfucker, regardless of
whether you're torturing someone or stripped
down to your urine-soaked tighty whities. Juan
leans in close and picks my chin up. As he does
so I bite on his nose and clamp down as if I'm
having ECT again.

His nose is one thick, blackhead-ridden piece

of disgusting skin and bone. I begin to grind with my teeth and can taste pus, blood, and skin run down the back of my throat.

The knife drops to the floor; self-preservation is now his sole concern. Whilst he's focusing on trying to stop me ripping his nose off, he doesn't even see my knee come up and connect with his nutsack.

So as he begins to crumple like a Chevy meeting a truck head on, I let go of his nose and tip the chair forwards. I'm now straddling him. By chance, my legs have pinned his arms to the floor. My piss-soaked groin is washing his bloodied face real pretty. Guess the ammonia is hurting Juan bad, as he is howling like a castrated coyote.

Sensing that it is very much now or fucking never, I begin to headbutt him like a crazed longhorn. After seven or eight blows Juan is out like a light.

The boot, as they say, is now well and truly on the other fucking foot.

He didn't say shit for three hours. Muffled cries and hard-ass looks, even when I started taking his toes off. The knife was real sharp. I'd snip one off, then spark his Zippo and jam the end onto the stump to cauterize the wound. All of them went in forty minutes, and aside from losing a sock size he didn't say shit.

Next up I started slicing the webbing between his fingers. I'd learned from his mistake, and had him strapped to the metal bed-frame in the room. He wasn't going anywhere. I ran the blade down between the fingers until it scraped the bone. By the time I got to Mister Lefty, he was on the verge of blacking out.

I gave him a break, let the wound seal up, then figured I'd quit fucking around. Woke him up with a right hook, wanted his full attention, told him to tell me everything. Last chance.

Nothing.

I slid the blade under his left eye, just above his nose, and worked my way round anti-clockwise. He most certainly did not enjoy that. When it was cut free, I placed the blade a little ways into the socket and started to lever it out.

Then, he finally fucking spoke.

Said that it was a list of instructions, how that inside everyone was essence which has been there since the universe was born. That we're all nothing but fucking stardust. After a cigarette, he calmed down and told me how to extract it, that you had to get a certain amount. The dimensions of this pot were all on there and, after I gave him a hit from his hip flask, he told me.

I asked him what it would do, and he said he didn't know. I was about to remove an ear when he said that it wasn't written down. I searched his jacket and found it, along with a pen and a notebook. I got him to translate every single fucking word, and I wrote it down.

Motherfucker was right; it didn't say shit.

Just as I was about to slash his throat open and pull his windpipe out, I notice that the bottom edge of the hide is a bit fatter. I wiped the knife clean on his jacket and carefully ran the blade along the end. I opened it up to see that there was more writing there. I asked him what it said, and he told me it said two things.

The first was: We are all one. Each is our kin and our own maker are we.

The second was: When the harvest is complete and the tithe is repaid, only then can you merge with the reclaimed and burn anew, as one.

My head was a little fuzzy. The words meant shit to me, but they sounded...soothing, like it was something I'd like to do, make up for the things I'd seen and done.

However, I am not a man who takes shit at face value. I am - *was* - after all, a man of ill repute. I had to know that it was true.

I dug my fingers into his eye-socket and pulled the ball and string out. I tried to yank it all out, but figured if I needed to ask Juan some questions after, I better not fully fuck him up. I sliced the stem off and took it over to the sink in the bathroom.

I'm not gonna lie, I thought it was the biggest pile of BS I'd ever heard, but what if it was true? This lil' puto had gone to such lengths to take this from me. It must be pretty important. Anyways, I put the plug in and lay the eye in the basin. Using the knife hilt, I smashed it up real good. Had the consistency of a pickle. I go at it until there's nothing left but this red and yellow jelly.

I'm gonna call bullshit on the whole idea when I go and light myself a cigarette. I'm about to knock the Zippo closed when I see something glisten in the mashed up eye. Looking closer, I see it. Not much, barely enough to put on the end of your pecker and be happy about it.

Motherfucker.

Figured ol' Juan owed me. He done near took me out of this world, and now he's given me a whole new reason to be a part of it.

So, he was the first volunteer. I wanted him

to stay with me as long as possible, so took it real slow. I started with--

ANTHONY ORTEGA: Pastor. Sir, sorry bu--

JIM DONALD GIMBAL: What the fuck are you doing here, Tony. You know not to interrupt me whilst I'm in my chambers.

ANTHONY ORTEGA: Sir, Senator Boulder...he was wearing a wire sir. It--

JIM DONALD GIMBAL: Stroke my balls again, Tony, say what?

ANTHONY ORTEGA: He's wearing a wire. Well, a transmitter, sir. We need to get out of here.

(GUNFIRE)

(SCREAMING)

JIM DONALD GIMBAL: Let's get out of he--

AGENT JEFFREY GOFF: Pastor Gimbal, put your weapon down.

(CLICK)

heXAgRAm

(GUNFIRE)

--Recording Ends—

DUNCAN P· BRADSHAW

"So we grew together,
Like to a double cherry, seeming parted,
But yet an union in partition,
Two lovely berries moulded on one stem"
- William Shakespeare,
'A Midsummer Night's Dream'

73 DAYS UNTIL THE END OF THE WORLD
SALISBURY WILTSHIRE UNITED KINGDOM
YESTERDAY

DUNCAN P. BRADSHAW

"Wow."

"She looks beautiful. Truly stunning."

"Agreed. I don't think she has looked this good in years. Brilliant work."

"Are you sure she's dead?"

Henry Phelps, owner of 'Dead End' funeral parlour, allowed a smirk to crack through his well-honed demeanour of sombre sincerity. "Thank you, gentlemen. And yes, Mrs Bentley is still as deceased as when she came into our care six days ago."

"But she looks…well, like she's just sleeping. How have you done that?" George Bentley, eldest son of the late Edith Bentley, enquired, studying his mother's vibrant features.

His brother Clive stuck an index finger into the neckline of the silver and purple sequinned dress and pulled it down. The image of health and vigour ceased as the surgical staples holding grey sallow skin together shattered the illusion briefly offered. "Urgh," he involuntarily exclaimed, stifling the rising bile with the back of his hand and a willpower befitting of someone who had given up smoking fifteen years ago.

Two months.

One week.

Four days.

Six hours.

And twenty three minutes.

Give or take.

The passing of his mother had reignited the cravings bad. He had resisted the nicotine pole dance so far, but his lungs were resigned to the inevitable relapse.

Henry Phelps delicately rearranged the dress, ensuring that the pattern was straight and true. "Yes, gentlemen, your mother is still deceased. The scaffold pole which went through her scapula may have been removed, but I can assure you that any practitioner of the necromantic arts has failed to work their spell on her."

The three brothers looked at each other with a mix of confusion and repressed male emotion. Robert, the middle child, sniffed back a tear and peered closer. "Are you sure? It's like she's got a glow to her, you know? An inner fire burning." He reached forwards to touch her face. Henry intercepted the hand and rejected it softly with a gentle shake of his head.

A hush fell upon the party.

Henry coughed gently. "I do have one question, gents…if it's no trouble."

Three gormless faces looked blankly back at him.

"The sequin dress? I'm guessing she was a bit of a dancer?"

A round of in-joke chuckling ran round the trio. A series of elbows in ribs elected Clive to be the family spokesperson. "Just one of those silly things, I 'spose,

Mum loved a bit of *Strictly Come Dancing*. Always tried to get our dad to give it a go. They went on a cruise round the Med a few years back, when he was still. Ya know…alive? Mum never took no for an answer. One night, they went to dinner. She made her excuses, came back a bit later dressed in that dress, suggested that they learn the Tango."

"Did your father give it a go?" Henry enquired.

Another round of infantile sniggering ruined the still aura of the funeral home. Clive piped up, "Did he heck. Mum got the hump and ended up dancing with some old Canadian guy. They didn't speak for a fortnight. When he died, Mum said she wanted to be buried in it. So that when they were together, she had all of eternity to change his mind…"

A consoling brotherly arm was flung round Clive's body like a fire-blanket on a smouldering chip pan. "It's alright, bruv, it's alright. She's at peace now. Thanks, we better be off. Got six loaves of bread to butter ahead of the wake tomorrow. You're welcome to…you know, come if you want?"

Mr Phelps inclined his head slightly. "That's very kind of you, Mister Bentley. We may well join you once our duties are complete." He held out a perpetually warm, yet soft, hand to each of the bereaved in turn, shook theirs firmly and then led the way out of the display room and back to the front of the building. After another round of handshakes and commiserations, Henry trudged back to the body of Mrs Bentley.

He scanned the body, ensuring that she was as perfect as she could be. As he removed a rogue hair from her eyelashes, he heard the door behind him open with an arthritic creaking. "Have they gone?" asked a thin reedy voice.

Henry, content with the arrangement, crossed himself and turned to the open doorway. "Yes, Esther, they have gone." He stood immobile, hands clasped loosely in front of him, head tilted slightly to one side in a welcoming, almost apologetic, manner. "Come in, please."

The door squeaked once more and a woman, whose frame could not have matched her uncertain voice more, stepped into the brightly lit room. The display room had a wall of flowers neatly presented in identical crystal cut vases. Though a myriad of colour, they were expertly arranged, and created a three dimensional flock wallpaper.

A delicate yet sustained perfume consumed Esther, taking her breath away momentarily. She squinted to adjust to the shower of light in the room. "Did they?" she asked timidly.

Henry smiled. It oozed warmth and care. "Yes, Esther, they did. It is a rare gift that you possess, managing to make the departed seem as vivid and real as if they were still with us in this world. You should feel proud of what you do, of what you give people. Come here." he beckoned the petite woman to him reverently.

Clutching her arm as if it was wounded, the hunched lady cast nervous looks around and then joined Henry by his side. As she ran her eyes over Mrs Bentley, she smiled. "That dress certainly is a statement, eh?"

With a mirrored smile, Henry turned around and gazed down at the body once more. Edith lay there with such tranquillity that it was as if the pair were intruding on her slumber. "Tell me, Esther, how do you do it?"

Esther stirred from the viewing, looked up at her boss and shrugged sharply. "I'm not sure, Mister Phelps. When I'm with them out back, it's like…you'll think it's silly…"

"Please, dear, tell me," he beseeched quietly, yet firmly.

Her bleary eyes looked up into his, and for a moment they were joined. "When I work on them, it's as if they communicate with me, pushing me one way or another, teasing how they want to look from me as if I were a loosely tied purse. I can't explain it…to me, Mister Phelps, it's as if they're alive, and for the time I am with them, that I *am* them. Like we're the same…" she trailed off. "Sounds silly doesn't it?"

He shook his head so slightly that it was almost as if the world trembled as he alone stood still. "No, my dear, it does not. I imagine you're quite the artist. If this is—"

The bond between them was severed violently as Esther looked away and into her hands. "No, Mister Phelps," she replied firmly. "I cannot paint. If you'll excuse me." She turned quickly and headed back towards the door whence she came.

"Esther," Henry called after her. "I meant no offence."

The scrunched up woman held the door open. Half of her body had morphed into the shadow skulking beyond the wooden frame. "None taken," she said disappointedly, before slinking into the room. The door cried its dismay upon rusting hinges and sealed the void.

The bus doors hissed themselves closed. The vehicle lurched from the sanctity of the bus stop into the road. It merged with traffic in a brusque manner, invoking a number of horn honks and expletive-laden remarks.

Esther peered out of the grimy window at a white-van-man gesticulating towards the bus driver and offering to stick the driver's cranium into a usually outbound only orifice. This was refuted with a raised middle finger and a retort in which several new swear words were created.

"Ha ha ha! You have a bag like my one."

The words snapped Esther from her people-watching and back to the dreaded confines of public transport. Buses were the preserve of the infirm, the young, the disqualified and the mentally imbalanced. At first glance, she put the intruder firmly in the latter camp. "Sorry?" she mumbled.

"Your bag is like mine," the man repeated, running a finger covered in blue plasters across his fringe, sticking a loose clump of greasy hair back behind his ear. The gaudily-dressed finger pointed to the bag clamped between Esther's feet, and then to the one he held out, as if it warranted some kind of in-depth search.

"Hmm," Esther mumbled. Her brain worked its way through possible excuses to escape this strange social interaction; she made a mental note to buy a new pair of earphones.

With no hint of invitation, the man plopped himself down next to Esther, pinching an inch of her side-bum between the threadbare, piss-stained seat and the man's equally attired and stained jeans. "Sorry," he muttered, patting her trousers with a hand which would make a virologist rub their NBC suit covered gloves with glee.

Just don't make eye-contact…only two stops…do not ask what is in the bag—

The man shoved the bag under Esther's nose. "Do you want to see what's in my bag?"

Balls.

Esther turned from the window to her seat companion, sighed, and replied, "It depends, it's nothing dangerous, is it?"

"Ha ha ha ha, no of course not. It's my special film collection. Tell me, lady, what's your favourite film?"

"I don't know…*Eternal Sunshine Of The Spotless Mind*?" she ventured.

"UURRR, wrong," the man buzzed. He looked at Esther expectantly. The bag was placed gently on his lap as he plunged his little finger into his ear.

Ignoring the wax excavation, Esther offered, "*Star Wars*?"

"UUURRRR, wrong again." The exclamation made his finger fall out; a ball of hair- and ear-debris fell onto Esther's sleeve. She swallowed the instinctive urge to vomit.

235

"I don't know. What *is* my favourite film?" she asked, getting ratty.

The man unzipped the sports bag and carefully withdrew a thick folder. As it left the inner sanctum he placed it on his lap, stuck his hands in his armpits and rubbed them within the dank folds. Daring a look at the cover, she saw the beaming face of *Hudson Hawk*-era Bruce Willis.

Opening the cover as if it were the Necronomicon, the man cleared his throat. "You could've gone with any of the following: *Mercury Rising, The Siege, The Jackal, The Whole Nine Yards* or *Die Hard.*" An approximation of laughter came out of the man. "Obviously."

Esther sighed. "So anything by Bruce Willis, I'm guessing?"

The man giggled as if tickled by a cat tail. "So wotcha got in *your* bag lady? Do you have Bruce Willis films, too?" Closing the DVD folder cover, he leant forward and reached for his bag's factory twin.

"DON'T" Esther shrieked, and dragged it to one side with her foot. her outburst caused a number of the bus patrons to place her into the 'mentally imbalanced' category. A chorus of tutting and eye rolling ensued.

Withdrawn into a sitting foetal ball, the man was petrified in time, a stringy fishing-line of saliva was cast from his agape mouth and onto Hudson's sunglasses.

"It's just...I don't like people touching my stuff," Esther said. "Now if you'll excuse me." She pushed her way past the chair golem and wobbled her way to the front of the bus, pressing the bell as she staggered between the single mums practising 'Parenting 101' by texting and rolling a cigarette at the same time, and the old ladies chatting about their latest affliction.

3

As Esther slid the key into the lock, she clutched the bag to her chest. Its weight and squishiness comforted her. "I'm home," she called out as the door closed behind her. The dingy hallway had the appearance of a haunted tunnel.

Placing the post onto the half crescent Argos telephone table, she dropped the keys into their usual home—the Brakspears ashtray she had liberated from her local when she was nineteen.

Esther pushed the living room door open with her foot. "Is anyone in?" she hollered again. The television was off and, aside from her breakfast accoutrements still sitting where she left them this morning, it looked like nothing and no-one had partaken in the room's mundane delights.

Walking into the kitchen, she placed the sports bag onto the faux-marble Formica worktop and looked at the pile of dishes residing in the fetid pond which also doubled up as a sink. By now, the exertions of ear-wax man and getting Edith Bentley looking her best had left Esther at a low ebb. A rogue thought of doing the washing up ran across her mind.

"Hey, sis, you took your sweet time, didn't ya?"

Esther smiled and turned around. "Had some weirdo

on the bus try to convert me to Willis-ology. Did you have a tough day, Stell?" she said, gesturing to the stacked up filth and crap heaps dotted around the immediate vicinity.

"Hey, it's not easy being a stay-at-home sibling, you know. I did loads of stuff…just not immediately obvious stuff from the small portion of the house you've currently visited. Idiot," Stella replied, throwing in a sense of indignation that her sister saw through immediately.

"Okay, well, I guess I can clean up some of this later on. We've got work to do first," Esther said, filling a swilled-out jam jar with water.

Stella twirled on the spot, clapping her hands. "Oohh, you got some more did you? Good girl. I knew there was a reason why you earn the big bucks and I merely exist in this hovel."

Esther opened her arms out wide to take in the house. "Yes, as it is clearly evident, I earn the big bucks. Now, come on, let's get going. This isn't going to mulch itself down, you know."

4

"Are you going to start with the lungs again?" Stella enquired, peering into the bin bag filled with human offal. Esther pulled out a pair of worn kidneys; forty years' worth of Malibu and Gin had given the organs the appearance of being in a bath for too long. She smiled at her sister, who replied with, "Spoilsport, you *always* start with the lungs," as Esther stuffed them into the blender.

The motor struggled at first to gain purchase in the dense rich flesh. After a bit of shaking it chugged into life and started to slash the kidneys first into a series of pulpy ribbons, and then into a thick deep red paste. "Whoa," Stella warned, "don't do it too much. It'll just slop through the pan otherwise. Remember Mister Petrakis? Half of him ended up going down the drain."

Esther chuckled and turned the blender off. She twisted the jug free from the base and pried the top loose. "Let's see how much we can get out of Mrs Bentley, huh?" Moving to the end of the wooden desktop, she poured the sludge into a sieve, which was resting on top of a one-time plastic salad bowl.

As she gently squeezed a bottle of filtered water over the gunk, bits of tough gristle and benign tumours were all that remained sitting atop the mesh. The solitary lightbulb above the work space made the chunks glisten like freshly polished gemstones. "Good job we don't eat people, sis. She would've been mighty chewy," Stella remarked, eliciting a giggle from her sister.

Having sieved the mashed up kidneys, Esther pushed the meaty lumps into the blender and whizzed them down into a finer consistency. After repeating the sifting process until there was nothing sizeable left, the pair smiled at each other. "C'mon pardner, let's go see what the old girl had in her," Stella said in her best cowboy drawl. She fired her finger-pistols at her sister and blew the imaginary smoke away.

Esther picked up the bowl and gently poured the watered-down goo into a larger prospecting pan. It had three quarter inch riffles on one side, to aid the retrieval of the precious material. Content that she had everything in the pan, Esther got to work with the efficiency of a Swiss watchmaker.

"Was she a big girl?" Stella asked as she watched her sister tip the pan this way and that, trapping particles of various sizes in the ridges.

"Not huge. A bit of a muffintop, but that was about it," Esther replied distractedly, lost in her work.

Stella tutted and peered back into the depths of the bin bag, at the remaining meat and veins they had to work through. "Shame. We get more from the fatties, don't we? Wonder why that is? You'd think that everyone would have the same amount. When you're created, we're all basically the same aren't we? Yet time and time again, whenever we get a big 'un, we always manage to get more."

Esther rested the pan on the worktop and plugged the dental suction pump into the grimy four-gang electrical socket resting precariously on the side. After checking that it was working, she began to suck up the crap from the bottom of the green plastic pan. Over the sound of slurping, she hummed the melody to 'Tiger Feet' by Mud.

With the visceral effluent removed, she bent down and, as if handling an ancient relic, placed a plastic Tupperware tub next to the pan. Esther carefully removed the lid with a series of clunky clicks and then lifted a small immaculately-clean hand trowel from a hook screwed into the breeze block wall.

"Wow, you forget how cool it looks don't you?" Stella cooed, her eyes transfixed on the humble container. Her words were met with a reverential nod from Esther.

Esther closed her eyes and mumbled a series of words under her breath. With her nerves steadied, she ran the tool along the raised pan riffles and teased tiny sparkling fragments of what looked like pearlescent sand onto the trowel. She carefully transplanted the dust into the plastic container, making sure to scrape every last trace from the corners.

With her free hand she pulled a small, firm hand brush from another hook. With the trowel over the tub, she carefully cleaned off any residual powder from the hand tool. Content that she had got the lot, she returned both implements to their respective hooks and replaced the Tupperware lid.

"Good girl. You've got nerves of steel, I tell ya," Stella said, suppressing her glee. "We've still got a way to go, though. Going to be a long night."

Esther nodded. "Don't have to be in till late, unless anyone comes in overnight. I've got nothing on tomorrow," she replied. After rinsing the pan and sifter in a small corner sink, she pulled out some more of Edith Bentley's insides and squished them into the blender, ready to repeat the process.

As she replaced the lid, her fingers resting on the dial, she asked Stella, "So how much stardust do we need then? We've been doing this for ages. Look at what we've got so far. We're going to be doing this forever if we're not careful."

She turned the dial to a low pulse and watched as the clumps of thigh muscle she had put in rotated slowly, like a surreal barber's pole. Stella crossed her arms. "I don't know, do I? Guess we need to read the book again. Problem is with ancient measures that they don't exactly translate well into pounds or kilos, eh?" she said defensively.

"I know what you're going to say…" Esther added.

"What? I still reckon we use the pot we found in the fireplace. There must've been a reason why it was there. I know you're still a bit sniffy about it, but it's half empty already. Makes sense to add what we have to it," Stella protested.

Satisfied that the blades had the better of the muscle and fat, she increased the power. The meat was turned to a thick slurry in a matter of seconds. The sound of silence was interrupted by her saying aloud, "Fine. You're right, we need to do something, Stella. I can't keep cleaning out the odd body here or there. At some point Mister

Phelps—"

"Your boyfriend," Stella interrupted.

Esther shot her a scowl. "He's not my boyfriend. You know I'm not a people person. As I was saying, at some point, someone is going to find me out. We need to up our intake, just not sure how."

Stella drummed her fingernails against her teeth as Esther poured the mixture into the sifter, watching as strands of coagulated blood and stringy vein got caught on the coarse plastic grid. "Well, I've been having some thoughts on that, though I'm not sure you'll like it…"

Returning the blender jug back to its base, Esther asked grudgingly, "Go on, though I am not going out looking for roadkill again. Grinding up people's guts is one thing, I'm not exhuming any more dead badger innards. The smell was bad enough, but their little furry faces—"

"Shut it weirdo. No, it's not roadkill. Something altogether a bit more avant-garde. We'll have to be a bit creative, though, and that means you getting your hands dirty," Stella said flatly.

As Esther trickled water over the coarse lumps, she replied, "If it helps us get more stardust, and quicker, I'm listening."

Stella clapped her hands with joy. "Excellent! Now, you know we get more from fat people? Well…"

5

Durrington sits on the edge of Salisbury Plain, a few miles from the city itself. Like any rural community, the town hall is the focal point for all kinds of events. From Bridge afternoons for old age pensioners, to discos for the under sixteens. If you need a cheap venue to hire, for a gathering of people, you'd be hard pressed to find a better place.

Wednesday evenings, for the past six years, have been the preserve of slimming club. 'Waist Management'. This evening's meeting, attended by the twenty regulars and five new attendees, was in full swing.

The night began in the usual fashion. They exchanged stories about the previous week, usually which food they had been craving the most.

After getting a tea, coffee or tap-water, they sat in a half circle around Maureen and her two whiteboards. After a brief talk on the virtues of eating less fried food, the dreaded part of the evening took place: the walk of shame to the scales and back.

Many decried the weighing implement as utterly faulty, or that a two-pound gain was a result of some long lost relative visiting, which ended in a three day binge of white wine spritzers and croissants.

Maureen herself was the by-product of the morning TV fitness experts from the early nineties. When Mr Motivator and his garish Lycra-clad body bid farewell to GMTV in 2000, she was unable to cope with the news. Gorging herself on Penguin bars and deep-fried sausage rolls, Maureen spiralled into an evil cycle of self-loathing and comfort eating.

In an attempt to get back into her old jeans, she formed Waist Management so that those who were in a similar situation could club together and try to guilt trip each other into losing weight. Her tactics were somewhat militant, and one of the whiteboards was always adorned with some witty quip about people's size. This week was a particular brain coup she had thought of whilst eating a Battenberg cake in one sitting:

YOU'RE FAT !!!

DON'T SUGAR-COAT IT

BECAUSE YOU'LL EAT THAT TOO

Underneath she drew a large chubby face with three chins and a toothy grin. Her logic of fat-shame people had been wholly unsuccessful. The other whiteboard was used to brainstorm suggestions throughout the meeting. So far, the only contribution had been;

SALAD, GOOD ??

...in green marker pen, which Britney had volunteered

after the weigh-ins.

"Now everyone, I want to talk about a weakness that a lot of us suffer from. The evil biscuit. For me, custard creams are straight from the food devil's kitchen, am I right? Well…" Maureen prattled on.

"Linda."

Esther looked to the woman next to her, whose arse cheek had invaded her side after the weigh-in. Her podgy face looked back expectantly. "Erm, hi?"

Linda beamed a huge smile back. She nervously glanced from Maureen vilifying the noble custard cream back to Esther, and looked her up and down. "You're a bit…well…*thin* aren't you? Is it an eating disorder? Do you…you know?" Linda, with all the tact of an enraged horned bovine in a pottery sales outlet, mimed the whole fingers down the throat motion.

Glowing red from embarrassment, Esther looked at her new friend and replied sheepishly, "Ha ha, no. I'm…Yvonne, and I'm a fat…slimming club organiser from Trowbridge. Thought I'd come along and, you know, get some tips."

Linda started to snigger. Seeing that Esther/Yvonne was being serious, she scrunched up her face. "Really? You came here to get tips from Maureen?" She nodded to the front of the audience, where the illustrious Maureen had produced a Vanilla Hob Nob Cream and an Oreo in separate hands, and had engaged them in mortal combat.

As the Vanilla Hob Nob Cream mullered the Oreo in a shower of crumbs and globules of creamy middle goo, she knelt down and held the winning biscuit aloft as if it were Excalibur. An awkward round of applause trickled around the group. "Next up, it's a Digestive taking on the might of the Bourbon Cream. Who shall reign victorious and get through to the semi-final?"

Esther mustered every ounce of resolve to stifle a laugh. "Yeah…erm, I heard good things about her, and our numbers are dwindling, so I thought I'd come round and check out—"

"The biscuit wars?" Linda interrupted. "She does this once a month. Do you notice how she's only using one biscuit each?"

Esther nodded.

"Where do you think the rest of the packet goes?" Linda again, oblivious to the fact that most people can process words without the need for a matching action, cracked her mouth open and poured an invisible packet of biscuits into it.

"I'm sure she means well," Esther said, looking on in dismay as Maureen jammed the Digestive into the cream of the Bourbon biscuit and started to lever it apart.

"Take that, you bastard!" Maureen shouted. She flicked the Digestive upwards and the top of the Bourbon flew across the room and hit the kettle.

"Anyhoo, give it another twenty minutes and she'd have started on the peach schnapps, which she hides in that Costa Coffee cup," Linda continued.

Esther smiled sweetly. "Would you just excuse me a minute. I have to…ya know, go—"

"For a slash?" Linda finished. She spread her legs and allowed a large satisfied look to appear on her face.

Esther kept the fixed smile on her face and made her way down the row of people towards a small hallway.

Checking to see that she hadn't been followed, she snuck down the corridor and walked past the communal toilet, which reeked of old lady piss and old man farts.

Opening a battered wooden door, Esther crept inside and turned on her pocket torch. The beam of light ran across the front of the boiler and she peered at the last service date. If it was correct, a trained engineer had last checked the surety of the heating device around the point Scrappy Doo was deemed 'cool'.

Thinking back to her internet searches, she wrapped a scarf around her face and elbowed the exhaust pipe until a crack prefaced a hissing sound. She started to feel a bit woozy, and opted to get out of Dodge.

She pushed the back door closed and jammed the wooden door wedge under the bottom. Content that it wouldn't budge, Esther stumbled round the building and searched for the flue.

She found it behind tinsel-like strings of ivy and picked up a discarded fast food paper bag. Filled with empty wrappers, she shoved it into the vent. She cast a quick glimpse at her watch and realised that if she hurried, she would be back in time for a repeat of *Friends*.

6

Twenty three died from carbon monoxide poisoning. Of the two survivors, Linda would spend the remainder of her time on the earth, just under sixty days, being kept alive by a machine worth more than she made in four years of miming on the streets of Wiltshire.

Maureen, after two weeks in intensive care, appeared on the local news. Though she remembered nothing of the incident herself—having been rendered unconscious along with everyone else. She sought to propagate the myth that it was she who raised the alarm and contacted the emergency services.

The truth, though, was far less glamourous. Two local boys, Ed and Mark, both twelve, were having a kick-about outside. When Ed went for glory with a half-volley, instead of seeing the imaginary net bulge with satisfaction, the ball went through a window in the town hall.

As they forced the door open to retrieve the present from Mark's dad, who died a few months earlier when he became trapped under a rather large donation of Lego to Eastern European child immigrants, they found everyone inside 'lying about the place'.

Initially believing that it had been Ed who had caused

everyone to pass out, they grabbed the ball and legged it. They only returned when Mark repeated the feat through another window and found that everyone was still either playing the 'Be Really Still' game, or were dead and/or dying.

The Salisbury Occasional went with the headline 'FATS WHY YOU SERVICE YOUR BOILER', which completely skirted round the wealth of physical evidence at the scene which hinted at foul play. The police were involved, but with no witnesses and two comatose survivors, leads were at a premium.

'Dead End' funeral services ended up dealing with just over half of the victims.

"Well, obviously I can't help you," Stella stated, offering her pale hands to her sister as some form of feeble proof.

Esther busied around the room, clearing away anything from the workbench that they wouldn't need. Four new blenders sat alongside her well-used one. All of them were plugged in and ready to go. "I've never had this many to do in one day before. I'm scared," she panted.

Stella offered a sympathetic smile, but it did little to assuage Esther's concern. "Do we have enough paper upstairs? Stell, I'm gonna be up all night doing them, aren't I? Let's say there are five to do tomorrow. That means I've got three nights of this. I don't know if I can do this. No, let's just skip it. Why are we doing this anyway? It's silly, I th—"

"Shhhhh," Stella whispered softly. "It's okay, sis. I get it." Esther began to sob. Her body quaked with emotion and dread. "Hey, Es, you know why we're doing this. It's the only way, isn't it? There's only one option, and, well, to be the brutally honest, bitch, it didn't pan out too well when you tried, did it?"

Esther looked up at her sister, then down to her arms. Stella traced her fingers in the air down a trio of pink ribbons across her sister's wrist. "See, I couldn't even do *that* right," she moaned.

"I'm glad, you dozy cow! If you hadn't done that, then we would never have found what we did, eh? It's given us a better way now. Once we figure out the last little details, we are gonna be sorted, huh?"

"I guess," Esther said softly. "Is there enough paper upstairs? I don't really want to spend any free time tomorrow scrubbing the walls."

Stella chuckled. "That was the first time, do you remember that? What was his name? Steven…something."

"Steven Burton. He had that purple cravat and the side parting. I still don't think I got his smile right, you know?" Esther replied, lost in the memory.

"Anyway, there's nothing more to do here. How you getting it all home tomorrow anyway? Won't fit in your bag, eh?" Stella asked. She scanned the room in search of alternate containers.

Esther pulled a granny trolley from the hallway. "Ta-da! This should do. Will get most of it in there, I reckon. I've lined it already, so just have to scoop it in there."

"Have you got the…ya know…in there ready?" Stella enquired, as she tried to peer into the semi-closed trolley.

"I have. Got a load on the way back from the town hall, after…*it*."

"Do you feel bad?"

Esther pondered the question. "I thought I would, but now it's done, not in the slightest. As you said, this is our only alternative. I can't say I'm too happy about those people dying, but we need to increase the output, or we are going to be doing this forever."

Stella winked. "Good girl. Another couple of them, and I reckon we could be nearly there, you know. Now, to sleep, perchance to dream…"

"Yeah, about dead people. Great."

7

"She looks serene," Henry commented reverently. He smoothed down the jacket lapel of Mrs Talbot and took a step back to admire Esther's handiwork. It had been a busy few days. Whilst the business was welcome, it had taken its toll on his mortuary cosmetologist. The dark bags under her grey eyes hinted that Esther was running on fumes.

"Why don't you take a break? There's only one to go. Ms Englund isn't due to be buried for another few days. Pretty sure she'll keep," Henry offered.

Esther looked at him as if she was an animal transfixed by a truck's headlights. "No," she insisted. "I need to get them all done today. Please."

Henry saw that the poor girl was clearly on edge. He didn't wish to push the matter further and make her ill. "Okay, but take tomorrow off. I insist. You've been working non-stop for the last couple of days. You need to recharge your batteries."

She nodded weakly at him and put the mug to her mouth. She tried to tip the tea down her throat, but despite going near horizontal, nothing came out. A quick check confirmed that she had finished it some time ago, dregs and all. "I'll get you a fresh cup, and bring in Ms Englund, if you're sure?"

Esther mustered a half smile which convinced Henry to make his exit and give the poor girl a break. Despite her working for him for almost a year, her guard was still up. He unlocked the wheel brakes and pushed Mrs Talbot out back to the fridges, where she would rest with the others.

Looking over the assortment of makeup brushes and hair accessories, Esther picked up a brooch, made to resemble a Geisha's open fan. "This looks really nice up close," she muttered herself.

The door behind her clicked and Henry pushed the gurney, the cold clammy body of Ms Englund lying prone upon it, into the room. Her thick arms were a pallid grey. Black veins ran under her skin like liquorice sticks. She had already been changed into a flowery kimono, which had large lotus flowers printed on it. Henry asked, "What was that?"

"Nothing…just think it's nice when people are laid to rest with things that mean something to them," Esther replied sheepishly.

Henry gently took the brooch and turned it around in his fingers. "I think so, too. Some would say it's a waste, but in my opinion, it is important we observe people's last wishes."

He looked at her. A clump of hair had come loose from her hairband and swished across her cheek. Esther caught his stare; her skin flushed with embarrassment.

Henry coughed nervously and looked away quickly. "Well, I'll erm…just go and start the paperwork. Here's your, erm…tea. Are you sure you're going to be okay?"

Esther nodded curtly. "Thank you, Mister Phelps. I'll let you know when I'm done. If you don't mind?" She gestured towards the door. Henry nodded, and left the young woman to her work.

She breathed out all the tension which had built up. After taking a moment to collect herself, she tiptoed to the door which led to the viewing room and pushed it to make sure it was shut. Content that it was, she slowly slid the small metal bolt across, so that if Henry decided to come back, it would at least buy her some time to hide her 'other work'.

Standing over Ms Englund, the lady looked like an old jelly bean that had been stuffed into a fancy Oriental sweet wrapper. Taking care to not crease the material, Esther began to untie the kimono until the grey torso of Henrietta Englund was exposed to the world.

Working from top to bottom, she snipped away at the thick sutures running down the woman's sternum. The puckered skin, like old orange peel, parted reluctantly; the smell of warming putrid flesh escaped through the gap.

She pulled on a new pair of latex gloves and gently teased the skin open so she could get better access to the tissue and organs within.

With a sufficient gap created, she held a scalpel in her palm and slid her closed hand up past the ribs to the inside of the left shoulder. Esther teased the sharp blade through her fingers and, with a deftness honed over the past year, she ran the razor-sharp edge along the bone, separating muscle, tendon and tissue from where it was attached. She worked quickly, but surely. In next to no time she had done one side, and repeated the process on the other.

The front was a piece of cake compared to the back. After death, gravity had pulled all the veins and organs towards the spinal column. By the time she had done her work there, her gloves were covered in clumps of black pulp, which had the consistency of pork pie jelly.

With the holdall open and resting atop Henrietta's untrimmed lady garden, Esther gently tugged on the stomach and hoped that she didn't rupture the guts. A few times now, in her haste, she had dug her fingers in so hard that when she pulled, the stomach split. Though she had become accustomed to the smell of dead organs, the smell of decaying food and crusty stomach lining was an acquired bouquet which she had yet to attain.

Fortune was on her side, and the skin sack, looking like a pair of deflated bagpipes shorn of pipes, slid into the bag, which had been lined with cut open carrier bags. The intestines were wrapped around her hand and elbow as if they were the electric flex to a lawnmower. They too were placed lengthways into the bag.

With the organs and as much tissue as she could scrape off the bone shoved into the bag, she ran a length of Clingfilm over the top before zipping it shut and placing it on top of the granny trolley.

Even though she knew the door was locked, she conspiratorially checked over her shoulder before she unlocked a cupboard beneath a spotless stainless steel sink. Esther moved aside bottles of bleach and assorted cleaning materials, and pulled out two blocky polythene bags, formed into two rectangles.

She made her way back to Ms Englund, carefully undid the top of one of the bags, and squeezed the polythene bag, loosening the material within.

Happy that it wasn't too clumpy, she poured in the first bag of sawdust, making sure that it was evenly distributed. "Gonna need another bag with this one," she mumbled to herself and retrieved bag number three from under the sink.

With the ballast inside the body cavity, Esther picked up the thick needle and surgical thread and proceeded to stitch the skin back together again, making sure to go through the holes already created when Ms Englund had been sewn up the first time.

With the chasm closed, she pushed and prodded the skin until it was as smooth as she was going to get it. Content, she carefully retied the kimono and smoothed it out so it looked smart. *Now the real work.* Esther sat down on a padded stool by Ms Englund's head, pulled in a lamp which was attached to a telescopic arm, and thought back to the previous night.

With the image clear in her head, she began to apply the make up to the body.

Within the next six weeks, another two slimming classes reported vastly reduced memberships. The Wilton Fat-Fighters lost thirty-one members, whilst the Amesbury Chubby-Checkmates lost eighteen. In total, thirty victims were handled by 'Dead End'.

By now, the police were well and truly on the case. The modus operandi in all three cases were near identical. In each the central heating systems were sabotaged, resulting in carbon monoxide poisoning.

A chill ran around Wiltshire. Talk of a rake-thin serial killer with prominent cheekbones, intent on offing the obese, caused salad scuffles in the High Street branch of Salisbury's Tesco supermarket.

Whilst the citizens of the county started to reduce their waistline and increase their lung capacity, Esther's and Stella's high yield source of material got cut off.

"Look, right here. It says that it needs to be in the pot," Stella argued back, pointing at the open page. The paper was yellowed and extremely fragile. One terse exchange had resulted in a number of the pages flaking away to dust in Esther's fingers.

Esther scrunched up her face. "But who is to say that it

is *that* pot? There are no exact measurements in there, eh? It has pretty much everything in there, *except* the damn pot measurements."

She closed the red leather-bound book and ran her fingers over the near worn away golden six-pointed star. "Diego Villa was a dumbass," she affirmed. "Idiot leaves his stupid book and his stardust in our fireplace and doesn't even bother to say for definite how much we need."

"But why would he come all that way with that pot, if it wasn't the right size?" Stella argued back. It sat in front of them on the coffee table, on top of a collection of old TV magazines and credit card letters.

"I just think before we go and sieve all the crap out of it, and then put all of ours in there, that we need to be sure it's the right bloody pot. If not, then it isn't going to work, is it? That half page we read said that it *has* to be the right amount. Considering what we have to do after, I'd rather be certain, eh?"

Stella pursed her lips. She knew arguing with her sister was pointless. She was never going to change her mind, and as much as she hated to admit it, she was right. They'd found the book and pot containing what appeared to be glitter a few years back, not long after they had moved into 97 Brown Street.

In a DIY-induced frenzy one Sunday, Esther had put a claw-hammer through the wall, and to their joy, instead of rupturing a water main, they had found a bible-like book wrapped in a dirty cloth and a clay pot half full of what they assumed was a glitter-suicide-bomb factory.

The book was fragile, but it reeled them in. Divided

into a number of sections, the first recounted how an unnamed man had discovered concealed text within ancient armour, after being dashed upon the rocks in a storm.

The story itself was an epic tale of how one man ruled over the native people, and how he had harvested some kind of mineral from them. They treated him like a god, and believed that he had fallen from the sky. And in order to ascend to his rightful place in the heavens, he needed sacred material which lay inside all living things.

The fate of the individual is unknown, as it cuts short following an event called 'The Feast of the Forest'. The book claimed that the man was driven mad by his own lack of faith and, after killing all of his followers, went into the darkest recesses of the forest where he still lives. Longing for the day when he is shown the true meaning of faith, and is able to complete his holy task.

The second part of the book, which took up over two thirds of the entire document, was written by a Father Rodriguez, who pulls apart the core story and, at times, examines in mind-numbing detail, each main event.

It took the sisters a month to read it, as in places it became rambling and incoherent. It was evident that Rodriguez had met this mythical man, perhaps in the forest, and his words had become etched upon his very soul.

Rodriguez believed that the minerals he found inside people was the work of God, and it was his sacred duty to harvest enough. So that he, along with his growing band of followers—the Church of the Saviour's Star—could resurrect God, and together they could sacrifice themselves and meld with the deity.

The last part of the book was originally left intentionally blank. Hand-scrawled notes, in a mix of English and Spanish, were dotted on each page. It was as if each person was encouraged to explore the text themselves, offering their own thoughts on how best to complete the ritual.

As they read it, they noticed a large number of assumptions and a number of key details missing. The story itself was evidently exaggerated, but to what end? Rodriguez mentioned a number of times that this man found some original document that he worked to, but from the vague words, it was highly likely that the priest himself never got sight of it.

Their argument was brought to an abrupt end when the front door rattled in its frame from a series of sharp raps. "Who's that?" Stella asked dumbly.

Esther sighed and pulled a cushion to her chest. "I don't know, do I? Go see who it is. Go on."

Stella got up and walked over to the bay window, which was next to the front door. Through the net curtains she saw a familiar figure. "It's your boyfriend, sis," she shouted.

"Shit," Esther grunted. She picked up the pot and put it on the hearth, arranging the fireplace condiments in front of it as the front door was knocked again.

She smoothed down her hair and reached for the handle, feigning a smile as she opened the door a few inches. Henry's kind face looked down at her. "Hi, Esther. Sorry to bother you, but I just wanted to check you were okay. The last month or so has been awfully busy, and I couldn't help but notice a few things."

The pause that followed bookended eternity. Esther was sure at one point that her heart had stopped beating. Finally she managed to stutter out, "W-wh-what?"

Henry looked expectantly at the fissure between door and the inside of the house. Reluctantly, Esther allowed him in. As he walked past her, she closed the door behind him and counted to ten. Henry glanced this way and that, trying to take in the unruly mess the house was in. From the dishevelled state, any attempt to tidy had been abandoned long ago, and whilst not quite on the same scale as some of the TV shows he had seen on hoarders, it grated against his own personal hygiene standards.

"Through there," Esther said, pointing a hand wrapped in a jumper sleeve to a doorway to his right. He smiled as best he could and stepped over a stack of old Index and Littlewoods catalogues, into the living room.

Henry inhaled deeply. He couldn't quite put his finger on what the aroma was, but there was something *very* familiar about it. Something that he was intrinsically linked with, yet alien in this domestic setting.

He looked around and saw that the living room was in as much of a state as the cluttered hallway. A leather armchair sat in front of an old CRT television, which had a film of dust and cigarette smoke coated to its screen. The matching sofa sat parallel to it; half of the cushions were covered in pamphlets and sealed plastic charity envelopes, their bags still incarcerated within, dates ringed on the side long since passed.

Esther appeared from one side. She sat cross-legged on the armchair, looking thoroughly awkward. It was as if he had come round to do a public reading of her teenage diaries. Henry contemplated standing but, after investigated the sofa, realised it wasn't too bad. He ran his sleeve across the top of it and perched on the end.

"So, I—"

"Thanks for—"

The two voices clashed. As one they looked at each other, then down into some unseen distraction. Henry plucked up the courage first. "I just wanted to make sure you were okay. I know we've been really busy recently, and you haven't had much of a break. When I spoke to you the other day, you seemed as though you were barely hanging on."

Esther pulled her legs up to her body and hugged them. "I'm fine, thank you. As you say, Mister Phelps, just been a long few weeks. Be glad when it goes back to normal again."

"Ha, normal! That'll be nice. Everyone is on edge at the moment, what with all the deaths. Strange, eh?" Henry asked. Esther swore that as he finished he shot her a funny look.

"Where are my manners? Cup of tea?"

Henry barely had a chance to say yes before the slender woman had stood up and rushed past him, into a room beyond a doorframe laden with post-it notes. "Milk, one sugar," he called after her.

Resigned to the fact that he was probably going to have to make do with tea without sugar, he looked around the room, trying to take in some of the vast array of visual stimuli on offer.

Random prints hung on the walls, a few family photos

nestled behind old calendars and job adverts cut from newspapers and stuck to the wall with Sellotape. Curious, he stood up and, after working his way round a collection of encyclopaedias, he peeled back the adverts and looked at the photographs.

He grinned as he recognised Esther as a little girl. He could tell straight away that it was her. She looked about eight and was standing awkwardly in the foreground; behind her, a man clamped hands onto her shoulder, whilst a woman stood a few feet off to one side.

They looked odd, disjointed, not even like a real family. For a moment, Henry wondered if this was perhaps an Aunt and Uncle. Only when he saw the same recurring faces, yet through the passage of time, did he realise that they must be her mother and father.

In each photo, the man and woman never stood together. They didn't even touch each other. No hand-holding, hugs or affection was shared between them at all.

Henry wondered if this was where Esther had got her stand-off nature from. In each picture she alone stood at the front, her parents behind her. The only thing that changed was the background, the clothing, and the hair styles.

Then the parents were gone altogether. Staring back was a picture of Esther on her own. At a guess, Henry reckoned she was eighteen. He peered closer and saw a melancholy in her eyes. A sadness, sown and nurtured in the earlier pictures, had been allowed to take root.

"Here you go, Mister Phelps." The words, delivered so close to his ear, caused Henry to jump.

"Thank you, Esther. I was…I'm sorry. I was just

curious. Wanted to see what you were like when you were younger. Are those your p—"

"Yes. They are. Can we talk about something else please?" Esther butted in.

Henry took the mug of tea and mouthed, "Sorry."

They took their respective places on the armchair and sofa and exchanged small talk until the tea cooled enough to be consumed. "I'm glad you're okay, Esther, and apologies for coming around unannounced. Just I…you know, wanted to make sure that you're okay."

Esther smiled slightly. "Thank you, Mister Phelps. I do appreciate it. I just…I don't get many visitors, and as you can see, this place is a bit of a mess."

She waved an arm around the room as if to demonstrate the bleeding obvious. "It's very…homely," Henry said politely.

"It's a craphole, let's be honest." The pair chuckled and the mood eased for the first time since he had been granted admittance.

"May I just use your toilet before I go? Is it over—" Henry motioned towards the back of the house, which caused Esther to bolt upright.

"NO. It's not back there. I mean, sorry, it's not working. You can use the one upstairs, though? Top of the stairs and…second on the right."

Henry nodded thanks and disappeared into the hallway; muffled thuds tracked his path to bladder relief. "Wow, you are the mistress of pulling, eh sis?" Stella mocked sarcastically, appearing from the kitchen doorway.

"Shut up. I've told you before, I'm not interested, am I?"

Esther picked up the still-warm mug and made her way into the kitchen. "It must be love. You actually had to wash a mug up for him. Awwwww, 'ickle Esther wants to get freaky with Mister Dead."

"Seriously, Stell, shut up. I'm not in the mood. What if he asked about…you know? He saw the photos."

"You shut up, you div. He doesn't know about me does he? And let's be honest, it's pretty obvious what happened to Mum and Dad, isn't it?"

"I don't want to talk about it."

"Therein lies your problem, Es. You bottle all this up—"

"Shut up."

"You need to talk to someone about it all, perhaps—"

"SHUT UP," Esther bellowed, before becoming acutely aware she wasn't alone in the house. She listened intently, and was relieved to hear nothing.

"Alright, don't shit the bed, sis. I'm only saying."

"Sorry. Just, you know, I don't like talking about it. Hurts too much."

Stella smiled. "No worries. I won't ask again." As she finished speaking, a thought crossed her mind. "Is it me or is lover boy having the longest dump in the world?"

"Oh no," Esther mumbled. She jogged out of the kitchen and bounded up the stairs two at a time. The door to the bathroom was ajar, and a quick check revealed that Mister Phelps hadn't passed out through straining too hard.

As she stood in the hallway, a knot swelled in the pit of her stomach. Willing it not to be true, she walked to her bedroom and pushed the door open slowly with her foot.

267

Her worst fears were realised when she saw Mister Phelps standing by the window with his back to her. The bed was unmade and the duvet pulled open, exposing the sweat-stained bedsheets. Stuck to the walls were drawings of people in various poses. There was no background to any of them. Instinct kicked in. "How dare you! Get out of my room, Mister Phelps," she demanded angrily.

Slowly, he turned to her. In his hand was one of the pictures. She swallowed. It felt as if a ball of fear and dread was pulled out of her guts by a chain.

Stunned, he looked at Esther and turned the picture around to face her. It was of a fifty-odd year old lady, unremarkable in almost every way, except she was wearing a silver and purple sequinned dress. Just visible on her neckline was a surgical staple. "What is…what—" Henry struggled to compose himself.

He coughed and asked firmly. "What is the meaning of this, Esther? I don't understand."

Esther backed into the door, which closed behind her. As it clicked shut, she sunk to the floor, defeated. She began to cry.

Henry knelt down by her and tried to comfort her, though his attempt was rebuked. "It's okay, my dear, I'm here to help you, not to make things worse. This doesn't make any sense. All of these people, they are…*were*, customers. This is how they looked when you finished with them. Look, over there is Ms Englund."

He pointed to a picture stuck to the wardrobe, showing Ms Englund posing in her kimono, the brooch prominently displayed on her breast. "And Mr Chan, Mrs Franks, and is that? Ha, yes, it's Miss Read! I'd remember that make-up anywhere."

Esther sobbed into the sleeves of her jumper. "You won't understand," she whimpered.

Henry, ignoring the state of the carpet, sat down opposite her. "Try me."

She searched his face for any hint of falsehood or deception. She found none. Esther took a deep breath…

"The first time it happened was when my grandma died. Cancer, I think. I was only seven, heard my Dad on the phone speaking about how she had gone so quickly. They'd had a falling out a few years back. I guess he thought he would have all the time in the world to make up with her before it was too late.

He never did.

We drove to his parent's house in Birmingham. The night we got there, we stayed over at my Uncle's. He lived in one of those big blocks of flats; they've knocked them down now I think.

I woke up in the morning and I had pen marks on my hands and arms, like someone had been doodling on me whilst I was sleeping. I turned the light on and I saw a drawing of my grandma. She was smiling and waving to me. She had on this dress with these little owls on it, and this woollen cardigan over the top. Her hair was all curly too.

I was horrified. If my mum or dad found it, they would go spare. Mum was always looking out for things I'd done wrong, even if I hadn't. I pushed the bedside table in front of it and thought nothing of it. Must've just been sleepwalking or something.

We had breakfast and my dad tells my mum and me

that we're going to the funeral parlour, that he wanted to see her one last time. I'd never seen a dead body before, and she was my gran, so figured I'd go see her.

The man at the funeral parlour takes us round back and there she is. Gran is lying in the coffin, and guess what she's wearing?"

"An owl dress and cardigan?"

"Bingo. Freaked me out. I ran out of there crying. My mum went mental, demanding to know why I was causing such a commotion. I lied through my teeth, didn't want her to find I'd drawn on the wall too and get a hiding. Anyway, it didn't happen again, not until…"

"It's okay, you don't have to say Esther. I get it."

Esther wiped her eyes. "They died in a car crash. Hit head-on by a delivery lorry, killed instantly, the police said. I felt glad in a way. Ever since what happened when I was born, Dad said that Mum never got over it.

I had just started university, was smoking weed in my friend's room when my mobile phone went. PC Dunn checked who I was and asked if my parents owned a blue Ford Escort. When I mumbled a yes, he told me what had happened. I barely said a word as I was completely caned.

He asked if I could come down to the station to make a positive identification. Couldn't take it all in at first. I went to my room and cried myself to sleep. Woke up in the morning and found that inside my brand new notepad were pictures of my mum and dad. Hand-drawn, yet their bodies were all…"

Henry pulled her in close as she broke down again. "It's okay, Esther, don't worry. It's okay. Shhhhhh."

As the number Fifty-Seven pulled out of the bus stop, Esther plopped into her seat and edged the holdall, containing the internal organs and viscera of Julian Robertson, between her feet. Using them as bookends, she peered out of the window and watched the world go by.

Though work, and the harvesting, had slowed down considerably, she had been enjoying the lull. The past few months had pushed her to the edge of the black pit. She knew that, in order to finish their work, she needed to put things into perspective. She needed to focus on what mattered the most.

Thoughts of Henry ran through her mind again and, despite letting out a smirk, she reminded herself of the practicalities over any feelings she might be harbouring for him. Since she had spoken to him about her parents and her 'gift' a week and a bit ago, the pair had grown closer. Conversations were easier, and Esther knew that it was purely because she had allowed Henry to pull down the barriers she had erected.

This is not the time for this. We still have so much to do, and we're missing pieces of the puzzle.

She watched the full gamut of bus-voyeur television. A

couple pushed a pram down the street, strain and lack of sleep painted on their expressions. One brief exchange led to a small outburst from the man. Though muted by the glass, she could tell that it was born out of fatigue. The woman rolled her eyes and continued to push the infant along the pavement, blanking his diatribe.

On a park bench sat two old men engaged in jovial conversation. Whilst one twirled a curved-handled walking stick, he smiled as his chum waved his hands around enthusiastically. Perhaps he was telling his friend how things around here looked so different when he was younger? Maybe he was recounting the latest trip to the doctors. Whatever it was, the gesticulating old gent finished speaking and the pair erupted in laughter.

Esther smiled. Joggers galloped past, eyes fixed on the horizon. Arms pumped in time to the music they were lost within. They ran around a stationary group of school kids, who were taking it in turns to go through their sticker collections. One excitedly shouted, "NEED," as he saw the missing shiny sticker of Romelu Lukaku that he required to finish off another team. The card's owner stood up straight, knowing that he held the upper hand in the negotiations.

She surveyed a group of girls showing pictures on their phones. That was when a familiar voice from the seat behind said, "It's you again, lady! Do you have DVDs in your bag today?"

Esther tore herself from the improvised theatre outside the bus and turned around to face the man. "Hi," she said as politely as possible, "No, still got no DVDs in there, I'm afraid. How about you? You still got—"

Sensing her question, the man quickly opened his bag up to reveal the folder of *Hudson Hawk* inside. "Ha ha ha, yes, always do. I'm sorry about last time, lady. I didn't mean to touch your stuff. It wasn't nice of me to try without asking."

Esther smiled, this time genuinely. "No worries. I was a bit on edge last time. Apology accepted. So what's your favourite Bruce Willis film then?"

The man's face lit up like a bonfire doused in petrol and activated by flare gun. "Mine? Well there are so many to choose from. I love *Die Hard*, obviously, who *doesn't*? Only *mental* people that's who." He punctuated this with a braying laugh which caused a number of people to tut. Esther laughed with him, for he was plainly in his element.

"Obviously," she agreed. "I think the first one is still the best, though, how about you?"

"Duhhh, of *course* it is. I like the other ones, but in the first one, Bruce has more hair, and I think he looks more manly. I'd say it's in my top five, but I don't have a favourite, as there are too many. I also love *Fifth Element*, I think that's just like *Die Hard*, but in space, and…" The man trailed off.

"What is it? Are you okay?"

The man gathered up the courage. "I think the lady in it is really pretty too. There's a bit at the beginning, where you…" he moved in closer, as if sharing his deepest secret. "…you nearly see her boobies." This caused him to laugh again like a happy donkey, and after the initial bout of embarrassment, Esther joined in.

"So apart from nearly seeing Mila Jovovich's breasts in *Fifth Element*, what else do you like?"

273

He placed a finger to his lips, which seemed to aid his thought process. After thirty odd seconds of dead air, he said, "Today, I'd have to say, *Bandits, Look Who's Talking Too, Death Becomes Her, Armageddon* and *The Pastor of Deathtown*." Content with his answers, he rummaged around his bag and pulled out a Choc Dip, which he tucked into as if he were a velociraptor and it was a chicken.

Esther scrunched up her forehead. "*The Pastor of Deathtown?* Never heard of that one? When was that made?"

"1985, a film made for TV, released on video in 1989. Although many of the newspaper people hated it, I really like it. It's about the Gimbaltown Massacre. Have you heard of it?"

Esther nodded. "Yeah, that religious guy went nuts and convinced two hundred of his followers to kill themselves, poor souls."

The man cocked his head sideways. "They didn't kill themselves, at least not in the film. In the film, Pastor Gimbal, played by Bruce Willis—obviously—he plans to kill them to harvest their insides. But when he kills this senator, who was really an undercover government agent, the army is sent in and they kill everyone, but then they make it *look* like it was the pastor who did it. It doesn't score very well on IMDb, but I like it. I'd say my favourite bit is when he kills this man over the wrong kind of Cola. It's really funny."

After a double-take, Esther asked, "Harvest their insides? That sounds a bit…"

"Yes, it is," the man agreed vociferously. "Bruce thinks

that there is this special sauce inside of people, and if you get enough of it together, you can call God. I think it's like *ET*, when the *Predator* or whatever phones home, but I never watched it, as Bruce Willis isn't in it. Only saw the mini film they show on television with the adverts."

Esther looked into the man's bag. "That sounds really good, like it could well be his best one. Would you mind if I borrowed it and watched it? I'd bring it back for you tomorrow?"

The man regarded her as if they were alone in an elevator and he had just detected a strange smell. His face exploded with laughter. "Of *course* it is, though I only get the bus on Tuesdays, so it'll have to be next week, and you'll have to wash your hands before you take the disc out. Deal?"

"Deal." The pair shook on it. "I'm Esther."

"Matt, Matt Morlock, but you can call me Bruce if you like?"

Esther chuckled. "Of course I can Ma…I mean *Bruce*. Thank you, you've made my day."

Blood-covered hands were wrung in a once-white cloth apron. The surgeon, smoking cigarette hanging from his lips, looked down at the body on the table. "Looks like the senate is no longer in session, Mister Boulder," he drawled.

Cackling like an evil scientist, the surgeon picked up a large meat cleaver. He ran a gloved finger across the edge of the blade. "Looks like there are some...*cuts* to be made to your budget," he quipped.

With his free hand, he ripped the shirt open. As he saw what lay beneath, his face became a knot of confusion, then realisation and fear. "No...but that can't be...they'll know what we plan to do. I have to tell the pastor."

"Eric Roberts is *really* good in this," Stella said sarcastically. Esther shushed her for the umpteenth time.

"...whilst we strive to be all we can in this crazy world. If people had seen the things that I have." Bruce Willis, complete with a full head of hair, pulled off his mirrored sunglasses and gripped the microphone tighter.

"To truly see what binds us all together is almost too much for us to take in. To be witness to the revelation of our creation is almost too much for the mind to comprehend. But now that I have, I know that there is only one thing that must be done." Bruce dug his hand into a terracotta pot, complete with petrified clay faces and tendrils.

He pulled out a fist of glittering dust and let it fall back into the receptacle. "To think that so many people made this, and all we need now is a few more and then we can join as one, and be...a *God*."

The hand holding the microphone slapped against the desk. The slow spooling of the tape machine was interrupted as the door was flung wildly open. "Pastor, we've been made. MADE I TELL YOU. That damn senator was wearing a wire. He must be working for the agency. THE AGENCY I TELL YOU."

"What an over-actor. Hello, Mister Roberts, here is some more cheese. Pffft."

Bruce stood up and placed a hand on Eric Roberts' shoulder. "How can that *be*? I only asked for him yesterday...this is all—"

Automatic weapon fire ricocheted around the room. Eric Roberts pushed Bruce to the floor as he took seven rounds to the chest. He shook like he was trying to rid himself of a wasp infestation.

Eric Roberts lay on the floor. A trickle of blood ran from the corner of his mouth. Bruce rolled over, scooped a hand under his head and lifted it up. "Shhh, it's okay now, Tony. You did good. You did real good."

Eric grimaced. "They've got me, Jim. Got me bad.

BAD I TELL YOU. I can feel it…it's…not…long…"

Bruce removed hair from Eric's eyes. "We got so close, Tony. We were nearly there. When I found that parchment, you were the only one who believed me and now—"

Another round of gunfire silenced him. Eric grabbed hold of Bruce's canvas jacket sleeve. "I'd follow you…to the end of the world….Jim…go…give them hell. Tell them that Tony sent you." With that, Eric let out a loud sigh as his head fell to the side. Bruce pulled him into his chest and rocked.

He set the motionless body of Eric Roberts on the floor and ran a blood-covered hand through his hair. "What have I *done*?" he muttered to himself, before raising his head to the heavens, and shouting, "WHAT HAVE I DONE?"

"It's a wonder this film isn't shown more often. It really is the height of quality acting," Stella mocked.

"…but sir, they're unarmed civilians, I—"

Telly Savalas slapped Matthew Broderick hard across the face. "Shut it, Agent Boemdekoempf! We've got our orders. No one gets out of here alive." Taking his cue, Telly raised his hands, an Uzi in each, and gunned down a group of men and women running away from them. Seeing a couple run hand in hand down the dusty road, he went to fire, but both weapons were empty.

"Go long, you bastards," he growled. Pulling the pin out of the grenade with his teeth, Telly Savalas lobbed the explosive, and it landed behind the pair. The blast sent both of them somersaulting through the air in slow motion.

He looked back to Broderick as he reloaded. "Now get to it, Boemdekoempf, or I'll have to make you a KIA." Telly Savalas struck the match off Broderick's cheek and applied the flame to his cigar.

A sudden roar made the two heavily armed men look behind them. A murderous Bruce Willis stormed out of a building brandishing an M60. Taking residence in the middle of the street, Bruce shouted, "I may not get to be God, but you folks will get to go ahead of me now." Laughing as if possessed, he pulled the trigger and loosed off a hail of bullets.

People fell like scythed chaff, clutching wounds and pretend dead children. Telly Savalas hurled himself to the floor just in time as a volley of bullets stitched Matthew Broderick from nipple to groin. He collapsed to the floor, panting. He looked down at his body and saw orange blood pour from his wounds. "Permission...to die, sir..." he gasped.

Telly Savalas pushed up the rim of his helmet as Broderick gasped and fell silent. Savalas blew out a ring of cigar smoke, and snarled, "Permission granted, son."

Gunfire was all around him. Telly Savalas threw off his helmet and stood up. He pulled a blade from the sleeve of his jacket and held it between his fingers. "Time for you to meet your maker, Pastor." He flung the knife and it spun through the air, end over end, until it finally slammed into Bruce Willis' neck.

Everything went a pale shade of blue, until Telly Savalas' bald head loomed large. "I...nearly...did it,"

Bruce gasped.

Telly knelt down and gripped his hand. "Sorry, son. I couldn't let you finish this. The world needs to think that you're the bad guy here. All I've done today…is my job."

Bruce smiled and looked up at the fatherly figure of Telly Savalas. "It would have been…beautiful. I… I… I'm…"

"What, son?"

Bruce coughed. "I'm home." With that he lolled to one side. The picture panned out, showing bodies lying dead all around the village. Intermittent gunfire sounded out as soldiers stalked the streets, taking care of the last survivors. The screen faded to black;

PASTOR JIM GIMBAL DIED ON 8 DECEMBER 1981.

HIS WORK REMAINED UNFINISHED, THE GOVERNMENT COVERED UP THE MASSACRE AND LAY THE BLAME AT HIS DOOR.

THE LOCATION OF THE PARCHMENT AND THE DIVINE POWDER IS STILL A MYSTERY.

HISTORY WILL KNOW ONLY OF HIM AS…

THE PASTOR OF DEATHTOWN

As the credits rolled, Stella yawned. "Bullshit."

Esther let the movie run and opened the browser on her phone. "See, the thing about all of that is that people take one thing and twist it to make it into so called entertainment. Yes, it has the whole stardust thing going on, but that was utter crap. Everyone knows Gimbal poisoned the lot of them, and was then taken out by one of his own. Eric Roberts, or Tony, whatever the hell his name was."

Esther turned the tablet around to face her sister. "Then explain this."

"Sole survivor of the Gimbaltown massacre publishes the notebook, which he says drove Pastor Gimbal to murderous lengths. Tu Manh-Tran survived, as he was in the local Quantico-Mart buying the pastor's requested brand of Lucky Strike cigarettes.

When he got back to the village, he saw that the area was cordoned off by what he called, 'army-dudes'. Eager to retrieve a pocketwatch, the sole possession left to him by his deceased father, Tu waited two days for the area to be vacated.

As he searched the camp, it became quickly apparent that everything had been taken by the mysterious soldiers. Unable to find his watch, he decided to search the pastor's quarters, in the hope of finding something he could sell.

Carrying a tape recorder out of the building, he slipped on a shell casing and dropped the machine on the floor. Whilst he was at first annoyed, he discovered a notebook inside which he said looked 'really old and that'. He took it to the local library and photocopied it, before handing it in to our reporter on the ground, Gail Blower.

Whilst we attempted to verify whether this was an elaborate hoax or not, Mister Tran was found dead in his hotel room. Police say that he electrocuted himself whilst trying to use a toaster and bathing at the same time. Inspector Doohan says they are not treating the death as suspicious, and that the original notebook has vanished. Doohan suspects that Tu sold this to fuel his drug problem," Stella read aloud. "And?"

Esther scrolled down. "What do you see on here?"

Stella huffed and read down the photocopied document. "Motherfucker…"

"How about this one?" Stella pointed at a large ceramic bowl with a shiny glaze and little flowers hand-painted onto the surface.

Esther shook her head as she examined a chamber pot. "No, has to be circular doesn't it? It's about the size of a skull, though, I'll give you that."

With the discovery of the photocopied notebook online, the pair had wasted no time in visiting the nearest antique shop. This was a three floored building next to the 'Cash 4 Ur Stuff' pawn shop at the end of Catherine Street.

Esther remembered being dragged around it as a kid by her parents. Time itself slowed to a crawl as she sat on the stairs, watching them pore over old cameras, thimbles and bejewelled hair pins.

The instructions themselves were pretty straightforward, which worried them. The pot had to be merely 'larger than a human skull', but the devil in the detail was that the chamber had to be perfectly circular. This was the sticking point. They had found innumerable pots which were big enough, but none which matched the interior specifications.

Esther tutted as she replaced yet another chamber pot

carefully back on the shelf. The signs dotted around each floor let everyone know, in no uncertain terms, that if you broke it, you paid for it. They'd already witnessed an old lady being harangued for £15.99 after her arthritic fingers had failed to hold onto a small china bell, and it had smashed to smithereens on the floor.

"This is hopeless, Es, There's nothing here. I think if we stay any longer we may as well get a blue rinse, smell of boiled to death cabbage, and take up bingo," Stella moaned, again. Esther noticed that the closer they got to their goal, the more she whinged. Or, she surmised, that despite allaying her fears over Henry, Stella was worried that he was coming between them.

"Okay, perhaps we're thinking about this *too* logically. The instructions don't say that it has to be made of a certain material, does it? Only that the 'divine material' must be stored in something round. Ha, perhaps we should get a football?"

Stella shook her head. "No good. I thought of that, but it wouldn't really be the best material for the last part, eh?" Esther nodded in agreement. Her sister continued, "You do know what you've got to do at the end, don't you?"

"Course I do," Esther replied defensively. "Always had my suspicions, but good that it's confirmed."

"And you're not scared by it?"

Esther replaced a stuffed chaffinch back on the shelf. "Is that what all *this* is about?"

"What do you mean?"

"You know, the way you've been since we found out. You're worried that I'm having second thoughts, aren't you?"

"No. Maybe. Yes. Fine, I am. It's pretty full on, Es. I wouldn't blame you for not wanting to go through with it."

Esther smiled at her sister. "You're such a dick. I know I'm going to be scared, but I also can't wait. When it's done, it means that me and you are properly...ya know—"

Stella held her hand up. "Don't, I know. You'll set me off if you say it. Can't believe we're this close. I've been thinking, I reckon we probably have enough, if we can just find this fucking pot we can clean up the lot we found behind the fireplace, add it to our lot...we're gonna be there—"

"Or thereabouts. I know, I thought the same."

"Funny that," Stella winked and chuckled. "Can't believe it, after all these years it's all going to go away and we'll finally be—"

"Woah, sis," Esther interrupted. "Do you reckon this will work?"

Stella closed her mouth and looked at the object her sister was revolving. "That is perfect. Does it open at the top?"

Esther stopped the globe spinning and looked at the top axis. "Got to be something, a hole in each end for the pole to run through or something to support it. How much is it?"

"Fuck a duck," Stella said out loud. "That's a bit on the effing vertical side, isn't it? I've seen GDP figures for Pacific Islands run to less than that."

Esther shrugged. "Doesn't matter, does it? If we have enough stardust, then we won't be getting the credit card bill through, eh?"

"Are you going to be able to get it home alright?" Stella asked, taking in the size of the wooden globe and its stand.

"Reckon so. We're only down the road. Be back in ten minutes, give or take. Then we need to work out how to take a bit of the top off, and plug the bottom."

A middle-aged shop assistant who had been eyeing Esther like a hawk since she came in walked up to her. "An excellent piece, isn't it?" Cataract-threatened eyes latched onto Esther. "Are you alright, young lady? Just you seem a little…lost."

Esther looked to Stella who was standing behind the lady, pulling faces and sticking fingers behind her head to give her horns. "Yes," she answered. "I'm just fine. Thank you."

12

"Careful, you idiot, you're spilling it," Stella warned. Esther shot her another withering look, and resumed the task of sieving the material into the Tupperware box. "Amazing how much crap and grit there is in there."

"Not surprising, I guess. Must've been behind the wall for what? A hundred years? It's the dead spiders that are freaking me out, urrghhh." Esther shivered. She tapped the side of the sieve against the palm of her hand and watched in awe as the fine glitter fell through.

"Still think it's mad that this dust is in all of us, and most don't even know about it. Guess we *are* all made of stars, huh?"

Concentrating on the task in hand, Esther managed a grunt in reply. Satisfied that all of the precious dust had been filtered out, she ran a finger around the sieve. "Is that, or *was* that, a beetle or something? Looks disgusting. Is that the lot?"

Stella peered into the pot and said, "Aside from some caked on bits, yeah. We just need to add in our lot now."

Esther tipped the assortment of crap from the sieve into a carrier bag, which had the breathing holes taped up. Discarding the sieve on the coffee table, Esther stood up and headed out to the back room. She returned with the Tupperware box, which was near full of the stardust they had collected. She knelt down by the table again and looked over to an expectant Stella. "Well, here goes nothing then. Are you sure you're ready?"

Stella nodded nervously. "Yeah. I mean, what choice do we have? It's this or we have to start nicking organs, or knock off some more fat clubs. Perhaps there are other depths of depravity we need to yet plumb?"

A hand gripped the edge of the bowl, poised to tip the contents. "Let's just do it, before I change my mind."

A sound like sand pouring through an hourglass sounded as the dust was mixed together. It looked almost identical, despite the age difference.

Almost sensing this, Stella muttered, "All those people..."

Esther nodded sincerely. "Yeah, their hopes, dreams, desires, all of it gone."

"I don't think so. Look, they're all here. Sure the methods by which they were taken may have been different. We got most of ours by what you would call fair means, but when it's all together, you can't tell if one was extracted a different way. I think it's kinda cool," Stella said.

"What do you mean?"

"If it hadn't been taken out of them, what would've happened to it? Either buried in a coffin and then taken into the earth, or cremated to nothingness. Least this way they get to live again, sort of. As long as our motives are honest, then surely that's the most important thing?"

Esther poured the last of the dust into the larger

Tupperware container. "Well, it won't matter soon, as we won't be in a position to judge. Though, no one will, will they?"

"Don't start this again," Stella warned. "We don't know for sure it'll take everyone else down with it, and if it does, so what? Look what we do as people. We've spent our entire time killing each other and everything else on this planet. We invented religion so that people can kill other people who believe in something different, or to offer some hint of better things when you've gone through your entire life serving those with power. It's bullshit. We're supposed to evolve as a species, yet it feels like all we do is go backwards. We find new and inventive ways of killing each other and ruining the planet. We don't *deserve* to carry on."

"But surely we shouldn't be the ones to judge?" Esther countered.

Stella pouted. "Sis, it doesn't matter. Really, it doesn't. We don't have to do this. We can go on as we have always done. Or we can see this through. What will be, will be. The important thing is that we will be together, properly, forever this way. We have the chance to do something which, what, how many people have tried to do over the years? Two? Three? If we weren't meant to do this, then we wouldn't be allowed to."

"Just because you *can* do something, doesn't mean you should."

"No, it doesn't. But our reasons are well intentioned. We're not using this as a weapon. We're doing this for something else."

Esther put the now empty box on the table, next to the

sieve. "You're right Stella."

They both jumped as a man's voice, somewhere behind them, said, "Who's Stella?"

13

Esther froze. She knew who it was before she turned around. "Henry? What are you doing here?" Shock quickly turned into anger. "And how the hell did you get in? I really don't appreciate people breaking and entering. It's not the way you do things."

Henry dangled a set of keys from his finger. "You left these in the lock. I had to talk to you anyway, but this just made things easier."

Esther gulped. "What do you mean?" She stood up and walked over to Henry. When she was within range, she snatched the keys from him and checked them.

"Something…something has come up, and I thought I'd best tell you in person, before they came round." Arms folded, Esther shrugged. Henry went on. "I had a visit from the police this morning. They exhumed one of the victims from the Durrington gas killings. They said that it looks like the bodies have been tampered with. That something was wrong with them. They questioned me for hours, and they wanted to know who else had access to the bodies."

"He's fucking grassed you up," Stella shouted. "The fucking snake. If I could, I'd rip his balls off and make them into Scotch Eggs."

Esther slumped against the back of the sofa, her hand clamped over her mouth. "They mentioned you by name. Something about an email to the organiser, Maureen something?" Henry added.

"Nice one, Brainiac. Told you to set up a new email address, didn't I? FUCK! Why don't you listen to me?" Stella chided.

Henry went to put an arm around Esther, who rebuked it forcefully. "No. *Don't*. Why are you here, Mister Phelps? Really?"

"I came to warn you. They're bound to be on their way. I had to let you know that it wasn't me that gave you up. You mean a lot to me, Esther, more than you know."

She shook her head, and mumbled, "It doesn't matter. Thank you for coming round, Mister Phelps. Now if you'll excuse me."

Henry stood like a scolded animal. "Please, Esther, what happened? You didn't have anything to do with that business, did you?"

Silence.

He sighed. "It's okay. We can sort something out. We can get you a good solicitor. They'll fight this, come up with a defence. It'll—"

"NO!" Esther screamed. "Yes, I killed them! But it's for something greater than all of this." She waved her arms around. "You wouldn't understand if I told you, and by the sounds of it, I don't have the time."

Sirens birthed into life, screaming louder and louder as they grew near. Blue flashes of light ran across the top of the closed curtains. "Please, Mister Phelps, you better go," she said softly.

Defeated, Henry sagged and headed towards the hallway. As he walked through the doorway, he stopped and turned back. "So, who is Stella?"

Esther stood up, chest puffed out, resolve running through her veins. "She's my sister, Mister Phelps. My twin. She died when we were still inside my mum. When she came out first, my parents thought we were both dead. Miracle baby, that's what Dad called me when I popped out ten minutes later. Mum didn't agree. She never got over it. She always thought that it was something *she* did, or *didn't* do. She could barely stand to be in the same room as me, said I reminded her too much of Stella."

She sat down on the back of the sofa cushions; Stella stood to one side. "The doctors said that she had been dead for a while, and that bits of her had dissolved away. Some went back into Mum, the rest must've gone into me. I've seen her my entire life. She *is* my sister, and we've grown up together, been through *everything* together. You should see her, Mister Phelps. She's...*beautiful.*"

"Shut up, idiot," Stella muttered.

Henry took hold of Esther's hands. "But *you're* beautiful Esther. You're like an angel; you just shine."

Esther broke free and rolled up her left sleeve, revealing an assorted tableau of pink scar tissue. "No, Mister Phelps, I'm the fuck-up, I'm the one who always got things wrong, the one who—no matter what they did—was always told off, or punished. Nothing I did was ever good enough.

All my life, I knew that I was the one that should've died, not her.

Me.

Stella had it all. The confidence, the charm. She knew how people really worked, not me."

"But she's not *real*," Henry said, desperate to get through to her.

"To me she is. She's right here," Esther gestured to Stella, who took a deep bow. "She's always been there. All I've wanted is for us to be together, somewhere where none of this can hurt me. Where nothing can hurt us."

"But people can help you. You just need to talk to someone about all of this. It's all in your head. Why can't you see that?" Henry begged.

"You've seen my gift, Mister Phelps. That comes from a place beyond everything we can see and know about. There is more to existence than this cheap flesh. All it is…is wrapping. The true us is inside here." She touched his chest gently. "If we had the time, I'd show you, perhaps even I could *convince* you. But we don't. So please, Mister Phelps, go. Tell the police that I'll be out in ten minutes, fifteen tops. There is just one thing I have to take care of before I go with them."

Henry shook his head vigorously. "No, we go out together. If you stay here, you'll—"

"What? Kill myself?"

The accusation hung in the air like a dirty secret finally aired. Henry struggled to find an answer. "No, just…yes, *fine*. I'm worried you'll do something silly. Please. Come with me now. We'll get through this together. I'll be with you every step of the way. I promise you."

Esther considered his words, then replied. "If someone like you had said this to me a few years ago, before I found out about everything, then I would follow you, Mister Phelps, honest, I would. But I can't. Please, just go, give me the ten minutes I need to make peace with something, and then I'll come out. We'll see how things go from there, okay?"

He wavered. Sensing his indecision, Esther pulled him close and kissed him. A sensation never experienced before ran through every fibre of her being. Every nerve ending tingled with anticipation and longing. Her heart skipped a beat. Stella coughed, "Jeez, get a *room*."

Esther stood back, the pair of them still lost in the moment and the whirlwind of emotion and feelings. "Thank you, Mister Phelps, really. You've been very kind to me."

Henry smiled back sheepishly. "You have no idea how long I've wanted to do that."

"Now please, go. Ten minutes. I'll burst through that door, nothing will stop me. I promise."

He smiled and edged towards the door. "We're going to get through this. I'll be with you every step of the way."

"I know."

Henry padded towards the door, took one last look back, and then left. As the front door was opened, the sirens and shouting increased, only silenced once the door was pulled shut.

"Esther and Henry sitting in a tree," Stella cooed, smiling.

"Shut up idiot," Esther said coyly. "We don't have much time. Let's get on with it."

Esther pulled the globe out from under the coffee table. She had affixed some makeshift feet to it, to stop it from rolling around the floor. Aside from plugging the hole in the bottom, she had also made the hole at the top slightly larger, so that pouring the dust would be easier. "Where's the funnel?" she asked, beginning to panic. "We're not going to have enough time. I knew I should have asked for longer. Why didn't I ask for *longer*, Stell?"

Her sister chuckled. "You're sitting on it, you eejit. Now will you please calm down? Us ghosts don't take too kindly to real people panicking and that. Makes us look bad."

"Phew, okay. I just hope we have enough, or we're going to spend the rest of our days driving each other insane inside a prison cell."

"Unless you haven't noticed, I'm dead already. I ain't going anywhere."

Esther pushed the end of the funnel into the hole on top of the globe. "Here goes," she sighed. She picked up the tub and carefully began to pour the powder into the hollowed-out wooden orb.

"Did you ever resent me?" Stella asked.

Esther sighed. "I'm trying to concentrate right now."

Stella huffed.

"Fine. No, I never did. How *could* I? You have to remember that when I was younger I thought you were real. It was only when Mum and Dad never set a place for you at dinner, or ever bought you anything, that I knew something was wrong. You've been there for me my entire life, warts and all. I'm just glad you stuck with me."

Stella laughed. "Where the hell else am I supposed to go? Don't think it works that way. Besides, not long now and we'll be together properly. Nothing will hurt you then."

Esther looked her dead in the eye. "I hope so."

"SHIT," Esther exclaimed, realising the funnel was backed up. She placed the tub on the table. There was still a pile of it gathered in the corner.

Taking care, she tapped the side of the funnel. Aside from a few granules sinking from sight, the rest remained. Esther pulled the end out and shoved a hand under it, putting it back into the tub, where it poured out of the end. Cautiously, Esther rapped her fingernails on the side of the globe, where France was painted. A dull thud sounded.

"We've done it," Stella said, surprised. Her sister nodded in agreement.

"MISS THACKARAY, THIS IS THE POLICE. WE HAVE THE BUILDING SURROUNDED. PLEASE COME OUT WITH YOUR HANDS UP."

Stella laughed. "They're playing our song, Es. Shall we dance?"

Esther smiled and nodded. She walked over to a stack of old newspapers, beneath pictures of her mum and dad on their wedding day. She stopped and ran her fingers over their happy two-dimensional faces. "We're out of here, Mum, Dad. I'm sorry if I did anything to hurt you. We both are.

It's time for us to go now.

We're leaving together.

For something better.

I hope that wherever you are, floating around whatever part of this universe, you'll keep an eye out for us.

We're coming home."

She brushed the paper to one side and pulled out a one gallon red plastic can, with a thick black screw top. Esther sat on the sofa, unscrewed the lid, and poured the petrol over herself. The smell took her breath away; as it ran into recent injuries, she winced from the pain.

The last drop fell from the tank onto her damp hair. It felt as if she had swallowed as much as she had covered herself in. Esther picked up the globe and clutched it to her chest. Bringing her knees up to support the weight, she jiggled around on the soaked sofa to get comfortable. She fumbled around her pocket for the BIC lighter. Noticing how sparkly the flint was, she looked up to Stella, who now loomed over her. "I'm scared," she said softly, petrol dripping from her chin.

Stella slowly knelt down by her and ran a finger across Esther's brow. The digit sunk through the flesh. "I won't miss that, I tell ya."

Esther laughed.

"I love you, Es. More than anything. Though I never got to do the things you did, I'm grateful that I got to see the world through your eyes. Thank you."

"ESTHER THACKARAY, IF YOU DO NOT COME OUT VOLUNTARILY, WE *WILL* ENTER THE PROPERTY."

"It's time," Stella said. She puckered her lips and kissed the space around Esther's head.

The lighter rasped against the flint, sending a small shower of sparks into the air. The flame swelled into a brilliant blue and yellow tear. The fumes at first retreated from the heat, but were then pulled towards it.

Fire ran around Esther's body like a force-field. The

pain caused her to drop the lighter, its job done. It hit the carpet and rolled under the sofa.

Having completely covered her huddled body, the fire took hold of the chair and rug. Esther screamed in agony, but held onto the globe even tighter. As the flames consumed her, the first embers of burning clothing found their way through the hole at the top of the world.

Like a barrel of gunpowder, it hissed like an angry snake. As melted skin sloughed off her bones, the fire utterly consumed the container and the sacrifice.

At first there was nothing except the fire. Then, with the stardust ablaze, the backdraft pulled what remained of Esther into the container itself. Stella blinked out of existence as her sister's essence merged with the harvested life-force.

Inspector Ford rushed into the house and saw the inferno. For the briefest of moments, he saw the lady from the photograph, and then she was a fireball.

The fiery orb floated, propelled into the air from the heat and from the energy bursting into life from the immolation. A chain reaction at the molecular level puffed the ball out by ten feet; the roiling surface, a mass of nuclear reaction and fire, reduced the policeman to a charred outline on the hallway wall.

Still the orb grew. With everything it came into contact with, its mass increased. Consumption and growth got faster and faster. Within twenty-nine seconds, the ball of fire had consumed the policemen and women outside. Henry went to run, but within the maelstrom, saw the face of the woman he loved. He stopped, smiled, and allowed himself to be devoured.

Still it grew, and soon all of Salisbury was nothing more than a charred wasteland. The ball moved further and further afield, yet a bridge had now formed between it and the earth.

As it fed on every living thing, it grew and burned brighter. Twelve minutes after ignition, the bridge between the earth and its destroyer was nothing more than a heat haze.

Tendrils of fire erupted from the fireball and wrapped around the planet. Like a predator snaring its prey, it pulled it into its violent creation.

The flames reduced everything to ash and, as the mass grew and grew, everything was pulled into the heart of the searing sphere.

And then…

"I have seen our end. It is in a swirling sapphire light, with smoke and fire."

DUNCAN P. BRADSHAW

starburst

From above, a burst of yellow light illuminated a patch of the night sky. Other stars, even the brightest amongst them, dimmed in comparison to the bloom of light. Slowly, but surely, the iridescent ball contracted, leaving behind another twinkling fleck of glitter in the galaxy.

"WOW," the girl exclaimed, her face filled with wonder and awe at the spectacle that had literally lit up her world. "It's beautiful."

Her father squeezed her hand a little tighter. "That is your star now, Terra. *Your* anchor in the universe. No matter where you are, and no matter what you face, that is the beacon that will guide you home. And when you're ready, and your days are spent, you will become one with it. Forever."

Terra realised that she was still beaming. "I think it's the most beautiful star up there, Papa."

"It is," her father agreed. "Yours and one other." His long finger traced a small trail across the heavens, to another which burned with renewed ferocity.

"Is that...?"

"Yes, Terra, that's your mother. When she was taken, your mother's essence managed to find its way to where it was meant to be. She has always looked down on you and

303

kept watch, hoping that one day you too would make this journey. So that, in time, you will be together again."

Terra squinted at the star which seemed transfixed on the pair, atop a mountain, one of hundreds looking into the sky. "Where's yours, Papa?" she asked, eyes flitting from one shining orb to the next, hoping she would recognise it.

"There is no star for me, my girl. My journey is spent getting you to this point, nothing more. But know that I will always live in you, even after I'm gone. For we are all connected. Time cannot keep us apart, for everything has already been. We are all one, Terra. We do not search for faith as we have certainty. We do not require belief, as our mere existence is all the proof we need. Go into your life now, and just be."

For a while, they lay there in silence. Other explosions of light caught their eye from time to time, but nothing compared to what they had seen.

Some were a baleful red, fearsome black-centred eyes stared down from the sky above. Their surfaces roiled with anger. Cracks of lightning shot from the Corona, visible even from where the pair lay atop the mountain. The girl looked from them quickly, holding onto her father's hand even tighter.

Eventually, Terra plucked up the courage to ask the question which burned within her the most. "What is my star made of, Papa?"

Her father looked from the heavens to his daughter. "Of love," he said softly, "and of hope and dreams."

DUNCAN P. BRADSHAW

WHO THE HELL WROTE THIS?

Duncan P(hantastic) Bradshaw, is possibly the best modest person you'll ever meet. His flaws are numerous, enough that if you were in a canoe - a one or two man deal, nothing too big – then they, along with his modesty combined, would probably help capsize us.

Though you'd never get him in the canoe to begin with, the inky depths of death do not appeal.

Aside from espousing his ism's onto the rest of the world, he writes down the things that scurry around his vacuous brain which was once the largest repository of weather trivia known to man.

Please, go over to Facebook and give him a like,

http://www.facebook.com/duncanpbradshaw

or, if you desire, check out his website,

http://www.duncanpbradshaw.co.uk

he'd be awfully grateful.

DUNCAN P. BRADSHAW

heXAgRAm

MORE TITLES FROM

DUNCAN P. BRADSHAW

DUNCAN P. BRADSHAW

PRIME DIRECTIVE

Some things are better left undiscovered.

The crew of the first manned mission to Mars, are in the final days of their expedition before they head home.

Shamed by a lack of discoveries and humiliated by her colleagues, geologist Dana Fischerman heads out to the Galle crater, eager to find something to make her own legacy. What she uncovers will not only threaten the safety of her colleagues, but also everyone back on Earth.

"A perfect mixture of sci-fi and horror this story plants the seed of fear in your head and makes it grow and grow until you close the book."
- Confessions of a Reviewer

"Prime Directive is filled with some fantastic comic situations and a premise that will rock your socks off."
- 2 Book Lovers Reviewers

CELEBRITY CULTURE

It's the thirteenth annual Lou Gehrig awards. Four B-list celebrity virologists vie to claim the Locked In Syndrome cup and get mulched down to form their disease for mass distribution.

A disease hipster takes centre stage on a night when a blast from the past threatens to turn his ordered, pus filled life upside down. In order to blow open a deep rooted conspiracy, he must team up with a disgraced one time child star who wants another shot at the big time, and clear his sullied name.

Together, they're going to show people the real meaning of a meltdown.

"You're completely at the mercy of his strange imagination and all the eccentric oddities that his curious mind can conjure up. Indeed, it quickly becomes apparent that the only way you'll be able to wade through the veritable quagmire of lunacy is by simply succumbing to the madness."

-   **DLS Reviews**

DUNCAN P. BRADSHAW

Hungover, dumped and late for work.

On an ordinary day, one of these would be a bad morning, but today Jim Taylor also has to contend with the zombie apocalypse.

Follow Jim during twenty four hours of Day One, as he and his zombie obsessed brother deal with the undead, a doomsday cult and maniacs in their quest to get to their parents, win his girlfriend back and for them to instigate 'The Plan'.

Worlds will collide and fall apart in a Class Three outbreak.

'This, ladies and gentlemen, is a classic. This is a book that all people who read horror stories need to have on their shelves. Horror. Yes. Comedy. Yes. Does it mix well? Absolutely yes.'
-   **Scream Magazine**

CLASS FOUR

Those Who Survive

The dead rule the world.

In the months after a deadly virus has swept across the planet, an eight year old boy and his appointed protector live from day to day. After a chance encounter they head for sanctuary. To get there, they will have to run the gauntlet of the inhabitants of this new world.

Ruled over by The Gaffer, a group of survivors holed up in a derelict factory struggle to maintain order and stability. Inside, those affected the most share their stories, hoping to come to terms with what has happened and what they've lost.

However, a clandestine operative in their midst lays the groundwork for an assault, the likes of which none of them have ever seen or could hope to prepare for.

These are the stories of those who survive.

"Action-packed, funny, and extremely brutal."
- Adam Millard, author of Vinyl Destination

313

DUNCAN P. BRADSHAW

CHUMP

Eight stories which take a different look at these reanimated denizens of death:

CURE WHAT AILS YA - When a snake oil salesman rolls into the Wild West town of Lobo, both he and the inhabitants are unaware of what is about to crawl out of the desert, hungry for brains.

1984 - Finally, after years of being subject to official censure, the true story as to why the Eastern Bloc countries boycotted the 1984 Los Angeles Olympics, is revealed.

RED SABRE ONE - An SAS team are tasked with extracting a high value target from their world famous home.

SENSELESS APPRENTICE - Step inside the mind of one of the undead, unable to do anything but watch on as his body acts on primal instinct.

DEAD DROP - A novella following a courier in the apocalypse. Ceepher's motto is simple; never look inside the package, and always be on time. His latest delivery will put both on the line.

CHARITY BEGINS AT HOME - Whilst out collecting for H.O.A.R.D. (Helping Orphans Affected by the Reanimation Disease), Sadie stumbles upon a middle age couple, who seem to have survived the apocalypse with their pristine house intact.

GONE FISHIN' - Bored, a son pleads with his dad to tell him, again, how his parents got together...one summers day on the lake.

WHACKOS - After 'Reclamation', a radio host and his sound engineer, follow a clean up team, as they confront the after-effects of the zombie apocalypse.

DUNCAN P. BRADSHAW

Lightning Source UK Ltd.
Milton Keynes UK
UKHW010037060119
335006UK00001B/131/P